PRAISE FOR *NO WAY TO TREAT A FIRST LADY*

"An exceedingly funny account of a White House scandal that doesn't bear the slightest resemblance—nudge nudge, wink wink—to one that took place there only five short years ago."
    —*The Washington Post Book World*

"This clever, gleeful satire . . . sets a high comic standard."
    —*The New York Times*

"Buckley has surpassed himself. . . . The result isn't humorous; it's hilarious. . . . Perhaps Buckley, in his bemusement at both right and left with the media and lawyers in between, has written the most discerning social history of the Clinton era that will ever appear. It is a feat that will be difficult to replicate."
    —*Los Angeles Times Book Review*

"Christopher Buckley must have had a great time creating this satire that is part legal thriller, part love story and entirely over-the-top funny. But those who choose to pick it up can look forward to smart writing, memorable lines and more than a few belly laughs. . . . [*No Way to Treat a First Lady*] doesn't have to be a guilty pleasure, it can be enjoyed and shared because it is simply smart and light and very funny."
    —*The Denver Post*

"[A] delightful romp . . . This Washington is teeming with barely disguised caricatures."
    —*The Wall Street Journal*

"Hilarious . . . I certainly laughed—a lot. Truth may be stranger than fiction, but fiction can be a lot funnier."
    —*Detroit Free Press*

About the Author

CHRISTOPHER BUCKLEY is the author of eight previous books, including *Thank You for Smoking* and *Little Green Men*. That would make this his, what, ninth? He is editor of *Forbes FYI* magazine and has contributed more than fifty "Shouts and Murmurs" to *The New Yorker*. He is also credited with bringing about lasting peace in the Middle East and with alerting NASA to significant problems with its Space Shuttle Automatic Re-entry Guidance System (SSARGS), thereby sparing several square blocks of Raleigh, North Carolina, a very unpleasant surprise. He is a regular contributor to *Martha Stewart's Inside Trading* magazine and informally advises the government of Argentina on debt rescheduling. He is the 2002 recipient of the Washington Irving Medal for Literary Excellence but has yet to actually receive it. He lives in Washington, D.C., with his saintly and long-suffering wife, Lucy, two children, and faithful Hound Jake.

Little Green Men

God Is My Broker (with John Tierney)

Wry Martinis

Thank You for Smoking

Wet Work

Campion (a play, with James McGuire)

The White House Mess

Steaming to Bamboola: The World of a Tramp Freighter

No Way to Treat

a First Lady

Christopher Buckley

No Way to Treat

a First Lady

A Novel

Random House
Trade Paperbacks
New York

This is a novel, that is, "a relatively long fictional prose narrative with a more or less complex plot or pattern of events, about human beings, their feelings, thoughts, actions, etc." (*Webster's New 20th Century Dictionary,* unabridged, Collins World Publishers, 1978). It is also satire, namely, "a literary work in which vices, follies, stupidities, abuses, etc. are held up to ridicule and contempt" (ibid.). Finally, and just to belabor the now obvious, all characters herein are *entirely* the work of the author's own twisted imagination and have absolutely nothing to do with actual human beings invented by, say, God.

Library of Congress Cataloging-in-Publication Data
Buckley, Christopher.
No way to treat a First Lady: a novel / Christopher Buckley.
p.   cm.
ISBN 0-375-75875-5
1. Attorney and client—Fiction.   2. Presidents' spouses—Fiction.
3. Trials (Murder)—Fiction.   4. First ladies—Fiction.
5. Widows—Fiction.   I. Title.
PS3552.U3394 N6   2002   813'.54—dc21   2002069926

Random House website address: www.atrandom.com
Printed in the United States of America
2   4   6   8   9   7   5   3   1

Book design by J. K. Lambert

FOR DON AND MEG GREGG,

WITH LOVE

No Way to Treat
a First Lady

Prologue

*B*abette Van Anka had made love to the President of the United States on eleven previous occasions, but she still couldn't resist inserting "Mr. President" into "Oh, baby, baby, baby." He had told her on the previous occasions that he did not like being called this while, as he put it, congress was in session. But she couldn't stop thinking to herself, *I'm screwing the President of the United States! In the White House!* Unavoidably, the "Mr. President" just kept slipping out.

Thrilled as she was, however, tonight Babette was ready for occasion number twelve to be over. It was after 2:00 A.M., and it was plain from the exhausted grunting noises and wheezes coming from her partner that he was straining to prove a point, more to himself than to her. God knows she had done what she could to make the evening exciting for him, but it had turned into an endurance contest. Where's the romance in that? Plus there was the fact that the First Lady of the United States was right down the hall. The President had assured her that his wife was sound asleep, but this was bold even by his incautious standards. The combination of his unamorous rutting and his wife's proximity made it difficult for Babette to relax and enjoy.

She concentrated on helping her commander in chief achieve bliss. It was work. Occasions one through four had been earth-moving experiences. Five through eight had been pretty exhilarating. Occasion nine—disaster. Ten and eleven were little more than awkward attempts to rekindle Eros' flame. Was he losing interest? The pressure was on.

Babette knew that she had to deliver or suffer the unthinkable—indifference. No more overnights in the Lincoln Bedroom at the White House, no more trips on Air Force One, no more golf or meals with world leaders, no more seat at the table. And just a few weeks ago he had dangled before her the prospect of a Middle East summit weekend at Camp David, the presidential retreat. Oh, to miss *that.*

Babette stirred from her reverie of trysting with the President in the Catoctin Mountains amid prime ministers.

There was a sound.

. . . bump . . . bump . . . bump . . .

It was the presidential head, striking the Lincoln bed headboard.

"Oh," she whispered, *"yes . . . yes . . . oooooh . . . .yessss . . ."*

Sometimes that got them off. Men loved an affirming sound track.

Babette sneaked a peek at the luminous face of her watch. Jesus Christ, he'd been humping her for over half an hour. Normally she'd be tickled to a puddle, but not tonight. The wife down the hall, Secret Service agents everywhere. She'd said to him, Tonight? Here? Is this *smart*? Navy men—they got off on risk.

He was sweating. He was hot to the touch. His breathing sounded labored. What was this new sound?

Unh, unh, unh, unh.

Grunting. Wonderful. It made her feel as sexy as a slab of meat.

She opened her eyes, then wished she hadn't. He had this *look,* like that of an exhausted bull salmon fighting his way up rocks to squirt his DNA over the roe so he could turn belly up and die. Isn't it romantic?

He was probably fantasizing about—someone else. Some body he'd seen in a magazine.

"Unnnnnnnnnh."

Finally, thank God.

"Ohhh," she lied.

Silence. The sheets were damp from presidential sweat. Babette liked clean, crisp, ironed sheets, the kind they had in British hotels, so much starch that they crackled. Now look at her bed. Lake Superior. What was she supposed to do, ring for the maid in the middle of the night to demand that they change the bed linen? Uch. She was going to have to sleep in them. Wonderful. She and her husband had donated half a million dollars to the party, and for what? To be on the receiving end of a joyless hump, with the risk thrown in of being walked in on by the wife, then to spend the rest of the night in damp sheets.

He rose.

He had gotten out of bed, without so much as a kiss or pat on the bottom, and was silhouetted against the window overlooking the South Lawn of the White House. He seemed unsteady.

She flicked on the bedside lamp. A vision greeted her: the President of the United States of America, naked but for knee socks, his face flushed like a Harvard beet, his most prominent feature still perpendicular from excitement.

"Nothing wrong with *you,*" Babette purred in her best Mae West accent.

The President looked down at his cantilevered anatomy, taking it in clinically. He grinned and made a satisfied, male grunt. He stooped to gather up his clothes, scattered over the floor. These were the only occasions when he had to pick up his own clothes. One of the perks of the office was to undress like a maharajah, tossing garments to the floor to be picked up uncomplainingly by reverent lackeys.

He pulled on his trousers but was unable to zip up. He seemed amused by this challenge, but then a look of distress took over his features and he backed into an armchair, where he sat, defeated, fly open.

"Would you like me to—"

Before Babette could finish her offer, the President lurched out of the chair purposefully toward her.

What impetuosity! She prepared to receive him, but he veered off in the direction of the nightstand. He grasped the leaded crystal carafe of ice water and with the other hand painfully bent the afflicted object downward and plunged it into the icy carafe.

Babette's mouth gaped as she viewed the presidential anatomy immersed in her ice water. A wonder there was no hissing of steam.

The immersion had the desired effect. The President was able to sheathe the afflicted limb in his trousers, though the zipping was done with extreme care, as if unstable nitroglycerin were involved.

Having finished dressing and combed his hair, he turned and flashed her a grin of triumph, with a navy-man wink. He opened the door, put his head out to check both ways down the hall, and was gone, leaving Babette to her damp sheets and unappealing ice water.

☆ · ☆ · ☆

Elizabeth Tyler MacMann, First Lady of the United States, lay awake in her own still crisp sheets, looking out the window toward the Washington Monument. Being married to America's most prominent symbol of virility, she was not blind to the irony of finding herself in bed alone, staring at the nation's most prominent phallic symbol. Not much had ever been lost on Beth MacMann, other than happiness.

Following the dinner for the President of Uruguay, Beth and the President had left their remaining guests and gone upstairs at 11:30. They'd undressed and gotten into bed. She'd fallen asleep.

She had woken up, at 1:42 A.M. by the digital bedside clock, thirsty for water, to find herself alone. Sometimes when a call came in the middle of the night, he went into his study so as not to disturb her. If it was a crisis of some sort, he usually went downstairs to the Oval Office. If it was really pressing, he would go to the Situation Room in the basement of the West Wing so that the press secretary could inform the press that the President had monitored the situation from the Situation Room. This sounded more impressive than "on the phone in bed."

The dark thought crossed Beth's mind, though she really—really— preferred not to consider the possibility, that her husband was down the hall in the Lincoln Bedroom. Surely he wouldn't pull something like that. Surely.

She knew the rumors and, moreover, knew the truth about her philandering husband of many years. But even if the rumors were true, this was the one night it was safe to assume that her husband and Babette Van Anka, actress, singer, party fund-raiser, were not engaging in bilateral relations.

Beth sat up in bed, straining to convince herself that her husband was at this very minute downstairs issuing orders to attack some Middle Eastern, or possibly Asian, country with stealth weaponry.

Just then she heard the click of the opening door as her husband, the President of the United States, came in.

She knew. Knew instantly, even in the dark. No surer radar than a wife's intuition has been invented.

Beth contemplated doing nothing, waiting until morning, when, after freshly squeezed orange juice, toast with butter and marmalade, and black coffee, she could calmly confront him with this latest installment in his serial infidelity. Then pour the coffeepot onto his offending parts. She contemplated this for five seconds, then flicked on the light.

He reacted like any creature of the night—raccoon, cockroach—suddenly bathed in unwelcome illumination. There was a rapid, lateral darting of the eyes, assessing avenues of flight. He was bent forward oddly, holding his jacket over his groin. Beth interpreted this posture as defensive. The body language shouted, "I've been screwing our guest!"

"Iraq," he said with a sigh. He rolled his eyes to show how grave and yet predictable was the situation.

It occurred to Beth that Iraq now stood in danger. He might well wait until she had gone back to sleep, then slink off to the Situation Room and order a few cruise missiles launched at Baghdad so that by breakfast time he could look her straight in the eyes.

The argument that followed was boisterous even by the standards of the MacMann marriage, currently in its twenty-fifth and final year.

☆ · ☆ · ☆

Beth awoke as usual at 6:15. She picked up the phone on her bedside table and ordered her customary breakfast. She got out of bed, slipped on her bathrobe, and opened the door to collect the morning papers, which had as usual been placed neatly on a side table, in the order she preferred to read them. In many ways, the White House was the Platonic ideal of the perfect hotel: twenty-four-hour room service, a concierge at the end of the line eager to provide anything at all, from theater tickets to an army on the march.

She scanned the front pages as she slipped back into bed. Nothing on Iraq. Surprise. An earthquake in Chile. The German foreign minister had given a speech saying that Germany had apologized sufficiently for World War II. A significant dinosaur bone had been found in Manitoba that paleontologists said might establish that dinosaurs had become extinct not because of a giant meteorite, but from osteoporosis. France, furious with the United States for imposing a 100 percent tariff on its Roquefort cheese, had agreed to sell China high-velocity nuclear torpedoes for its submarines. The head of Mexico's antinarcotics police had just built himself a third "palatial" villa, on a salary of $48,000 a year. With the presidential election "only" eighteen months away, "unnamed party leaders" were "concerned" that the President's "message" was not getting "out there."

Sophie Williams, the White House maid who always brought the First Lady her breakfast, knocked softly and entered. She and Beth exchanged the usual pleasantries as she placed the breakfast tray, with freshly cut orchid, over Beth's lap.

It was at this point that Sophie said to the First Lady softly but with alarm that the President's eyes and mouth were "wide open" and that he was "looking awful still."

This remark set in motion a series of events that culminated seventeen days later with Elizabeth Tyler MacMann's indictment for murdering the President of the United States of America. Had hers been an ordinary marriage, the charge would most likely have been second-degree murder. But since the husband in question was who he was, the plainly embarrassed attorney general explained that he had no statutory choice but to charge the now former First Lady with the monstrous crime of assassination.

Chapter 1

$\mathcal{H}$is secretary announced simply, "It's her."

There was no ambiguity as to who "her" might be, not after the force twelve media storm of the previous weeks. The country was convulsed. Seven-eighths of the nation's front pages and the evening news was devoted to it. If war had broken out with Russia *and* China, it might have made page two.

"Shameless" Baylor had spent much of the previous seventeen days wondering if Beth MacMann would have the balls to call him.

He was, at age not quite fifty, the top trial attorney in the country. He had been the first lawyer to charge $1,000 per hour, which—for too long—had been considered the unbreakable sound barrier of legal billing.

There were half a dozen second-best trial attorneys each of whom, naturally, considered him- or herself the top trial attorney in the country. But none of them had been simultaneously on the covers of all three weekly newsmagazines, none had been portrayed in movies by a famous British actor pretending to be American. None owned a professional baseball team. And, to be sure, none had been married and divorced four times. The previous record had stood at three. That he had any assets left after such serial marital wreckage was perhaps the greatest testament to his courtroom skills.

He hadn't been baptized "Shameless." In fact, up to the moment he set out to become the best trial attorney in the country he had been the soul of decency, what used to go by the name of "Christian gentleman," a veritable poster boy for all that is good and sunny in human nature. His real name was Boyce, and at his baptism, his godparents firmly rejected Satan on his behalf. The rejection lasted until an event that occurred to him just before he graduated from law school.

The nickname had been given to him by a federal judge early in Boyce's controversial career, after he had persuaded a jury that his client, the Cap'n Bob Fast Fish Restaurant chain, was unaware that its popular Neptune Burgers were made from black market Japanese whale meat. Since that stunning victory, Boyce had successfully defended traitors, terrorists, inside traders, politicians, mobsters, blackmailers, polluters, toxic-waste dumpers, cheats, insurance frauds, drug dealers, horse dopers, televangelists, hucksters, society wife batterers, cybermonopolists, and even fellow lawyers. An eminent legal scholar who wore bow ties commented on public television that if Shameless Baylor had defended Adolf Eichmann after he had been kidnapped and brought to Israel and tried for crimes against humanity, Eichmann would have been not only acquitted, but awarded damages. It was not said admiringly. But if Boyce's fame had long since reached the point where shoeshine men in airports asked for his autograph, the public was largely unaware of the actual motivation for his remarkable career.

And now—a quarter century after his career began—his phone rang.

He reached for the button, then paused. He thought of telling the secretary to tell her to call back. Sometimes he put new clients through a ten- or fifteen-minute wait before picking up. Softened them up. Made them all the more eager.

Should he, to her? No. He had waited twenty-five years. He was too impatient to begin this beguine.

He felt the kettledrum in his chest. Good Lord. Was his pulse actually quickening? He, who never broke a sweat, even while arguing before the Supreme Court?

He picked up.

"Hello, Beth. What've you been up to?" This was nonchalance carried to operatic heights.

"I need to see you, Boyce."

Her voice was all business. Cool as a martini, no more emotion than a flight attendant telling the passengers to put their seats in the upright position. He'd have preferred a little more raw emotion, frankly, even a stifled gasp or sob. Some clients, even burly men who could break your jaw with one lazy swipe of their paws, broke down the first time they spoke to him. Boyce kept a box of tissues in his office, like a shrink. One new client, the head of a plumbers union who had been taped by the FBI on the phone ordering the car bombing of a rival, had blubbered like an eight-year-old. He later blamed it on medication.

But even now, placing a call that must have humiliated her, Beth was in her own upright position, not a trace of begging or desperation in her voice. Boyce stiffened. His pulse returned to normal. *Okay, babe, you want to play it cool? I'll see your thirty-two degrees Fahrenheit and lower you five.*

"I could see you tomorrow at ten-thirty," he said. "For half an hour."

It had been a long time since anyone had said something like that to Beth MacMann.

The two of them began the mental countdown to see who would blink first.

. . . seven . . . eight . . . nine . . .

"Fine," she said.

"Will you be taking the shuttle?" He'd be damned if he'd send his own jet to pick her up.

"No, Boyce. I'll be driving. I don't relish the thought of being stared at for an hour on the shuttle."

As a former First Lady, she retained Secret Service protection, another of the ironies in which she and the nation found themselves: prosecuted by the government, protected by the government. A *Times* columnist had mischievously posed the question: If in the end Beth MacMann was executed, would there be a shoot-out between the Secret Service and the lethal injectionist? *So* many delicious questions were being posed these days.

"Ten-thirty, then."

Boyce leaned back in his leather throne and imagined the spectacle in all its many-pixeled splendor: hundreds of TV cameras and reporters outside his Manhattan office, clamoring, aiming their microphones like fetish sticks as the Secret Service phalanxed her through to the door. And there he would be standing, gorgeously, Englishly tailored, to greet her. His face would be on every television set in the world tomorrow. Peasants in Uzbekistan, ozone researchers in Antarctica, Amish farmers in Pennsylvania would recognize him.

He would issue a brief, dignified, noncommittal statement to the effect that this was only a preliminary meeting. He would smile, thank the media for its interest—Boyce was the Siegfried and Roy of media handlers—and usher her in. How satisfying it would be, after all these years. They were already calling it "the Trial of the Millennium," and there he would be, at the red hot center of it. And maybe— just maybe—to make his revenge perfect, he would deliberately lose this one. But so subtly that even the Harvard Law bow tie brigade would hem and haw and say that no one, really, could have won this one, not even Shameless Baylor.

Chapter 2

*I*t was a bigger zoo than he'd expected. Outside Boyce's Manhattan office were sixteen satellite trucks with seventy-foot telescope microwave dishes to supply the live feeds, as well as over three hundred reporters and camera people and twice that many onlookers. Even he was impressed.

The police had to block off one lane of westbound traffic on Fifty-seventh Street. It was the Client-Attorney Meeting of the Millennium. By the time this was over, one pixel pundit said, the word *millennium* would be so overworked that it would have to be mothballed until the year 2999.

Beth quietly fumed in the elevator until she and her Secret Service retinue had reached Boyce's office on the northwest corner of the fiftieth floor looking toward Central Park. He called it his "thousand-dollar-an-hour view."

"That was truly humiliating," she said. "Thank you."

He knew right away that there was no use pretending it hadn't been he who had leaked the news of their meeting. But he found himself hoping that she hadn't figured out to whom. Perri Pettengill, Boyce's current girlfriend, was the host of the Law Channel late night talk show *Hard Gavel*. She was blond, smart, and ambitious, talked fast, and wore bifocals and tight sweaters. She had the best ratings on the Law Channel, which tended not to attract many viewers in the periods between spectacular murder trials, though a highly classified in-house research report showed that roughly one-third of her viewers watched her with the sound off. Tom Wolfe had mentioned her in an essay, calling her "the Lemon Tort."

Perri and Boyce had met six months earlier when she moderated a panel at the Trial Lawyers Association in New Orleans on jury selection entitled "Peremptory This!" Boyce had been on it. She had introduced him as "not only the best but the most exciting trial attorney in the country" and that night after dinner had given him the most memorable evening he had ever spent in New Orleans, which was saying a lot. She had moved in later that week. Their relationship had been cemented in **boldface** type by the New York gossip columnists. She was smart enough not to have brought up the subject of marriage just yet, but the question was there every morning, fluttering over the breakfast trays like the Dove of Damocles. Boyce did have an excuse: four previous wives. It did give Perri pause. No romantic woman dreams, in her heart of hearts, of becoming Mrs. Number Five.

Boyce had called Perri after getting off the phone with Beth. She'd nearly hyperventilated. *What* a scoop. Her ambition sometimes made Boyce wary, as, to be honest, did her extraordinary ability in bed. Confronted with a truly skilled partner, a man had to wonder, even as he gasped and whinnied in ecstasy: *Where did she learn to do that?*

But now his thoughts were of Beth, upon whom he had last laid eyes a quarter century ago.

"You gave it to that woman, didn't you?" she said. "Sweater Girl."

"That's right. I wanted a big crowd down there today. I wanted to send a message to the U.S. government—"

"You did. It read, 'Boyce Baylor is a flaming egomaniac.' "

He was—stunned! It wasn't the sort of romancing Boyce expected from supplicant clients.

"I got up at five o'clock this morning," Beth said, "and spent four hours on I-95 feeling like O. J. Simpson in the Bronco, being chased by a half dozen Eyewitness News teams. Then I arrived to your welcome wagon from hell. So if you'll excuse me, I'm in no mood to kiss your ass."

With that she sat down and began pulling off her gloves. Beth had always worn them, for the uncomplicated reason that they kept her hands soft. When she became the wife of a presidential candidate, and no shrinking violet, the media seized on the gloves for a convenient iron-hand-in-the-velvet-glove metaphor.

Boyce couldn't help himself watching her take them off finger by finger in an incredibly sexy Barbara Stanwyck let's-get-down-to-business way. He couldn't take his eyes off her. Men are men and fools to a man, but it amazed Boyce, seeing her this close, that Ken MacMann had needed to screw all those other women when he had this waiting for him at home, warm in his own bed at night. She was a few years younger than he, and looked perhaps a few years younger than that. She had aristocratic cheekbones and black hair with streaks of gray that made the black richer and more lustrous. Her eyes looked straight at you in an evaluating but not unfriendly way. Her figure, unmarred by childbearing, was full and handsome. If she'd been an actress, she would have gotten the part of the take-charge businesswoman who turns out to be an absolute panther in the sack. He remembered how every time he walked behind her and saw the lovely sexy sway of her bottom, his mouth went dry and his heart soared with possession.

And so here she was, twenty-five years later, in his office, a client.

"Coffee, skim milk, one sugar." She crossed a black-stockinged leg. He heard the siren song of nylon on nylon. "So how are you, Boyce?"

It now dawned on Boyce Baylor, lion of the American Bar, that in less than thirty seconds he had been reduced to the status of coffee boy—in his own lair, with a view that God would envy, amid walls hung so thickly with honorifics and photographic testimonials to his greatness, his hugeness, that the very Sheetrock cried out under the strain. No no no no. This would not do. Not do at all. He must assert control, quickly.

He buzzed for the coffee and, sitting down opposite, said, "Not so bad. Haven't been indicted for murder."

She gave him the hint of a smile.

"Why," he said, "didn't you call me sooner?"

"I was waiting to see how bad it was going to get. I thought it might not get to this point. And I didn't want to make it appear worse by hiring a lawyer."

Boyce shook his head silently, wisely. How often he had heard this.

"Anyway," she said, "here I am. On bended knee."

Boyce used this as an excuse to look at her knees.

"The reason they're bent," she said, "is from four hours in the back of a Secret Service SUV. But I could say they're bent for your sake, if you'd like."

Toying with him! Intolerable.

"You must be in a world of hurt," he said, "to come to me."

"I've been indicted for murder. That's one definition of 'world of hurt,' I suppose."

"Why me? There are lots of good lawyers who'd love to have this case."

"Boyce," she said, "if you want me to say, 'Because you're the best,' I will."

"Beth"—he smiled—"I *know* I'm the best. Don't take this the wrong way, but I'm past the point where I need your approval."

"Oh, you've done well. No question. It's why I'm here, isn't it?"

He was thinking, *You waltz in here after screwing me over and sit there with those incredible legs crossed, putting out—attitude?*

Boyce decided right there and then to take the case.

"On the way up here," she said, looking down at her lap, "somewhere between Baltimore and Wilmington, I promised myself that I was not going to apologize. Then when we got to the New Jersey Turnpike, I decided I *was* going to apologize. Then in Newark I went back to my nonapology posture."

"How'd you feel going through the Holland Tunnel?"

"Like turning around. Only that's tricky in a tunnel. Annoys the oncoming traffic."

"Well, we can talk about all that some other time."

"Maybe we should talk about it now. I think I'd rather know your state of mind going in. I don't want to find out during closing arguments that your heart wasn't really in this."

She was a canny one.

"This isn't *Casablanca*. And this"—he waved at his Wall of Ego, which still, Beth noticed, held an official framed photograph of his former father-in-law Prince Lupold of Bad Saxony-Wurtburg—"is not Rick's Café. I moved on. And I've done just fine. The truth is I got over it pretty quickly."

"I don't flatter myself that I ruined your life."

Flatter herself? That she ruined *my life? Dammit . . .*

"I have a very good life." He nodded in the direction of the Wall of Ego. "As you can see."

She looked at the wall. "I see. I . . ."

"What?"

"I did reach out to you. After we got to the White House. You didn't answer four invitations. To state dinners."

"Must have gotten lost."

Beth smiled. "Boyce, dinner invitations from the White House don't get lost."

"I may have been in the middle of a trial. When I'm trying a case, to be honest, an earthquake wouldn't register."

"Then you must have been in the middle of four trials, because we invited you four times. I was going to put you next to Princess Caroline. Knowing how you like princesses."

"She was related to my wife. Somehow. All goes back to Queen Victoria." He was mumbling.

"The protocol office said they'd never heard of anyone not answering four White House state dinner invitations. You're in the *Guinness Book of World Records*."

"One of my fathers-in-law died in the middle of the MicroDot trial, and I was so wrapped up in it that I didn't even attend the funeral."

He heard the little computer voice in the cockpit saying, *Pull up, pull up!*

"So," he said crisply, "shall we talk about my bad manners, or the case?"

"I'm not sure," said Beth, "that I've satisfied myself as to your state of mind. If you're going to handle this, I need to know that you're on board, emotionally."

Boyce snorted. "I don't deal in emotions, only motions."

"I don't believe that for a second."

"What makes you think I've decided to take this case?"

"Boyce"—Beth laughed—"whatever the situation is between us, I really can't believe that you wouldn't take this case."

She was smiling. My God, the woman was smiling in triumph.

"I mean," she continued, "the very idea of you *not* being involved in this case—they're calling it 'the Trial of the Millennium.' It doesn't make sense."

She had him, had him by the short ones. All he could do was pretend that he was the absolute lord and master of the corner that she had artfully backed him into.

He gave her his best gaze-blank-and-pitiless-as-the-sun, the one he reserved for his most withering cross-examinations. And she just stared back at him until all he could do was try not to laugh at his own helplessness.

"All right. I'll handle the case."

"Thank you."

"But I want it understood, understood without ambiguity, that I'm in charge."

"Naturally."

"Oh no. Raise your right hand and say, 'I, Beth Tyler MacMann, do solemnly swear that Boyce Baylor shall be completely, wholly, totally, and one hundred percent comprehensively in charge of my defense. So help me God, Jehovah, Allah, Buddha, Vishnu, and all and any other gods not herein specified."

"Swear."

Boyce rose, his pride assuaged. "There's a basement garage so you can avoid your fans in the media."

"Don't you want to know if I did it?"

"Obviously, you never practiced law. The *last* thing I want to know from my clients is did they do it."

Beth had the disconcerted look of the bright girl in class who had just been singled out for saying something foolish.

"I'll fly down to D.C. tomorrow morning and we start."

Chapter 3

*H*arold Farkley had long dreamed of becoming president of the United States, but thrilled as he was finally to get the job, he wished the circumstances had been different. It was one thing for a vice president to assume the mantle of greatness because of a dramatic assassination, a sniper's bullet at high noon with all the world watching. But to be the beneficiary of a marital spat gone tragically awry . . . Harold Farkley could almost hear the gods sniggering. He could certainly hear the media tittering. Tittering—hell, they were howling. Openly. Hysterically. Wetting themselves with laughter.

He looked at the newspaper on his Oval Office desk, open to the editorial pages. Harold Farkley fumed. John O. Banion—that insufferable, bow-tied prig—had written in his widely syndicated column, " 'President Farkley.' Try, if you can, to wrap your mind around that stunning oxymoron." Boiling, he read on. "Harold Farkley was the second-born in his family, went to a second-rate college, where he graduated second in his class. Thus equipped with a second-rate intellect, he went into a second-rate profession. Eventually, he clawed his way to becoming the second choice of the voters in his party. This in turn got him the number two spot on the presidential ticket. Now fate has intervened in a most bizarre fashion, for only a bizarre chain of events could have propelled a Harold Farkley to the number one position. The universe is temporarily unbalanced. Some cosmic intervention may be necessary to realign the heavens."

Oh, for the days of real executive power, when a ruler could have his opponents thrown into a dungeon.

Harold Farkley forced himself to read the rest of the column, for even a second-rate mind knew that it was prudent to know how the enemy was thinking.

Banion, a contrarian, refused to accept the charges against Beth MacMann. President MacMann, he wrote, had been the victim of "bathetic happenstance"—a pun on bathroom. The President, Banion stoutly maintained, had gone in to use the bathroom in the middle of the night, slipped, crawled back into bed, and died. The strange markings on his forehead could be explained as a "dermatological anomaly." The First Lady had been unfairly accused. That weekend, Banion had announced with customary pomposity on his new television program, *Capitol Bang,* that the government was conducting a "witch-hunt even more unseemly than the kind conducted in Salem, Massachusetts, in the 1690s."

President Harold Farkley read Banion's opinion with the impotent fury of a second-rate mind and the fervent hope that it would remain in the minority. So far, so good. His own pollster confirmed what the media were saying: Most Americans thought she had done it.

The First Lady had been controversial from the start. From the moment she set foot in the White House, she made it abundantly clear that she did not plan to "spend my days going over menus." It was a far cry from Hillary Clinton, who contented herself with taking care of her husband and giving the occasional tea for congressional wives.

Beth's declaration that she would be a substantive First Lady was met with grumbling and mutterings of "Who elected *her*?" She attended cabinet meetings, where she not only spoke up but sometimes corrected the secretary of defense or commerce on a point.

A few months into the new MacMann administration, a report appeared in *The Washington Post* about an alleged "shoving incident" involving the First Couple. The White House spokesman dismissed it as "rubbish." A few weeks after that, the President appeared at a Rose Garden event wearing a bandage on his nose. The spokesman averred that the President's wound had been the result of "walking into a door." Washington murmured that it was more likely that the door had walked into the President. In the two and a half years of the MacMann presidency, the White House spokesman had dismissed a total of seven incidents, with indignation ranging from "totally untrue" to "I have nothing further for you on that."

So on the morning that the country awoke to the news that its leader had suddenly expired in his bedroom, in the company of the First Lady, it connected the dots before noon. Even the First Lady's supporters were at pains to exculpate her. It did not help Beth when one of her staunchest allies, the head of the National Organization for Women, went on TV that afternoon to defend her and said, "If something violent occurred, I'm sure she was provoked." Thanks a lot!

When the first public opinion poll was taken, three days later, the TV screen flashed the news that nearly 70 percent of the American people thought that Beth was "implicated" in the death.

This was the thin consolation available to Harold Farkley. He was determined, in his own quiet, number two–ish sort of way, to do whatever he could to ensure that he would go down in history as the collateral beneficiary of a murder, not merely a wet bathroom floor. He lay awake at night tormented by the vision of elementary school teachers a hundred years hence asking their children, "Now what vice president became president because of a bar of soap?"

And there was this: Harold Farkley detested Beth MacMann. She had managed to inspire in a second-rate temperament a genuinely first-rate passion. He loathed her.

During the primary campaign between himself and Governor MacMann, there had come a moment when it looked as though Harold Farkley might just break through the membrane of mediocrity that had bound him for so long to the earth and become—number one. He was ahead, though by the weensiest margin. His advisers counseled, Go for it, sir! Be bold! Pull out all the stops! Do what must be done, and greatness will finally be yours!

Harold Farkley, the taste of victory meltingly on his tongue like a chocolate caramel, gave in to the zealous urgings of his handlers. Here, they said, is MacMann's Achilles' heel: his pushy wife. Their polling showed that just enough MacMann male voters were wary of her to provide Farkley with a winning margin if they came over to his side. So Harold Farkley, daring greatly if not judiciously, crossed the invisible line and—criticized his opponent's wife.

"It is not him who worries me," he said memorably and ungrammatically in his fateful speech to the Michigan autoworkers. "It's her. I think the American people have a right to know whom will be wearing the presidency's pants."

Within two hours, feminists, soccer moms, and even happily unliberated housewives were clamoring for Harold Farkley to withdraw. You just don't go after a man's *wife*. It's un-American!

And so Harold Farkley's karmic parabola, having temptingly arced toward the stratosphere of greatness, curved steeply back toward the dismal earth. Only by furious backpedaling and a massive eleventh-hour media buy did he manage to hold on to his number two status. At the party convention, Beth assented to Farkley's being named to the ticket only after her husband's advisers convinced her of the inexorable electoral math warranting his inclusion. If they were to win in November, they would need Harold Farkley's fifty-four electoral votes. Anyway, the advisers said, it would look magnanimous. American voters love magnanimity, however you spell it. Beth was the very picture of magnanimity, right up through election day. Then she took a sharp knife and quietly removed Harold Farkley's testicles.

She froze him out. And when she couldn't freeze him out, she put him next to the kitchen. At state dinners, Harold found himself seated next to the non-English-speaking wife of the finance minister of the visiting head of state. "How are you enjoying your visit to Washington?" After interminable translation, the answer came back, "She say Washington very *hot* in summer." Harold found himself dispatched to represent the United States at their funerals before the foreign dignitaries had even died. He was appointed to commissions on "uninventing government." Around Washington he became known as Vice President Whatsisname. Indeed, his name recognition dropped below 23 percent. More Americans knew the name of Canada's Prime Minister than their own Vice President's. Editorials once again surfaced in the nation's newspapers asking if the vice presidency was really necessary. A year and a half before reelection time, it was all but certain that Harold would be unceremoniously dumped in favor of a new running mate. And it was Beth who had her hand on the lever of the trapdoor.

Then—this.

The gods who had for so long laughed in Harold's face had suddenly intervened on his behalf. Here, on a silver platter, was his chance to achieve what any politician most cherishes in his heart of hearts: payback.

But it must be done subtly. Harold Farkley had learned from his disastrous attack on her. This time he would be artful.

His feud with Beth MacMann was no secret. The media were ready to pounce on President Harold Farkley at the first sign he was using the incident as an excuse to prosecute his grudge against the First Lady. Hypocrisy is a prerogative of the press but must under no circumstances be tolerated in politicians.

So when the FBI director reported directly to newly sworn-in President Farkley that there were inconsistencies in Beth's statements, when the director of the Secret Service reported to him that an argument had been heard that night by one of the agents, Harold Farkley knew that he must dare to be cautious. He was out of the country on the day she was formally indicted.

Upon his return, he went on TV to address the nation. It was all he could do to keep from tap dancing. Before his address, he practiced his expression in the bathroom mirror prior to going on television, arranging his second-rate features into a look of overdone gravity, a vaudevillian attempting Shakespeare.

He told the nation that this was, indeed, a dark hour, "not only for the country as a nation, but for me personally, as a human being."

He said he had "every confidence that justice will prevail and that Mrs. MacMann will be cleared of the awful—indeed, horrible—charge against her." Thanks, Harold.

Since her indictment, Harold Farkley had been in a covert state of bliss. He happily attended to the affairs of state—the affairs of state that were now all *his*. In his quiet moments, he tantalized himself with day-dreams of Beth weeping, begging for a presidential pardon. Of Beth sizzling in an electric chair, hooded with a noose around her neck, dropping through the trapdoor, tied to the stake, the flames reaching higher and higher and higher—

"Mr. President?"

Dammit, the way they just walked in.

"What is it?"

"It's on the news. Mrs. MacMann has hired Boyce Baylor."

Suddenly the pleasant images shattered like glass struck by a sledge-hammer. Harold Farkley heard a voice pronouncing the awful words: "We find the defendant not guilty."

Chapter 4

Normally Boyce would have flown down to Washington on his private jet, a sporty Falconetta 55 with enough range to get him to Paris for dinner. But since he would soon be impaneling a Washington, D.C., jury whose primary source of news came from television, he not only took the commercial shuttle flight, but also carried his own garment bag and briefcase. His office had called the media ahead to let them know what flight he'd be on. They were waiting for him as he stepped off the ramp, with enough light to illuminate twenty Hollywood premieres.

"Boyce!"

"Mr. Baylor!"

"Are you—"

"Will you seek—"

"Possible to—"

"Yo, Shameless, over here!"

Boyce stood in the basting glare, trying not to blink—or melt—with an appropriately grave look and waited for the insect whir and hammer click of cameras to subside. He was used to media, God knows, but this *was* a turnout. There must be over a hundred.

He gave a curt nod to indicate that the orchestra should stop tuning their instruments. The conductor was ready. The symphony was about to begin. And he had brought them a little something. He always kept them well fed.

"I'm here," he said, "to help an old friend. With respect to the charges, I have this to say. I personally admire and respect the attorney general. So I regret all the more that he decided, in the face of massive evidence to the contrary, to sacrifice an innocent widow on the altar of his own burning ambition."

The attorney general of the United States, watching in his office at the Justice Department, said to his deputy, "That asshole. That *goddamn* asshole."

"Looks like war," his deputy said.

"Finally," Boyce said, "I would ask all Americans to remember something in the days ahead. Yes, the country has lost a president. But a beloved First Lady has lost her husband."

Beth, watching from her new temporary headquarters in Cleveland Park, a few miles from the airport, muttered aloud to her TV screen, " 'Beloved'?"

"That's really all I have to say at this time. Thank you." He always said this before proceeding to take questions.

"Boyce! Were you and Beth MacMann lovers?"

"Jesus Christ," said Perri Pettengill's senior producer, "those two? Used to *do it*?"

"Um-hum." Perri nodded, continuing to watch.

"That's perfect."

"They were in law school together. She screwed him over."

"So why's he helping her?"

Perri looked at him. "Harry, it's the Trial of the Millennium. Of course he's going to represent her."

"You gotta get him on the show tonight. We gotta have him."

Boyce had told Perri he wouldn't do her show, at least for a while. "It wouldn't look right." In retaliation she told him fine, no sex. They compromised: sex and monster leaks.

"Let's save him for something big," Perri parried.

"It's *all* big," Harry said. "You've got a mass of hot air over Washington, a cold legal front coming down from New York, and media from all over the world converging. It's *The Perfect Storm* all over again. *'Perfect Storm'!* We could use that."

"Yes, Harry. That's good. Use it."

"I'll Chyron it."

Boyce had been ready for the question. He paused to give the impression that it had taken him by surprise. "The First Lady and I were at law school together. It was a long time ago." He added with nice faux self-deprecation, "You'd know it was a long time ago to look at me, maybe. Not the First Lady."

Through the plate-glass window in the airport terminal where Boyce was standing, he could see in the distance the towers of Georgetown University. A quarter century ago, he and his fellow third-year law student Beth Tyler had one night found themselves in the auditorium for their first moot court. They were so nervous they shook, and this was in the days before beta-blockers.

A rumor had been going around for days that the presiding judge would be a Bigfoot. When that day the door opened and out walked Chief Justice Henry Adolfus Wiggins of the Supreme Court of the United States, a gasp went through the standing-room-only auditorium. A month before, Wiggins had ordered the President of the United States to turn over his secret Oval Office tape recordings. That led swiftly to his historic resignation. The Georgetown Law School dean—he had clerked for Wiggins years ago—had pulled off a coup getting him to come.

Beth groaned to Boyce, sitting beside her, "We're dead."

She was to play the part of the U.S. solicitor general and argue the government's side before the Supreme Court. Boyce was her deputy. He whispered back, "He doesn't look happy."

Indeed, Chief Justice Wiggins wasn't happy, not at all happy. He'd been sandbagged by the dean, his former clerk, who had not told him until the last minute that the mock case tonight he would be presiding over would be the very same one he had so historically decided a few months ago. It bordered on impudence.

Beth and Boyce had pulled two consecutive all-nighters to prepare. They looked like extras from the movie *Night of the Living Dead*. Her argument for letting the President keep his tapes was that the Supreme Court justices lacked the proper security clearances to hear what was on them. They were armed with precedents, but now, looking at the imperious, pinched-looking Wiggins taking his seat before them, they felt a presentiment of doom. In effect, their job tonight was to persuade him that he had been wrong. And chief justices, generally, did not like to be told that they were wrong.

"Oyez, oyez, oyez," the dean intoned, grinning at his triumph. *The Washington Post* and *The New York Times* had sent reporters. "All persons having business before the honorable, the Supreme Court of the United States, present themselves."

Boyce began humming Chopin's "Marche Funèbre." Dum dum de dum *dum* de dum de dum de dum.

"Shut *up*," she hissed.

Beth stood. Justice Wiggins did not return her smile. In his robes, spectacles, and blue, bloodless lips, Justice Wiggins looked as though he were yearning to sentence everyone present to death by hanging, or preferably by some more prolonged, medieval form of execution.

Beth stood mute at the lectern. Five seconds went by, ten. Fifteen. Wiggins, accustomed to brisk kowtows and beginnings, frowned, a formidable sight.

People exchanged glances. The dean's smile vanished. The silence that descended on the auditorium had an Old Testament quality, the kind that preceded the Voice in the Whirlwind announcing, *I am the Lord God Almighty, and I am very, very wroth.*

"Your Supreme Honor—"

Off to a good start.

"With all due respect, I—we, that is, the government of the United States—do not believe that you—that the Court—has jurisdiction in this matter."

Wiggins, who had just earned himself his own chapter in the legal history of the United States for a written opinion that was being hailed as the most consequential legal ruling since Maimonides, glowered at Beth like a malevolent owl contemplating a mouse. The Wiggins Supreme Court felt that it had jurisdiction over everything, including what time the sun was allowed to rise.

Boyce felt his insides loosen, along with the cold scalp prickle that augurs calamity.

Wiggins let her continue another two and a half sentences, whereupon he assumed his accustomed role of grand inquisitor. It was merciless. It was scathing. It was so bad that no one could bear to watch. Four hundred pairs of eyes looked down. Never had the auditorium floor been so closely examined. It was so awful that finally Boyce decided there was nothing left to lose. He scribbled on an index card and slid it in front of Beth as the judge continued to blowtorch her for her abominable—no, worse, abysmal!—understanding of the Eleventh Amendment. It read:

He's wearing panty hose underneath

To keep from laughing, Beth sucked in her upper lip and bit down on it so hard that it stayed swollen for two days.

Boyce's note saved her from annihilation. Chief Justice Wiggins, who deep down was really more angry at the dean than at an intellectually frisky third-year student, saw this young woman in front of him apparently about to burst out crying and ceased his attack. He became even moderately magnanimous. He concluded by telling her that her argument was "without merit," but was without merit "in an original way." For Wiggins, this was tantamount to a compliment.

At the reception afterward, another third-year student named Kenneth Kemble MacMann, six feet four, lean, with Kennedyesque hair and soulful, hooded eyes, approached Beth to say how impressed he had been by her performance. Boyce knew him slightly. He was older than the other students. Word was he'd been to Vietnam. If you were a vet in the 1970s on an eastern college campus, it was not something you broadcast to your fellow students or teachers, who would be only too glad to accuse you of crimes against humanity.

☆ · ☆ · ☆

A few days later, Beth showed up in Boyce's dorm room with microfiche copies from *The New York Times*, *The Washington Post*, *Time*, *Newsweek*, and an official U.S. Navy publication, page after page of news stories about a navy ship called the *Santiago*.

"What's this?" he said.

"That guy, the third-year the other night we talked to—read this."

Boyce read.

The *Santiago* was a fast navy electronic surveillance vessel assigned to monitor Russian shipping in and out of Haiphong Harbor. Its captain had taken it inside the twelve-mile limit, probably on orders. A North Vietnam MiG attacked. Everyone on the bridge was killed except for Lieutenant (jg) MacMann. Wounded, he had assumed command and—as the citation that she for whatever reason had dug out of the archives put it—at great personal risk attempted to drive the *Santiago* into undisputed waters while simultaneously directing aid to the wounded and the destruction of classified materials. The *Santiago* was overtaken by North Vietnamese gunboats. Lieutenant MacMann ordered abandon ship and evacuation of the wounded but remained on board himself. While continuing to receive enemy fire, he successfully scuttled the *Santiago,* which sank to the bottom of the Gulf of Tonkin.

He was picked up by the gunboats and endured three and a half years of torture, starvation, inadequate medical care, and solitary confinement at the Hanoi Hilton. Upon his release, Lieutenant K. MacMann was awarded the Purple Heart, Distinguished Service Medal, Navy Cross, and Congressional Medal of Honor. He'd been personally decorated, in the Oval Office, by President Richard Nixon, otherwise known among the eastern academic elite as the Antichrist. (Not that the eastern academic elite believed much in Christ.)

"He's a hero, Boyce."

"Boy," Boyce said. "I'll say."

"Listen to this." She read: " 'Following Lieutenant MacMann's release by North Vietnam, he was returned to the United States and spent two months at the Naval Hospital in San Diego. Subseqently he received an honorable medical discharge from the Navy with the rank of Lieutenant Commander.'

"I wonder what the reason was," Beth said.

☆ · ☆ · ☆

The first indication that something was wrong came a few days later when from a distance Boyce saw Beth heading into Habeus Sandwich, the Georgetown Law student hangout, with Kenneth Kemble MacMann. Boyce followed them and, finding them both sitting cozily in a booth, announced himself with a "Hi." Beth appeared clearly disappointed.

"Mind if I join you?"

"Absolutely," Ken MacMann said heartily, displaying more ivory than a Steinway piano.

Beth looked even more disappointed.

They made small talk until the French fries arrived, when Boyce, feeling more and more leery, decided to plunge in.

"So Beth tells me you had to quit the navy for medical reasons."

Beth stiffened.

"Yeah," Ken said.

"Must have been serious."

"Nah. Navy regs, is all."

"So what was it?"

Beth kicked him. "He doesn't want to talk about it, Boyce."

"Just asked."

"You know what the worst part of it was?" Ken said. "Saying good-bye to those navy nurses."

"But you had to leave, is that it?"

"Boyce. Will you stop?"

"It's okay. I could have stayed in, but it would have been a desk job."

Boyce wondered if a penis was considered essential equipment for line duty aboard a navy ship.

Awkward silence descended on the table.

Ken said, "If you really want to know—"

"Oh God," Beth cut in, "seven forty-five!"

"Is the world scheduled to end?"

"I have to get back to the library."

"Well, go ahead," Boyce said. "I want to hear about Ken's wound."

Beth's eyes narrowed.

"I took a tracer round through the stomach. It kind of never fully healed."

Beth turned to Boyce. "Why don't you tell Ken about your squash injury. The one that kept you from being sent over there?"

On their way back to the library after Ken had left them, Boyce said, "You had to bring up my knee?"

"You were being a dick."

"I was trying to get you an answer to the question that clearly had been tormenting you."

"Good *night*." She peeled off.

A week before finals, Beth knocked on Boyce's door. She was flustered.

"I guess we need to talk."

"We are talking."

"Okay," she said, exhaling, "Ken's asked me to marry him."

Boyce stared. "Did you tell him you were already engaged? To me?"

"Uh-huh."

"So, then?"

"I told him yes."

"How can you be engaged to two people?"

She kissed him tenderly on the top of his head, the blow-off spot. "I'm so sorry, honey," she said. "It just happened."

"Is that supposed to make me feel better?"

Beth and Ken were married two months later, by Chief Justice Wiggins.

Chapter 5

*D*id you have to say that about the attorney general sacrificing me on the altar of his burning ambition?"

"You missed the key word," Boyce said. "Sacrificing a *widow* on the altar of his burning ambition."

"I don't think of myself as a widow."

"Start."

"But why piss him off? I bet he's ballistic by now."

"Worried he might get really mad and indict you for murder? I *want* him mad. I want them all mad. Mad people make mistakes. We need the other side to make mistakes, since you've made so many of your own so far."

"Such as?"

"Where do I start? Like talking to the FBI without counsel present. People who rob convenience stores know better."

"How would it have looked? Hiring a lawyer."

"Smart."

"Boyce, I was in shock, for heaven's sake. Have you ever woken up in bed with a dead spouse?"

"I've gone to bed with some." He sighed. "I'm frankly surprised at how you screwed this thing up."

"Is abuse included in your thousand-dollar-an-hour fee, or do you bill separately?"

"Separately, under 'photocopying, telephone, facsimile, and messenger services.' " He read the FBI report. "Why did you refuse the polygraph? It was the right thing to do, but since you did everything else wrong, I'm curious."

"It was insulting," she said hotly. "I'd just come back from burying him at Arlington. I thought it was grossly inappropriate to ask me to take a lie detector test."

"Your outrage is convincing. I almost wish we could put you on the stand."

"I want you to put me on the stand."

Boyce laughed. "Under no circumstances are you taking the stand. What's the matter with you? Have you forgotten everything you learned in law school?"

"I want to tell the truth."

"Boy, you have forgotten everything. Including the most important rule of all: The truth has no place in a court of law."

"I don't remember being taught that."

"In the real estate business it's location, location, location. In a trial, it's perception, perception, perception."

"Perception," Beth said. "Look at this." She held up the *New York Post*.

REUNITED AND IT FEELS SO GOOD!
LADY BETHMAC AND SHAMELESS BAYLOR

It was a photo of the two of them from the mock trial at Georgetown.

Boyce shrugged. "They've been calling you that for years."

Beth slammed her palm down on the conference room table. "Well, it's not pleasant."

"Look at you. And you want to take the stand? By the way, how come you didn't wipe your fingerprints off the Paul Revere silver spittoon after you hit him with it?"

"Nice try."

Boyce smiled. "Good girl. We'll use the fact that your fingerprints were all over Mr. Spittoon as evidence that you didn't murder him, since a murderer, even a moron, would have wiped her fingerprints off the murder weapon. But forget taking the stand. Or I'm on the next shuttle back to New York. I'd forgotten how uncomfortable commercial aviation is."

"Oh, spare me. Your little jet would fit in the lounge of Air Force One."

Boyce chuckled. "Why didn't you just tell the FBI that you threw the spittoon at him?"

"I panicked. I was scared. There he was in bed next to me, dead. If I'd told them what happened, it would have looked . . ."

"Like you killed him."

"But I didn't kill him, Boyce. I chucked the spittoon at him. It did hit him, on the forehead. But it wasn't *that* hard. He barely flinched. Well, he went back a bit. But he didn't fall down."

Boyce stared.

"I've thrown heavier things at him, you know."

"That'll sound good to the jury, when you take the stand. 'I've thrown heavier things at him, you know.' "

"I'm telling you, it didn't make a dent. He just called me a bitch, went to the bathroom, got into bed, turned off the light, and went to sleep. Next thing I knew, I'm having my breakfast and he's—dead."

Boyce looked at the D.C. medical examiner's report and Bethesda Naval Hospital autopsy report in front of him. "Cause of death, epidural hematoma resulting from blunt-force trauma. Time of death, between three-fifteen A.M. and five A.M. Tell me this: After you ki— After you both went to sleep, did you wake up in the night to get a drink of water? To pee? Walk the parapets? Rub the blood off your hands?"

"I slept right through. I always sleep like a rock after I've clocked him."

"Don't forget to mention that, too, to the jury, when you take the stand. This Secret Service agent, Woody Birnam, who claims to have overheard an argument between you and the decedent—"

"Why don't you just call him Ken? It's not like you didn't know him."

"Huh!"

"If you're still churning about it, I think you owe it to me to say so."

"*Owe* you?"

"Boyce, I'm going to need all of you in court. Not just all of you minus the ten percent that's still seething."

"If I were still seething and churning, why on earth would I have taken this case?"

She looked at him. "First, so that you could finally get the whip hand in this relationship."

"I always have the whip hand in the attorney-client relationship."

"Second, to show the world that you're so goddamn magnanimous, you'd defend the woman who du—who broke up with you back when."

"Magnanimity is for wusses."

"And third, in order to lose the case on purpose—in such a way that everyone would say, 'Oh, even Shameless Baylor couldn't have gotten her off,' so that I'll end up in jail or on death row. Just to get even with me."

"I cannot believe," Boyce said, affecting chagrin, "that you think that I'm capable of that. Is this what politics does to a person's soul?"

Beth laughed. "Oh dear, that's good. Look, I need to know. Are you in or out? Psychically."

So much for the whip hand. "I'm in."

"All right, then."

"For the record," Boyce said, "the decision to break off our engagement was mutual."

"Of course it was."

Dammit. There was no winning with her.

"Why were you so sure that he'd been doing push-ups with Babs in the Lincoln Bedroom?"

"The look on his face when he came in and I flicked on the light. He didn't look like he'd been in the Sit Room deploying aircraft carriers."

"His philandering, was it as bad as the rumors and reports?"

"Worse. What's so funny?"

"I was remembering how worried you were that his willy had been shot off by the Vietnamese. But if you knew he was having an affair with Van Anka, what—pray—was she doing as a guest in your house?"

"I know, I know," Beth said, defeated. "It's so—God, the *deals* you strike."

"I have to explain it to the jury. I mean, here's this hump-happy husband and you're allowing him to bring bunnies in for sleep-overs down the hall."

"I didn't invite her. I can't stand her. I don't like anything about her. Even her singing, much less her quote-unquote acting."

"So what's she doing there in Abe's bed, pumping the commander in chief?"

"It's . . . she's a star. She draws. Her husband, Max, is a huge financier, major donor to the party. They're a power couple."

"Okay, so why not have both of them over? You could do a foursome."

"Screw you, Boyce."

"Just trying to be helpful."

"We did have them both over. But neither of us really liked Max. He's a bore in that way that some financiers are. Then there was some heat in the papers about some of his business connections. Anyway, he sort of stopped coming. Babette was the friend, anyway."

"I'll say."

"She put on fund-raisers. Raised a lot of money for us."

"A jury averaging twenty-five thousand of income a year will be thrilled to hear it." Boyce studied the Secret Service log. "Jesus. She spent more nights in the Lincoln Bedroom than Lincoln. Fifty-six visits in two and a half years? Did she get miles?"

"We had an arrangement. Ken wasn't to sleep with her when I was in residence."

"This was an interesting marriage you had."

"Who are you to talk? Four marriages, the last one, to that Victoria's Secret model, lasted how long? Six months?"

"We were blissfully happy the first two months."

"Boyce, you're the Elizabeth Taylor of trial lawyers. Do not lecture *me* on how to conduct a happy marriage."

"We still have to sell it to the jury. You have an arrangement—somewhat unusual by the standards of the American presidency, you may admit. He breaks the arrangement and the next thing you know, kaboom on the noggin and they're saddling the riderless horse for the trip to Arlington. Forgive me, but we have some explaining to do for Mr. and Mrs. Jury."

"I didn't kill him. I *know* I did not kill him."

"Fine, but you whacked him with the spittoon and next morning he's Mr. Frosty. Reasonable human beings, including the FBI, the Justice Department, the attorney general, the media—"

"The media? Reasonable? Human?"

"—and, according to the latest poll, sixty-eight percent of the American public, two-thirds—think you killed him."

"Whose side are you on?"

"For a thousand dollars an hour, yours. But you want to start with the jury's worst suspicions. It's always the best baseline. Okay. So he could have slipped in the bathroom and gotten back into bed and died. But that's not much in the way of an alternate narrative. For one thing, there's the Paul Revere hallmark they found stamped on his forehead."

Boyce studied the photograph of the President's forehead. "It's kind of pronounced. We'll do some computer enhancing . . . we can probably make it look ambiguous. Get some friendly skin experts in, make it . . ." He grunted. "Maybe if we showed it upside down. . . . Well, we'll figure something out."

He tossed the photo aside and gave Beth an assessing look. "You're looking good these days."

"Thank you," Beth said in a businesslike way.

"Do you work out?"

"When I can. What does this have to do with anything?"

"Do you *exercise*? Pump iron? Treadmill? Tae-bo, whatever it's called?"

"A trainer used to come four times a week. Why?"

"Because the jury is going to be wondering if you were strong enough to lift a"—he glanced at the autopsy report—"two-hundred-and-eight-pound dead president off the floor and into bed. I see the War God put on a few pounds over the years. What do you weigh?"

"Hundred and thirty-eight."

"We start jury selection in four months. I want you down to one twenty."

"You want me to look anorexic? The media's going to see through that."

"It's not for the media. It's for the jury."

"The prosecutor will find a way to point out that I've lost weight since the incident."

"And we'll say, 'You insensitive swine, of course she's lost weight. She lost her husband. This is a grieving widow, look at her, and you're putting her through this hell.' "

"I'll lose the weight."

"Look on the bright side—you can take up smoking again. You used to love to smoke after . . . wards. The maid, this Sophie Williams, who brought you a hot breakfast while War God was cooling beside you, does she like you?"

"Like me? I suppose."

"No, no, no, do not 'suppose.' When she takes the stand, will she, a black woman, convey to a substantially black jury that you are a wonderful, kind, thoughtful employer who remembers staff birthdays and whose kid broke his arm and whose aunt just died? The sorts of things that thoughtful big people do for the little people?"

"I should think. Yes. You know, the Lady Bethmac thing was never—that was unfair. I'm not a bitch."

"Hm."

"I am *not* a bitch, Boyce. Just because I fired some people on the White House staff."

"Why'd you give them the sack?"

"In one case because the staffer was giving my husband blow jobs on Air Force One."

"He was head of state. How many did you sack?"

"Over the two and a half years? Nine."

Boyce groaned. "This is going to be such an easy sell to the jury. You didn't kill your husband, despite the fact that he was humping the guest down the hall, as well as half the employees on the federal payroll. What really happened was he got up in the middle of the night, consumed with remorse for his cheating ways, decided to commit suicide by smashing himself in the forehead with an antique spittoon, and just before dying, tucked himself back in bed. It's so obvious. We'll move for summary dismissal."

Chapter 6

$\mathcal{B}$abette Van Anka had been in the public eye for over two decades now, since her spectacular film debut in *Expensive—And Worth It,* as the suburban housewife who secretly moonlights as a prostitute to support her family after her stockbroker husband is shot by a commuter train conductor upset over the bad stock tips he had given him. At the time of the President's death, her career had been in decline. She was now getting more press coverage than she'd ever had.

Their "special relationship" had been the subject of unremitting news stories ranging from sober headlines in the *Times* (ACTRESS SPENT 56 NIGHTS IN WHITE HOUSE, subheadline "Wealthy Financier Husband Was Also a Guest—Four Times") to the more exuberant ones in the supermarket tabloids (BAB'S NIGHTS OF BLISS WITH KEN). Inside one of the tabs, someone was quoted saying, "Babette Van Anka, she's so bad you wanna spanka."

Babette lived in Bel Air, the moneyed enclave in the hills looking down on Los Angeles, with her third husband, Max Grab, the international financier. He advised a number of sultans of the oil-rich archipelagoes of Southeast Asia. He was said to have, as it is put, "ties" to influential Chinese.

The Grab–Van Anka mansion was large even by Hollywood standards. The grounds included a private hippodrome and his and hers helipads. The hippodrome had caused controversy. When their neighbors complained about their plans to blast away half of the side of one of the Hollywood Hills in order to accommodate it, there was a stink. Since Babette passionately embraced environmental causes in addition to peace in the Middle East, some delicacy was required. They hired Nick Naylor, who had once been the chief spokesman for the U.S. tobacco industry.

Naylor produced a letter from an organization that taught handicapped children to ride horses. The letter praised the Grab–Van Ankas lavishly for so generously offering them unlimited use of the new hippodrome. The enraged neighbors never regained the public relations offensive.

The blasting proceeded, the hippodrome was finished, complete with chandeliers and potpourri instead of sawdust, Max Grab having an aversion to the smell of horse by-products. Max also had an aversion to handicapped children, as it turned out. The organization was quietly presented with a check by Naylor and a note suggesting they seek other facilities. The Grab–Van Ankas were no amateurs when it came to the art of spin.

But even Nick Naylor, veteran of a hundred seemingly hopeless public relations challenges, was at a loss as to how to cope with Babette's new starring role as the President's mistress or, as one glib pundit put it, frequent guest in the Lincoln Head Room.

Max had been complaisant about his wife's relationship with the late President. His physical ardor for Babette had long since given way to the more exotic refreshments provided by Los Angeles's leading madams. He had even built a separate bungalow on the property, referred to by the household staff as "the Pump House." It had its own driveway so that Madam Vicki's pageant of international talents could come and go without having to pass a tight-lipped Babette on her way home from a grueling day of making not very good movies.

Max had found it quite pleasant to be a friend of the President of the United States. It certainly impressed his patrons overseas. But this kind of publicity was disastrous. It wasn't as though he were CEO of a cor-

poration listed on the New York Stock Exchange. Max was an entre-
preneur with "ties" to rather exotic people. Now that his wife had become notorious, he found details of his previously quiet business
dealings leading the evening news. He was not pleased by this. He was
not pleased that three dozen cameramen had permanently encamped
outside the gates of Hanging Gardens, their estate. Thank God for the
helipad. He was not pleased by the visits from the FBI, the Secret Service, and those grim-faced helots from the Justice Department. He had
hired every lawyer in Los Angeles to handle it.

☆ · ☆ · ☆

"Whatever strategy we adopt," Nick Naylor said over his untouched
lobster tarragon salad, "we need to be very consistent with the testimony that Babette will be offering on the stand."

It was a beautiful, cool, perfect sunny day in Bel Air. The garden
blazed with hibiscus and bougainvillea and jacaranda, the air thrummed
with the soft sound of procreating hummingbirds. Yet Nick, Babette,
and Max sat inside. The Grab–Van Ankas had not enjoyed an outside
meal on their patio since the tabloid television show *Crime Time* had
one day trained long-range parabolic microphones on Babette and Max
as they lunched outside, calling each other names not found inside
preprinted Valentine's Day cards.

"However," Nick continued, "we need to get our message out."

"What message?" Max said. "That she wasn't humping him?"

"Max," Babette said.

Nick pressed ahead. "I'd like to gin up some press stories about
the many other aspects of Babette. Her wonderful charity work, for
instance."

"What, with the cripples and the retards?"

"Well, among others."

"I knew that was gonna come back and bite us on the ass."

"You and Babette have been powerful forces for change in the Middle East," Nick persisted manfully. "Your donations, the hospital, your

company that generously provides Sidewinder missiles and cluster bombs to the Israeli Defense Forces at significant discounts, the prefab houses for the West Bank settlements, Babette's Concert for Peace in Jerusalem."

"Peace," Max snorted. "They threw rocks. It was a *rock* concert." He chuckled and forked avocado and lobster into his already full mouth. "That's good. Rock concert. *You* should have thought of that. You're supposed to be so good with the words."

"An international film star and singer, willing to put herself in harm's way, to bring Arab and Jew together—"

"They came together. They tried to kill each other."

"The larger point is that the concert was a milestone in"—what?— "Babette's commitment to the peace process."

"I wouldn't push the concert."

"But—"

"She wanted the concert, not the Israelis. I hadda pay that putz minister a quarter million up front, just to—"

"*Max.*"

"Forget the concert. Trust me. You don't want those vultures digging into the concert."

The sound of a helicopter rattled the French doors.

"Is that one of yours?" Nick asked.

Max wiped a glob of tarragon mayonnaise that had been on his chin for twenty minutes and with disgust hurled his napkin on the table. It was one of the few dramatic gestures left to powerful men.

"I've *had* it with these helicopter pricks. Is there no fucking privacy left in this country? I'm going to the island," Max announced.

"Island?" Nick asked.

"None of your business. None of *anyone's* business."

"It's off the coast of Panama," Babette said.

"Don't tell about the island. Jesus Christ, you tell *everything*. That's why we're in this to begin with. What do I have to do, have your tongue removed surgically?"

"Max," said Nick, "I'm not about to tell anyone about your island. But how is it going to look if you go off to an island and leave Babette to face the music?"

"*She* made the music. *She* can sleep in it."

"The Shah of Iran used to own it," Babette said. "Max bought it from the Shah. Well, the wife. After he—"

"What are you, *Architectural Digest*? Shut up."

"Max," Nick said, "isn't there some other place you could go to get away?"

"You got something against the Shah of Iran?"

"Personally, no, but—"

"Let me tell you something. I did business with the Shah of Iran for fifteen years. Tankers, oil, caviar, helicopters, army uniforms—the best uniforms in southwest Asia. Did you ever see pictures of his generals?"

Nick sighed. "They looked sensational, but—"

"The first shopping mall in Tehran? *I* built it. The Shah of Iran was an honorable man. Maybe not the brightest world leader I have met, but you could do business with him. These mullahs? Try bribing them with a bottle of whiskey. They'll cut off your hand. And this is a pity. This was a beautiful country. I had many friends. What happened to them? Tragic. I can't even talk about it."

"I've got to get myself out there," Babette said.

"To Iran? They'd eat you alive."

"On *television*. Get myself on television. It makes no sense. Connie Chung, Barbara Walters, Diane Sawyer, *begging* me for interviews. And I can't even return their calls? What sense does this make? I should go on television."

"I'd really, really wait until after the trial," Nick said.

"The lawyers said no interviews," Max said. "You're not doing interviews."

"But I wouldn't talk about the case. I would talk about the Middle East, about the Kyoto Protocols."

"You think they want to hear your views on Gaza and exhaust emissions? Would you explain to her? They wanna talk to you about *schtupping* the President."

"You've never taken me seriously."

"Did I pay for your peace concert? Do I pay for your whatever you call them, issues advisers?" Max turned to Nick. "Issues advisers she has. On my payroll. One of 'em's a dyke."

"She is *not* a dyke."

Max rolled his eyes. "Whatever. Two hundred grand a year for the three of them. Do you know what they do? They read the newspapers and write 'briefings' for her so she knows the difference between the West Bank and an ATM machine."

"I am a personal friend of Shimon Peres!"

"Wonderful. Have him over for dinner. I pay for her to go to Davos in the jet? To Davos she goes every year. To *network*. She comes back and tells me we have to do something about debt relief. To her, debt relief is me paying her bills."

"Excuse me! Excuse me if I care about global warming and hunger and peace while you're buying up golf courses in Arizona for the Sultan of Brunei."

"Where's dessert? I want dessert."

"You could never stand it that Kenneth MacMann cared about what I thought about the Middle East. He valued my input."

"Input? The only input he wanted with you was inputting his—"

"Don't talk to me. You and your escort services. Do you know what his American Express bill was last month? I saw. Twenty-eight thousand dollars. He puts it on his American Express so he gets points. How smart is that? Mr. Genius International Financier!"

At such times, Nick yearned for the simpler days of going on television to denounce the latest medical evidence that smoking was bad for you.

"Why don't I get back to you in a day or two with some concrete proposals?"

☆ · ☆ · ☆

Perri Pettengill and Boyce lay in bed in Boyce's Fifth Avenue apartment with its view of Central Park, New Jersey, Pennsylvania, California, and the Pacific Ocean. Scented candles burned on both bedside tables. She had on a cream-colored teddy, no panties, thigh-high stockings made of real silk, drops of Outrage perfume in just the right places.

Thrilled as she was that Boyce was defending Beth MacMann, Perri wondered. Beth McMann was an undeniably attractive woman. She and Boyce had been engaged. A long time ago, but still.

So tonight, after taping *Hard Gavel*, Perri had come straight back to the apartment to make sure everything was ready when he got back from Washington on the last shuttle. Dinner had been waiting, his favorite, *linguine alla vongole*, with the teeny-tiny clams, bought that morning at an ungodly hour by Fung, Boyce's butler-cook-concierge, along with a glass of crisp, chilled Orvieto. Boyce permitted himself one glass of wine a night, nothing while trying a case.

The Billie Holiday CD was on, Manhattan twinkled expensively through the window. During dinner she slipped off her shoe and stroked his ankle with a stockinged toe and made purry allusions to the waiting bed. A little squeezy-squeezy on the way into the bedroom, where the candles were already lit, the bed turned down like the Bower of Bliss, Eros' trampoline.

She popped into the dressing room to turn herself into a Vargas Girl, and as she was putting on the finishing touches, dabbing Outrage on her inner thighs, what sound did she hear coming from the bedroom? Moans of anticipation? No. The TV.

She emerged, looking hot enough to induce an erection in a three-thousand-year-old Egyptian mummy, and he's on the bed, shoes still on, flipping through the channels with the remote.

Hard Gavel came on. At least he was watching her show. That day she'd interviewed C. Boyden Gray, the very tall, distinguished Washington attorney who had been White House counsel in a previous administration. He said he was relieved that something like this hadn't happened on his watch.

Boyce flipped past her show. She couldn't believe it. He flipped until he came to *The Geraldo Rivera Show* and stopped. Geraldo. Her competition.

Geraldo's guests were Barry Strutt, Bill Howars, and Alan Crudman, an unholy trinity of trial lawyers. Each thought of himself as the best in the business.

The fourth guest, piped in via remote from Harvard Law School, was Edgar Burton Twimm, the tweedy Wise Man still waiting for some president to nominate him to the Supreme Court. He was on to provide gravitas and to shift uneasily in his seat when the other guests said something provocative.

Perri stood there, an Aphrodite in silk. And what did Boyce do? Asked her to bring him sparkling water. With ice.

This left her with a choice of going into the kitchen and inducing a collateral erection in Fung or putting on a bathrobe. She was mad enough to get completely dressed and leave. But seeing Boyce intently watching Edgar Burton Twimm interjecting thoughtful harrumphs and cautioning against "throwing out the Fourth Amendment with the bathwater," Perri wondered if he would even notice that she was gone.

They'd been seeing each other for six months now. If he was trying a case, you could pour lighter fluid on yourself and light a match and he wouldn't notice. But the trial hadn't even started yet.

Well, he was Boyce Baylor and she was television's up-and-coming law honey and he had just signed on to the Trial of the Millennium and that made him her ticket to certain stardom.

Take a deep breath. Get him his (damned) ice water.

As she turned to go, Alan Crudman spoke up. Alan Crudman, the noted San Francisco attorney, was riding high these days. He had just gotten his latest client acquitted, an NBA basketball player who after a three-day cocaine binge had driven his Lexus off a raised drawbridge over the Intracoastal Waterway, demolishing the top deck of the yacht that was passing through at the time, killing two people and maiming four others. Crudman described his client as "a terrific human being."

Crudman told Geraldo that while he, Alan Crudman, tried not to get emotionally involved with his clients, it wasn't always possible.

"How Boyce Baylor," he said, "is going to handle the fact that he was once engaged to his client and she dumped him is anyone's guess."

Perri said, "I thought you dumped her."

Boyce grunted.

William "Billable" Howars, the exuberant Memphis, Tennessee, lawyer, said that Boyce would probably make Babette Van Anka out to look like "the whore of Babylon" on the stand. This brought a soft cough and concerned interjection from Edgar Burton Twimm about the presence of television cameras in courtrooms.

Barry Strutt had won a dramatic court-ordered exhumation of President Kennedy's assassin Lee Harvey Oswald that had established finally and irrevocably, beyond a shadow of a doubt—absolutely nothing, but he was triumphant about it. He said that it would be bad strategy for Baylor to try to cast doubt on the testimony of Secret Service agent Woody Birnam, who said he had overheard the President and First Lady arguing that night. He said that a Washington, D.C., jury—the phrase was now understood to be code for "predominantly black"—tended to respect the Secret Service and wouldn't like it.

Geraldo broke for a commercial. Perri went and got the sparkling ice. Geraldo was back on by the time she returned. Boyce was snoring. She thought about pouring the ice water on his lap, then got into bed and turned the channel back to her own show.

Chapter 7

$\mathcal{B}$oyce and Beth sat together on the observer side of a one-way mirror as Boyce's team of pollsters prepped seventy people on the other side of the glass for the focus group that was about to begin.

Normally, Boyce did not invite his defendants to participate in these sessions. Often, being in jail, they were unable to participate. But Beth had asked to come. She seemed genuinely eager to hear what people thought of her.

The focus group began. Part one consisted of the pollster reading aloud a series of statements about Beth. The group pressed buttons on the consoles in front of them. The body sensors measured their sweat, breathing, and heart rates to determine the honesty of their responses. The first question was: "Do you believe that Beth MacMann killed her husband?"

Beth looked at the computer screen in front of Boyce. A bar column of lurid electronic red rose vertically. The number 88.32 appeared above it.

"Is that—"

"That," Boyce said, "is where we start."

☆ · ☆ · ☆

Three and a half hours later, after the last person had been unhooked, thanked, handed a check, and reminded that he had signed an enforceable confidentiality agreement not to reveal even that the session had taken place, Beth looked as if she had just been sentenced to death.

"I think we could both use a drink," Boyce said.

Beth nodded wanly. They went to Boyce's hotel suite.

He felt for the first time since taking the case a sense of pity for her. Large crowds used to cheer when she took the stage. Now she had just spent the afternoon listening to a majority of seventy people call her a murderess and, into the bargain, a scheming, manipulating, power-grabbing bitch. It wasn't the steely Lady Bethmac sitting across from him staring into her Scotch, but a frightened woman facing the death penalty.

"I tried to be a good First Lady. I pushed through initiatives on child care, prescription drugs for the elderly, the environment, a lot of things."

"I know," Boyce said. "The bastards ought to be grateful, instead of getting all bent out of shape just because you killed their president."

Beth gave him a horrified look.

"So shall we dispense with the self-pity and get to work?"

She nodded. "Fair enough."

"We heard some bad news today. But we also heard some good news. Many of them, at least the males in our group"—Boyce looked at the screen of his laptop computer—"think that the President and the entire government hate you. I'm *very* pleased with that."

"You are?"

"Yes. We can accomplish wonderful things with that."

"Was there any other wonderful news?"

"Two-thirds thought Babette Van Anka's last movie stank. The one where she played the Israeli female tank commander. That's excellent news. *And* you did very, very well among certain demographic groups. Males twenty-five to forty-nine want to have oral sex with you."

"Why would you *ask* such a thing? It's mortifying."

"It would be mortifying if they didn't."

"Why"—Beth blushed—"that particular category?"

"Our research indicates that ninety-seven percent of heterosexual men want to have sex with attractive women. So this tells us nothing useful. But men only want to have oral sex—to perform oral sex—on women to whom they are especially attracted. This is great news for our side."

"I don't even know how to process that information."

Boyce scrolled. "We didn't score well with pet owners. They didn't like the fact that you didn't have a dog in the White House."

"You want me to go out and buy a sheepdog?"

"We could get you a puppy, but it's kind of late. Gays liked you, especially the hard-core lesbians."

"I score well among hard-core lesbians?"

"They love you. Probably because you crushed your husband's skull with a spittoon."

"I *didn't*."

"Whatever. We'll be getting some deeper analysis on those numbers. Among the former military, we did not do well. Not at all. No surprise there, since you—since they think that you killed one of the nation's great military heroes. By the way, everyone—even the hard-core lesbians—thought you were a little dry-eyed at Arlington Cemetery during the burial."

"What was I supposed to do, start wailing and tearing my hair? Leap in with the coffin?"

"If you had called me when you should have, instead of playing Mrs. Why Do I Need a Lawyer?—"

"We've been through this."

"—I would have rubbed onion juice on your sunglasses before the funeral."

"That's awful."

"I had a client once, she blew her husband's head off with his twelve-gauge Purdey shotgun—a forty-thousand-dollar gun—in the living room, in front of guests, on the white carpet—"

"I don't want to hear this."

"Ooh, this was one *tough* cookie. Hard like a rock. Sigourney Weaver played her in the movie. She blew two holes in him the size of grapefruits, then reloaded and kept blasting. At the funeral, mascara—down to her cleavage."

"I'm not listening."

"White onion is best. Not red. We went for temporary insanity. The jury was out in under two hours. She was out of the mental hospital in less than three years. She's a tennis pro in Boca Raton. By the way, I want you in black for the trial."

"Isn't that a bit obvious?"

Boyce shrugged. "I'm not saying wear a *burqa*. Look, most women in New York wear black, and they only dream about killing their husbands."

He scrolled down.

"Now, these numbers about the late President's policies. There's stuff in here we can work with. African Americans were not happy with his last Supreme Court appointment, plus he criticized the Reverend Bones for having that love child with the head of his choir *and* deducting her on his income taxes."

"Bones called again yesterday," Beth said. "He wants to come pray with me."

"I'll bet he does. And they call me Shameless."

Boyce scrolled.

"They thought your late husband was squishy on affirmative action. You gave a speech about that, didn't you? You disagreed with him. Was that a good-cop, bad-cop routine you two worked out to keep the black vote mollified, or did you actually mean it?"

"Screw you, Boyce."

"Pardon my cynicism. I thought you and he might have other arrangements, in addition to the one about his not banging actresses when you were in residence."

"You didn't used to be like this."

"No, I didn't. I was quite trusting, actually. Then I got screwed by someone I trusted. So now I have no illusions about people. I not only expect the worst from them, I demand it. Is any White House staffer likely, on the stand—under oath—to derogate or otherwise cast doubt on the integrity of your coming out publicly against your husband on the issue of racial quotas?"

"Is that what you think of me?"

"The witness is directed to answer the question."

"No. Amazing as it may seem, I was speaking from the heart."

"It's not that often I get such principled clients."

Chapter 8

Three days before the start of jury selection, Boyce was filing his seventy-fourth pretrial motion—a personal record—this one to suppress the evidence of Beth's fingerprints on the Paul Revere spittoon on the grounds that her voluntary submission to fingerprinting by the FBI had constituted a "flagrant and unconscionable" violation of the Fourth Amendment to the Constitution, which prohibits unreasonable search. It was a long shot, but Boyce was already in his mind mapping out pretrial motion number seventy-five, on the even more daring premise that the traces of French-made hand moisturizing cream in the fingerprints would unfairly bias jurors who felt that an American First Lady should use only American-made beauty products.

The TV was on. He watched with one eye.

"Good evening," said Perri Pettengill, wearing a clingy sweater and trademark eyeglasses, "and welcome to *Hard Gavel*. My guest tonight, one of America's great trial attorneys, Alan Crudman. Welcome."

Alan Crudman was in fact a fine attorney, one of the best, yet even in his late forties he still carried on like a twelve-year-old clamoring to be acknowledged as the smartest boy in class. In law school it was said of him that he had come out of his mother's womb with his hand raised. He had gotten acquitted some of the most loathsome human beings on the planet and yet, not content to shrug and say that he had simply been upholding the purity of law and rights guaranteed by the Constitution, insisted on going an unnecessary further step and proclaiming in front of cameras that his smirking client, shoes still sticky with his victims' blood, was "totally innocent." Even colleagues who hadn't lost a minute's sleep after a lifetime career of defending the dregs of humanity shook their heads in wonder at Alan Crudman's amazing protestations on behalf of his clients. Could he really have convinced himself of their innocence? Impossible. Too smart. It had to be more complicated: he had graduated to telling the big, big lies, daring God to challenge. This fooled no one, but the media ate it up. The television talk shows loved it. It got them callers galore. And Alan Crudman was never too busy to go on television, on any show, to comment about anything at all. If the Weather Channel invited him to go on to talk about the legal implications of a low-pressure system over Nebraska, he'd be there as long as they sent a limousine for him. A short man, he demanded big vehicles.

Crudman loathed Boyce Baylor for four deeply held philosophical reasons. One, Boyce had gotten more guilty people off than he had. Two, Boyce was richer. Three, Boyce was taller and better looking. Four, Beth MacMann had chosen him over her.

He had placed a call to Beth within an hour of hearing the news that she was a suspect in her husband's death—and *she had not returned his call.* This hadn't happened to Alan Crudman in two decades. Who did she think she was? So now he despised her as well. He lay awake at night pleasuring himself with visions of the jury foreman pronouncing, "Guilty!" He saw her stunned expression, saw them drag her off. Saw her in bright orange death prison garb, struggling as they inserted the needle, shouting, "Get me Alan Crudman!"

"Thank you, Perri. Always good to be here."

Perri disliked Alan Crudman for one deeply held philosophical reason. She had invited him on one of the early episodes of *Hard Gavel* and he had treated her like a dumb blonde instead of a former assistant district attorney. At one point he'd airily informed her that she had "totally misconstrued the deeper meaning" of *Plessy* v. *Ferguson.* After the show, he had invited her to his hotel room—a lavish suite at the St. Regis

Hotel, charged to *Hard Gavel* along with the limo—for a drink. She had gone with one purpose in mind. Over drinks, she'd sat opposite him while he'd talked about his greatness, her miniskirted thighs parted just enough to provide a glimpse of the heaven within. Having brought him to a state of painful arousal, she had looked at her watch, announced she was running late, and left him to quench his ardor with any means at hand.

As *Hard Gavel*'s ratings increased, Alan Crudman's attitude toward her became less and less condescending. He now addressed her as he would a Supreme Court justice.

Perri had asked him on the show tonight because she was mad at Boyce. Boyce was refusing to feed her details about the case.

"So how do you think the defense is shaping up so far?"

"I wouldn't want to second-guess Boyce Baylor," Alan Crudman lied, "but I'm frankly surprised that he hasn't put together a top-level *team*. All he's got is associates from his own firm, most of them younger people. This is, as I don't need to tell you, going to be a very tough case. Even I would find it a tough case. And I certainly wouldn't try to do it all myself. So it's either remarkable, or daring, or both, that he seems intent on trying this case all by himself."

"You're acknowledged as being the best in the business"—she knew this would infuriate Boyce—"when you take a case of this profile—"

"Perri"—Alan Crudman smiled, not one of nature's prettier sights—"with all due respect, there has *never* in history been a case of this profile."

"—you usually partner up with other distinguished attorneys. It's not like you're saying, I can't handle this all by myself. Right?"

"Absolutely. In the J. J. Bronco case, as you'll recall, there were—what?—six of us. I, of course, was lead counsel, but I had Barry Strutt to handle the bloodstains, Lee Vermann for hair samples, Kyle Coots, who as you know is *the* authority on slash wounds—he wrote the book—so we had a good, solid team. And of course justice prevailed."

"On that, any progress in the search for the real killers?"

"I—there's—I understand he's pursuing it. But as far as the MacMann case goes, yes, I am surprised that Boyce Baylor seems determined to do it all by himself. I'm sure he has his reasons."

☆ · ☆ · ☆

Beth too was watching. She had developed a curiosity about Perri Pettengill.

Listening to Alan Crudman, whom she had loathed since he had pronounced on television that J. J. Bronco was "one hundred thousand percent not guilty" of the grisly murders, confirmed her decision not to return his call during the first days of her nightmare. Yet the lawyer in Beth was wrestling with the fact that he *was* Alan Crudman, a lawyer of great ability. Even if she discounted his palpable jealousy of Boyce, his comments did make her wonder why Boyce was so intent on going into court solo. She'd asked him why he hadn't assembled the mother of all defense teams. He'd said he didn't want to overwhelm the jury with too many expensive suits. The fourth time she'd asked, he'd gotten huffy and reminded her that he was in charge. Two possibilities lurked in her mind: one, he was playing single-combat warrior to beat the odds and win back her heart; two, he wanted to lose this case to punish her for what she'd done to him. She didn't like either scenario, though the first was preferable.

Chapter 9

If it wasn't going to be easy to impanel a jury in *United States* v. *Elizabeth MacMann,* finding a judge was presenting its own challenges. There were thirteen full-time judges on the U.S. District Court for the District of Columbia. Four had to recuse themselves because they had been appointed to the bench by the late President MacMann. Two more had to drop out because they had been appointed by the previous president, whom Ken MacMann had defeated. Another had been overheard by a caddie telling his golf partner on the seventh hole of Burning Bush Golf Club that the President "got what he had coming." The caddie sold the quote to the *National Perspirer* tabloid for $10,000. Scratch judge. Another judge had been on a panel with Boyce at the Trial Lawyers Association convention years ago and had called Boyce "the worst human being on the planet" while discussing the topic "Getting Hitler Off: Rethinking Nuremberg Defense Strategies."

The media combed through the court transcripts and biographical profiles of the remaining judges to see what nuggety chunks of mischief might be embedded in their pasts. One judge, fresh out of college, had spent a summer working for a congressman who had insisted that Beth's husband had been brainwashed in captivity and referred to him publicly as "the MacManchurian Candidate." He was out. Another had protested against the Vietnam War in which President MacMann had so valiantly fought. Out. The gavel of yet another had to be pried from his fingers after it was reported that he had gone on a blind date twenty-five years ago with Babette Van Anka, whose name then was still Gertrude Himmelfarb. By now one dyspeptic columnist at *The Washington Post* suggested it would be simpler just to take Beth out back of the courthouse and shoot her.

In the end, it came down to the one remaining judge on the bench. His name was Sylvester Umin, known to his colleagues as "Dutch." He had been appointed to the bench two months before by President Harold Farkley. Up to then, he had been a senior partner in the distinguished Washington firm of Williams Kendall, specialists in impeachment and negligence law.

Dutch Umin was in his early sixties. He had drowsy but watchful eyes and the Cheshire cat physique of a gourmet and oenophile. His vertical collection of Château Petrus made dinners at Mandamus, his Virginia mansion, memorable occasions. He collected Dutch master artwork, the source of his nickname.

He was a man of formidable intellect who had clerked for the great Potter Stewart on the Supreme Court and over the course of a distinguished career had won impressive victories for clients ranging from left-wing firebombers to cocaine-snorting major-league baseball players to international grain corporations accused of using powdered insect dung to give a popular children's breakfast cereal its distinctive crunch. But he had yet to try a single case as judge, and now by process of elimination he was—it. Overnight, he became the most famous jurist in the world. Within weeks, he would have name recognition among aborigines and Seychelles islands fishermen. He was not altogether delighted by this abrupt propulsion to celebrity. His glasses had developed a tendency to fog.

☆ · ☆ · ☆

Judge Dutch Umin's first official duty in *United States* v. *Elizabeth Mac-Mann* was to convey his dismay over the witness list that Boyce had submitted. It included 281 names, including the directors of the Secret Service and the FBI, the President of the United States, and most saucily of all, the deputy attorney general, who was prosecuting Beth. One columnist remarked that it was a wonder he had not subpoenaed Paul Revere to attest to the authenticity of the spittoon.

The atmosphere in chambers was tense. Sandra Clintick, the deputy attorney general—who had not at all hungered to have this prosecution handed to her—had taken exception to Boyce's demand that she herself testify. She was so mad that she avoided eye contact with Boyce. Never, she told the judge, had she heard of more appalling—make that atrocious—ethics. It was beyond insulting. The gloves were off, and they weren't even in court yet.

"Counselor?" Judge Dutch leaned back in his armchair, which gave off the creak of expensive leather. Knowing that the ordeal ahead would tax all his reserves, he had resolved to be as laconic as possible, even to the point of Zen.

"Your Honor," Boyce said, smiling, as if he were presenting the most reasonable proposition since Newton's last law, "one of the foundations of our defense will be that this prosecution, *ab initio*"—he turned to the deputy AG—"sorry, 'from the beginning'—"

"I know what it means."

"It's Latin."

"I know that."

"I wasn't sure they still taught Latin when you—"

"Your honor."

"*Counsel.*"

"A significant part of our defense, Your Honor, will be that Madame Deputy Attorney General here—"

"The name is Clintick. I don't work in a whorehouse."

Boyce snorted. "I'd say *that's* a matter of opinion."

"Your *Honor.*"

"Counsel."

"We will establish that Mad—that the deputy attorney general is merely the smallest cog in a larger government conspiracy machine to bring murder charges against the former First Lady to further their own political agendas. Their evidence is disgraceful. Worse than disgraceful. I will annihilate it. Having done that, I will show by direct and cross-examination that Ms. Clintick conspired, along with other officers of government, to crucify Elizabeth MacMann on the altar of their own ambition. I understand, Your Honor, that this is a foul charge. I use it reluctantly, having no other recourse." When Boyce got going, his language became florid in a nineteenth-century sort of way.

Judge Umin tried not to smile. He concentrated on thinking about the crippling price he had just paid for his latest acquisition, a still life of a pear and eel by Govingus Koekkoek (1606–1647).

"I won't sit here and listen to this," said the deputy AG. "I will certainly not sit in court and listen to it."

Judge Dutch creaked in his chair. "Why don't I decide what we'll do in court?"

"Of course, Your Honor. I meant . . ."

Bingo. Boyce always tried to rattle them before going into court, to see where their stress points were. This one's stood out like rivets.

"I'm hard-pressed to think of a precedent," Judge Dutch said.

"I can't think of a precedent, either," Boyce interjected. "The executive branch conspiring with directors of the nation's top security and law enforcement agencies to frame the widowed wife of a president in order to conceal their own rank animosities and evil designs—"

"Steady, Counselor."

"I apologize, Judge. I forgot myself. But I feel myself stirred."

"Give me something concrete, not a Patrick Henry speech."

Boyce handed him a loose-leaf binder full of press clippings highlighted in bright colors, neatly tabbed.

"As you know, Mrs. MacMann was no passive First Lady. She did not confine herself to serving tea to other wives and organizing Easter egg rolls on the White House lawn for the children of . . . cabinet officers."

The attorney general, father of five, had been conspicuous with his brood at the recent White House Easter egg roll.

Boyce continued. "Beth MacMann was the most substantive First

Lady in our history. This did not sit well with some. On occasion, as the documents in that binder will show, Mrs. MacMann was vocally, if always cautiously, critical of the FBI and the Secret Service. The former for what she viewed as incompetence for hiring a man with the middle name of Vladimir to head up its counterintelligence operations. The latter for its hiring practices, which she viewed as discriminatory. We will contend that these two agencies, which played so critical a role in her being dragged by the hair to the dock, were predisposed to exact revenge on her by concocting the evidence against her."

"Evidence, Counsel, evidence. These are press clippings."

"With all respect, you're putting my client in a classic Catch-22 position. She cannot produce evidence without putting her accusers on the stand, yet you will not permit her to put them on the stand without first presenting evidence."

"I'll consider it. But for your client's sake, I wouldn't put all your eggs in that basket. As for calling the President to testify, visualize a snowball. Now visualize the same snowball in hell."

Boyce smiled. "I am at the mercy of Your Honor's wise and learned judgment."

Chapter 10

There are few spectacles more pathetic than a roomful of otherwise responsible people trying to squirm out of a civic duty enshrined in Magna Carta as one of the signal boons of democracy. On the other hand, who in his right mind wants to serve on a jury?

Impaneling a jury for *United States* v. *Elizabeth MacMann* was more daunting. When the prospective jurors entered Judge Umin's courtroom with the downcast shuffle of the damned, most of them took one look at the judge, Boyce, and the deputy attorney general and uttered the same silent cry: *Oh God, no—not* that *case!*

Boyce and his jury consultant studied their faces intently. It was easy enough to spot the ones who were horrified at the thought of spending the next year in some ghastly motel with seventeen of their "peers."

Others positively radiated delight, either at the thought of becoming part of history, or at the prospect of all those lucrative book deals. *Juror Number Five: My Story.* Film rights to Warner Brothers for seven figures. A top New York publisher had been quoted in the *Times* saying that a book by the first juror to be dismissed would fetch at least $1 million. But a juror who held out against the other jurors, either for or against conviction—*that* juror, the publisher said, could go start pouring the concrete for that dream house.

"This is a capital murder case," the judge began on the first day of jury selection. "Capital means that conviction carries a potential penalty of death. Normally a case like this could take months to try." Groans came from men and women in expensive suits who looked as if they measured their time in minutes. "But this is not a normal case, so it is difficult to predict. It could take up to one year. It could take more. Especially"—he glanced sideways at Boyce—"since an extensive witness list has been submitted by the defense." Gasps, groans, chests were clutched, bottles of nitroglycerin tablets rattled.

Boyce and his jury consultant watched the faces of the jury pool. Boyce's jury consultant was a man named Pinkut Vlonko. Before going into the lucrative business of advising trial lawyers on jury selection, "Pinky" Vlonko had been for over twenty years the CIA's top psychological profiler. His job was to figure out which of the CIA's top people were most likely to be selling secrets to the Russians or Chinese; also, to determine whether Saddam Hussein was technically a malignant narcissist or simply a fruitcake. Pinky had worked with Boyce on many cases. Between them, they had the best juror "radar" in the business. Boyce was fascinated by psychology. After being dumped by Beth, he had taken a master's degree in applied psychology.

The two of them had prepared a juror's questionnaire extensive even by their standards. It consisted of eight hundred questions. Number 11: Did you vote for President MacMann? Number 636: Are you regular at bowel movements? During his years at the CIA, Pinky had discovered that defectors and moles—switchers of allegiance—tended to be constipated.

The questionnaire had occasioned another heated session in Judge Dutch's chambers. Ms. Clintick, the DAG, had pronounced it an abomination. Boyce had thereupon produced a questionnaire used by the attorney general's own pollster when he had run unsuccessfully for governor years ago. It was 120 questions long. He'd waved it in the DAG's face. A compromise was struck. Boyce's questionnaire was trimmed to 650 questions. This was more or less the number of questions he and Pinky wanted to begin with. Boyce's rule since childhood had always been, Ask for a lot more than you need so that you end up with what you want.

Boyce's amiable but relentless grilling of the jurors, carried live on TV—Judge Dutch had decided it would be more complicated not to allow cameras in the court—led one pundit to venture that the only jury Boyce would be satisfied with would be one consisting of blind deaf-mutes with an IQ of 75. Not at all, Boyce countered cheerfully. All he wanted was "a level playing field." Was it unreasonable to seek out jurors whose minds had not been "hopelessly polluted by the daily diet of deplorable lies, innuendos, and vilification manufactured by the government's agents of smear and malediction"? If finding an unbiased jury required a little patience, who could object?

A "little patience" ended up taking four months.

Chapter 11

*Y*ou should have been there," Boyce said. "I thought he was going to stab me with a Dutch letter opener. This is going to be fun."

"I'm glad you're enjoying yourself," Beth said.

Boyce put his hand on hers. "I'm just trying to get *you* to relax."

Beth looked anything but relaxed. She'd lost the weight Boyce had ordered her to shed. Her cheekbones were more prominent now, and the eyes had the darty intensity of someone dreaming of deep-crumb coffee cake. Looking at her, Boyce suddenly felt guilty. He wanted to pull the motorcade over and rush in and get her a chocolate milkshake.

"You okay, kiddo?"

"Fine."

"You look great, for someone who hasn't eaten in six months." The beauty magazines had tracked Beth's change in physical appearance. *Vogue* had done an article entitled "Diet of the Millennium." It quoted a leading Hollywood "aesthetic consultant"—formerly "makeup man"— saying, "If this is what killing your husband can do for you, then more women ought to considering clubbing their husbands to death."

Vanity Fair magazine pined, "If only Natalie Wood were still alive to play her in the movie. That limpid sexuality, the steel hidden beneath the puddly dark eyes, the tragic glamour."

Variety reported that Catherine Zeta-Jones was "desperate" to play Beth in the movie. Further, that Joe Eszterhas, the dramatically hirsute and extravagantly compensated screenwriter, was holed up in a bungalow on Maui pounding out draft number seven of his script, entitled *Spittoon*.

All this Boyce had tried to keep from Beth. He needed her focused. She rolled down the window.

"Ma'am," said Hickok, the Secret Service agent in the front passenger seat. Hickok was jumpy these days. The death threats had been increasing.

Beth ignored him. The air was June—humid and sweet with moldering blossoms. She'd been a virtual prisoner since last fall in the house in Cleveland Park, under permanent surveillance by a press camp that never dropped below fifty people, even during the Christmas holidays. The house, built by a friend of George Washington, had the happy name of Rosedale but had been renamed Glamis by a pundit, after the castle in *Macbeth*.

Beth left the window down. She'd be damned if they'd deprive her of a few gulps of fresh air on her way to be tried.

They drove along Pennsylvania Avenue to the United States District Court for the District of Columbia at Third and Constitution. She thought of the January day three years before when she and her husband, freshly sworn in as President, had walked past the spot, waving to cheering crowds. Normally this would be enough to make a couple happy. Not the MacManns. The night before, at Blair House, Beth picked up the phone to make a call and heard her husband on the line talking to a well-known society woman in New York, the trophy wife of a billionaire. They were making plans for an afternoon hump at his New York hotel while Beth was across town at the United Nations, addressing a conference on the role of women in the new millennium. She reflected that the role of women in the new millennium seemed to resemble the role of women in the last millennium: on the wrong end of the screwing.

She put down the phone, went into the next room, picked up a lamp, and was about to conk him with it when a vision made her stop—the vision of herself twelve hours later holding the Bible as Ken took the oath of office, looking at him adoringly, his head wrapped in a bandage. She put the lamp down. And Ken smirked. If she was dry-eyed at his funeral, she was drier still at his swearing-in.

Now the motorcade pulled up in front of the courthouse. This was Boyce's idea.

"Okay," he said, "remember, we're going to walk in there like we own the place. By the time we're through with these jerks, they'll be the ones on trial."

Boyce didn't quite believe this, but going into court was like taking the field in a game. You had to pump up your players. You had to pump yourself up.

There were so many satellite trucks, it looked like a NASA tracking station. It was a scene. Media, cops, and demonstrators with signs— ASSASSIN!, FRY THE BITCH!, FREE BETH!

She was wearing a black pantsuit copied from one of the leading designers, with enough changes so that the media wouldn't be able to say that she had looked "stunning in Armani." Half a dozen designers had called Boyce offering to dress her for the trial. Boyce had turned them all down. What's more, he'd informed the media that he had. On the first day of her trial, Beth looked stylish but sober: a smart-looking woman in her early forties on her way to a business meeting. The white blouse, Boyce joked to her, symbolized her innocence. It was open enough to draw the eyes of the male jurors without offending the women. The string of pearls had been a gift from Ken, bought by his secretary when he forgot her birthday.

"Okay, here we go," he said. "Got your mantra ready?"

She gave him a tight smile. The mantra, devised by Boyce, was "When we walk in, there'll be one single thought in your head: *I have come to accept their apology.*"

That night, after the first day of the Trial of the Millennium, her entrance into the court was shown on an estimated 72 percent of the world's television sets. Her swanlike serenity, amid a clamor that would have rattled a professional wrestler, was widely commented upon.

☆ · ☆ · ☆

Boyce was cheered by DAG Clintick's opening statement. She delivered it in an earnest more-in-sorrow-than-in-anger tone. He was so delighted that he decided to break his rule and depart—slightly—from his own memorized fifteen-thousand-word opening statement.

The essence of the United States's case against Elizabeth Tyler MacMann, Ms. Clintick averred, was straightforward: The President was found dead in his own bedroom. The autopsy established time of death between 3:15 and 5:00 A.M., and that death had resulted from an epidural hematoma caused by blunt-force trauma to the skull five centimeters above the right eyebrow. Photographic enlargement of the bruise revealed the distinctive imprint of the hallmark of an antique Paul Revere silver spittoon. The spittoon, used as a wastebasket, was found not in its usual place in the bedroom, by the First Lady's side of the king-size bed, but by the door, on its side. The jury would hear testimony from a Secret Service agent who would testify that he had heard a violent argument coming from the presidential bedroom between 2:10 and 2:20 A.M. They would hear from numerous people who had attended the state dinner that night that the President had been in fine spirits and health, no bruise or Paul Revere hallmark on his forehead. An overnight guest in the White House would testify that she said good night to an unbruised President at 12:30 A.M. They would hear testimony from numerous friends and associates of the First Couple as to the turbulence of their marital relations.

When all this evidence was presented, the jury would have no choice but to conclude, beyond a reasonable doubt, that Beth MacMann had callously and cold-bloodedly murdered her husband as he slept, in their own bed. A husband who, as it happened, was President of the United States of America. They would therefore have no choice but to find her guilty not only of murder in the first degree, but of assassination, the gravest crime in the land. This litany of villainy took slightly under two hours to deliver.

☆ · ☆ · ☆

Boyce rose, buttoned his jacket, and walked toward the jury box. He rested his hand on the edge of it as he walked from one end of it to the far end, as if it were a banister. He had learned this from Edward Bennett Williams, the great trial attorney: Show them you're not afraid of them, show them you're comfortable everywhere in the courtroom, show them it's *your* courtroom.

He turned, faced them, and said in a quiet but commanding voice, "Good morning." His jury consultant, Vlonko, noted that eight out of eighteen returned his greeting. Resting one elbow on the jury box, he began. No podium, no notes—unlike the DAG. He then launched into his imitation of a lawyer speaking from the heart, one of the great dramatic roles.

"Ladies and gentlemen, that was a pretty good speech you just heard by the deputy attorney general. She was, as you know, appointed to her office, a sacred trust, by her boss, the attorney general, who got his job from Mrs. MacMann's late husband. She and her superior, the attorney general of the United States, seem to have held on to their jobs, despite the change in administration." Pause. "That is unusual. But not irrelevant to this case. It is also highly unusual for a deputy attorney general of the United States to personally prosecute a case. Extremely so. One might ask, *Why* is she prosecuting this case, when she could be doing what a deputy attorney general does? Namely, keeping the nation safe. Working on behalf of those whose civil liberties have been violated? On behalf of those whose livelihoods are threatened by giant monopolies? On behalf of those who are persecuted for the color of their skin, for their sexual orientation—"

"Objection."

"Proceed, Counsel."

"Now, ambition in itself is not a bad thing. All of us, all of you, have ambitions. To move up in the world. To earn the respect of your fellow citizens, to save money to send your children to college—"

In the press section, heads turned. Someone said, *"Oy."* There's no more suspicious sound than that of a lawyer proclaiming the decency of his fellow man.

"—to make better lives for ourselves. That is ambition, and there's nothing wrong with it." Pause. "But . . . *but* when ambition consists of exploiting a tragedy and the misery of a widow"—this would be the first of 1,723 mentions by Boyce of the word *widow* during the trial—"in the service of a conspiracy by the same government whose sworn duty it is to protect us, then, ladies and gentlemen, decency shudders, honor flees, and darkness has surely descended upon the land."

The deputy AG rose. "Your Honor, this is intolerable."

"This is a court, Mr. Baylor, not a church."

"Well, there I agree with the deputy attorney general. I agree that it is intolerable that a woman who has dedicated her life to public service, to feeding the poor and underprivileged, caring for the elderly, seeing to it that working men and women have jobs and portable health care—while also making sure that business and entrepreneurs are not over-taxed and over-regulated by government"—a little something for the Republicans on the jury—"I agree that it is intolerable that such a woman be vilified and unjustly charged with a heinous act." Pause. "Simply because she dared to speak out against injustice and wrong-doing. Yes, I would say that the deputy attorney general has it exactly right. It *is* intolerable. And after the facts have been presented, you too will find it so. This case is designated *United States* versus *Elizabeth MacMann*. Well, that's about the size of it. The government, the entire United States government . . . versus one single woman."

Boyce walked slowly over to the defense table and stood near Beth. She hadn't quite anticipated a *J'accuse!* of this amperage. She tried to conceal her embarrassment by staring blankly at the table.

Having placed himself next to the Widow MacMann, Boyce continued.

"There is a philosophical principle called Occam's razor. It goes like this: Never accept a complicated explanation where a simple one will do. Smart man, Mr. Occam. The prosecution—the government—would have you believe that the explanation for President MacMann's demise is more complicated than landing a person on the moon. They will bring in charts, timelines, computer-enhanced photographs, to convince you of a scenario so wild, so convoluted, so unbelievable, that to process it, to take it all in, would require the intellectual capacity of an Albert Einstein or Martin Luther King. You recall that the judge here explained to you during voir dire that this case might take some time to try?" Boyce chuckled. "Well, brace yourself, ladies and gentlemen, because it might just take *years* for the deputy attorney general to convince you of the preposterous scenario upon which her case depends."

Boyce sighed deeply at the monstrous injustice of it all. He aimed his next burst of rhetorical flatulence at the heavens beyond the ceiling, where surely God and His archangels were listening, sharpening their swords of righteousness.

"Be prepared for arguments that would make Jesus weep and Einstein's head spin. Be prepared to hear that a mark on the late President's forehead was put there . . . by Paul Revere."

The correspondent for *The New Yorker* magazine leaned over and whispered to the *Vanity Fair* reporter, "I love this guy."

"That's right," Boyce continued. "Paul Revere's silversmith mark. Supposedly from a spittoon Mr. Revere made about the time of the American Revolution. Well, sit back and get comfortable. They're going to bring in photographic blowups of a tiny spot on the President's forehead. Experts—that is, they call themselves experts—with expensive, government-supplied laser pointers, will point at these photographs like they were aerial reconnaissance maps of Afghanistan. They'll say, 'See this teeny-tiny part here? We know it's hard to see, but that's Paul Revere's initials on the President's skull. Can't you see that? Are you *blind*? Why, any *fool* could see it!' Well, ladies and gentlemen, that's exactly what the government thinks of you—fools. To be manipulated! Um-*hum*."

Jurors seven and nine were nodding along as if it were a Baptist sermon. *Say it, brother!*

Boyce shook his head bitterly in wonder. The next words exploded from his mouth with such force that the front row of jurors recoiled.

"A *spittoon!*"

The stenographer started.

"The so-called murder weapon. An antiquated device going back to the days when men chewed tobacco. How fitting, ladies and gentlemen, that the government's chief piece of evidence should be a receptacle . . . for *spit.*"

The *New York Post* headline the next day was:

SHAMELESS: I SPIT ON YOUR EVIDENCE!

"Ladies and gentlemen, you will learn that there is a far, far simpler explanation for the President's unfortunate and untimely demise than that his devoted wife of twenty-five years awoke out of a deep sleep in the middle of the night and seized a historic antique—she, a lover and respecter of antiques, you'll hear testimony to that—crushed his skull, then went back to sleep, woke up, and cheerfully ordered breakfast in bed, with the corpse still cooling. The simple truth is . . ." His voice dropped.

Reporters, jurors leaned forward in their seats.

"Accidents happen."

Boyce turned directly to the jury, his back to the rest of the court and the world, as if this weighty matter were just between them.

"Planes crash. Cars crash. People fall down stairs, slip in bathrooms. Who among us—who among you—has not felt a wet foot go out from under us—"

Boyce pitched forward, grabbing the jury box rail.

"—and caught ourselves in the nick of time? Has that ever happened to you?"

"Objection."

"Sustained."

But three jurors were already nodding at him. To hell with the prosecutor and the judge. This was between them!

"Who among us, saving ourselves from snapping our necks or going down with our head on the tiles, has not felt a vast *wave* of relief and gratitude and thought, *Whew! Thank you, Lord! That was a close one!*"

Boyce walked over to the prosecution's table, where the deputy AG and her team sat, glaring at him. Boyce loved to end his opening statements here, in their territory, in their faces.

"A death by happenstance, by accident, is no less tragic, perhaps, than any other kind of death. But"—withering glance at the prosecution—"it is *not* murder. It is *not* assassination. And it is *no* excuse—none!—to charge horrendous deeds to a woman whose only crime, if you want to call it that, was to have loved her husband too deeply, and too well."

He'd timed it to the minute. It was 4:43 P.M. Judge Umin had announced at the outset that he would adjourn every day at 4:45. His opening statement would marinate in the jury's minds all night, barbecue sauce seeping into meat.

Boyce sat down and bowed his head prayerfully, as if he had just taken Communion.

Chapter 12

You know what they're going to call it, don't you?" Beth said in the car on their way to the post-trial conference in Boyce's hotel suite. "The 'shit happens' defense. You've staked my life on a wet bathroom floor."

Boyce was pumped. Oxygen was roaring to his brain, as if he'd just run five miles. Oh, the poor mortals, the nonlitigators, the timid souls who would never in their lives know this feeling, the thrill of owning a courtroom. A symphony orchestra conductor, a stage actor, a tenor, a great orator, an athlete at his or her peak—they knew something of it. But their stakes were relatively trivial: art, a home run, a moment of up-lift for the paying audience. This—this was life or death! This was the Colosseum. He was floating in endorphin soup. All was well with the world. He was in a state of grace. This was going to be his greatest triumph ever, the crown in a shimmery career. He even forgot about his secret plan to lose.

He looked at Beth, and she looked pumped, too, for the first time since this had all begun. He was seized with the urge to kiss her. No. Not yet, and anyway, not in the car with Agent Hickok up front. Boyce wondered about the agents.

She had a large detail—a dozen. Athletes with Uzis. Were they spying on them? He wondered. They were professionals and honorable. But in a few days they were going to hate Boyce's—and her—guts so badly, their trigger fingers would itch like bad cases of poison ivy. The temptation to fight back would be hard to resist.

Watching the back of Hickok's head, Boyce felt a pang of regret. It would pass. He had read that Ulysses Grant, commander of the Union Army during the Civil War, would stay in his tent during the ghastly battles lest the sight of all that ground-drenching blood soften his resolve. Boyce had learned that if you were going to win, win at whatever cost, you had to reach inside your head and flip the on/off switch on the conscience console. And look what you saved on electricity.

His three connecting suites at the Jefferson Hotel, once owned by his idol, Edward Bennett Williams, had been transformed into a command post. One room was full of television screens and young associates monitoring the media. A section of the room had been turned into a remote TV studio so that Boyce could comment live, if need be, at a moment's notice. Another room had been converted into a fitness and meditation center, complete with exercise machines and a boxing bag. During a trial, Boyce liked to hang upside down by his ankles and with boxing gloves beat a hundred-pound bag full of sand. Marvelous for the circulation and wind. There was a massage table, meditation mat, juicer, and oxygen tanks. When Boyce had turned forty-five he'd noticed that it was taking him eleven minutes instead of ten to do London's *Sunday Times* crossword puzzle. Suspecting diminished mental capacity, he had submitted himself to a battery of neurologists and cognitive and memory experts. They'd found no slowing down but suggested that he inhale pure oxygen for ten minutes a day. He went them one better. During trials, Boyce slept with an O_2 tube in his nose. At home in New York, this impeded amorous relations with Perri, who during the wakeful wee hours liked a bit of spontaneous num-nums.

Another room, fitted with special locks and a 24/7 armed guard, was designated GZ (ground zero). This, Boyce confided to Beth, was mostly to psych out the prosecution. Since the thrust of his defense was that Beth was the victim of an insidious conspiracy, Boyce put out the word to his "friendlies" in the media that he was concerned about spying. He told them that he had the GZ "swept" for electronic bugs twice a week. He'd contemplated installing retinal scanners at the door to admit only those whose ocular profiles had been programmed, but in the end he'd balked at the cost.

Boyce wasn't so paranoid as to think that the government was tunneling under the Jefferson to spike his computers, but he did not want them learning about JRTRE, or "Jeeter." This was the juror real-time response evaluator. No one outside a very small circle knew about JRTRE. It was something he'd devised with input from the excellent Vlonko. Every day in court, Vlonko and an assistant intently watched the faces and body language of the eighteen jurors. They entered their individual responses into laptop computers, which also generated a real-time transcript using voice-recognition software. Responses included FAVORABLE, UNFAVORABLE, AMUSED, ANNOYED, BORED, NODDING, ASLEEP, RESTLESS, ANGRY, INTENT, SMILE, SCOWL, LAUGH, CRY, HAPPY, AROUSED, RAPID BREATHING, HEART ATTACK, and forty-five other conditions experienced by jurors. Among them was GET ME OUT OF HERE.

At the end of each day of the trial, Boyce had a real-time log of each juror's apparent response to every second of the proceedings. Correlating all this raw human data with the biographical information on each juror required a team of eight analysts working through the night in shifts. But by the morning, Boyce went into court with a printout that told him which jurors he needed to concentrate on that day—and what they wanted to hear from him. Simple, really. It amused Boyce that none of his chest-thumping peers had thought of it. It did rather add to the cost of a trial, but he'd figure out a way to bill it to one of his corporate clients.

"How'd we do?" he asked Vlonko.

"Fucking better than expected." Years of debriefing Russian defectors had left Vlonko, himself a naturalized Hungarian, with the tic of inserting the f-word in otherwise prosaic sentences. Apparently, the f-word relaxed Russian defectors. "Jurors two, six, seven, nine, and ten through thirteen were wetting themselves during your finish. One and five were sphinxy, but"—he hit keys on his laptop—"aha, yes, I was not incorrectly remembering: Number one is one-quarter Scottish, and five liked to play chicken on railroad tracks as a child, so they wouldn't give us a reaction if you took out your cock and banged it on the defense table."

"I'm saving that for closing statements. Keep your eye on those two. How'd we do with fourteen? Thought she looked uncomfortable when I hit the spittoon line."

Vlonko called up number fourteen's biography on his screen. "Fucking straight. Father died of emphysema. She probably has the unpleasant associations with tobacco and spit."

"Make a note of that in tomorrow's brief, would you?"

Boyce cursed himself. Of *course,* juror fourteen's father had died of emphysema. Idiot! How could he have forgotten?

Frowning, one of his associates approached with a piece of paper.

Boyce read it.

"God-*dammit!*" he bellowed.

"What?" Beth said anxiously.

"We're estimating that the trial will go to the jury in two hundred and eleven days. And the goddamn moon will be full in two hundred and eleven goddamn days."

He said to his team, "We're going to have to stall. File some more motions."

"You gave me a heart attack," Beth said. "What's the problem? Are some of the jurors werewolves?"

"The last time one of my juries deliberated under a full moon, do you know what happened? I *lost.*"

"Is this a superstitious thing?"

"A full moon affects moods, Beth," he said crossly. "Gravitational forces are altered. Water is redistributed. Do you want your fate decided by twelve human beings whose *water* has been redistributed?"

"I hadn't factored that in."

"Well, that's your luxury, isn't it? I *do* have to factor 'that' in."

Boyce turned to an assistant. "Find out from Vlonko if he has data on the menstrual cycles of jurors two, eight, ten, and fourteen. Do they co-incide with the lunar cycles?"

The aide scurried off.

Boyce said to Beth, "Would you *poll* during a full moon?" He scowled and stormed off to his exercise room to beat his sandbag.

Beth said to an aide, "Is he always like this during a trial?"

"He hates to lose."

☆ · ☆ · ☆

Babette was alone in Hanging Gardens—that is, not counting the seven servants.

Max had made good on his threat to decamp and was ensconced on his island off the coast of Panama, deep-sea fishing and cornering the world's market in a mineral that was going to be on the cover of *Time* magazine in two weeks because of an about-to-be-released study showing that it might retard Parkinson's disease. His huffy departure aboard his private jet from the Burbank airport had been recorded in all its glory by half a dozen telephoto lenses and splashed across the front pages under headlines like MAD MAX and MAX: I'M OUTTA HERE!

Nick Naylor, now working more than full-time as the Grab–Van Anka PR man, had done what he could to spin Max's abrupt departure as an "environmental excursion" during which his client "hoped to experience some of the thrilling marine life of the San Blas islands." He left out the part about hooking the marine life and reeling it aboard so that Manolo could club it to death and serve it to him for dinner with lime juice and shaved coconut.

Nick had been working hard of late. When not trying to spin Max to the media as successor to Jacques Cousteau, he'd been acting as an ad hoc record producer—yet another new role for him—trying to put together a music album showcasing Babette's lifelong commitment to Middle East peace, working title "Babette Does Jerusalem." A better title might have been "Mother of All Headaches."

Babette was a wreck. She hadn't been out of bed since the visit to the deputy attorney general's office. A nightmare. Up until then, they had been pleasant, these people. Then suddenly comes this summons— that's right, summons—to come to Washington—the next day. Not "Oh, Ms. Van Anka, so sorry to bother you, would you mind terribly popping in at your convenience, and by the way, we *love* your work," but "We will expect you in our office at ten A.M. on Tuesday." The cheek of these people. Ken MacMann would have fired them all.

She showed up all right, with not one, not two, but three lawyers. Of course she was there to cooperate in any way. That ice queen deputy attorney general prosecutor, without even asking if she'd like a cup of coffee, began the grilling. Do you stand by your statements to the FBI agents the morning the President was found dead? Excuse me, for this I flew three thousand miles? To be insulted? You could have asked me this over the phone. Do you stand by your statement, Ms. Van Anka? *Yes.* You told them you said good night to the President around twelve-thirty. If that's what I said. That is what you said. Excuse me, am *I* on trial here? Silence. Morris, Howard, Ben, explain to the deputy attorney general.

Ms. Van Anka, you told the FBI agents that you went to bed at twelve-thirty. Is this a correct statement? That's what I said. I watched some television and fell asleep, I wake up, the President is dead and now *I'm* on trial. What is this, *Gaslight*?

Ms. Van Anka, were you and the President on intimate terms?

Intimate terms? Do you mean did he *confide* in me? Did I confide in him? Did he rely on me for input about the problem of the Middle—

Ms. Van Anka, were you and the President intimate physically? Did you have a sexual relationship?

What kind of question is that?

A direct question, Ms. Van Anka.

Who do you think you are, the *National Perspirer*? That's a grossly invasive question. And you, a woman, asking it. Because I enjoyed a warm relationship with the President, you assume he was interested in my body. It's an insult. Talk to my lawyers. Take your pick, I have three. And I can get more. We have nothing but lawyers in L.A. Next time I'll charter a 747 and fill it with lawyers. Don't think I wouldn't. Money is not an issue with us.

Ms. Van Anka, we have to ask these questions. If you testify at this trial, you will be cross-examined. You'll be cross-examined about the statement you gave to the FBI agents that morning. Moreover, you will be cross-examined by Boyce Baylor, Mrs. MacMann's attorney. You've heard of him? He will ask you these questions and many other questions. Your lawyers here know that.

So, why do I have to testify, anyway? I didn't *see* her clop him on the head with the spittoon. I'm not a witness. Why do you even need to involve me in this?

Because, Ms. Van Anka, you were a guest in the White House the night the President died. You were one of the last people to see him alive. If we don't put you on the stand, it would be tantamount to saying that we don't believe the testimony that you gave to the agents. And Mr. Baylor will call you as a witness. And if there are inconsistencies, any little holes in your original statement, he will drive trucks through them, Ms. Van Anka. Eighteen-wheelers.

I do not understand. You've got the murder weapon, the Secret Service man heard the shouting, you've got her fingerprints and the dent in his skull from the spittoon. Why do you need me? Do you have any *idea* what my life has become? I doubt it. Do you know what stress this has caused? This could affect my career. Let me tell you all something: *This could affect the peace process in the Middle East.*

Upon Babette's return from Washington, the city she had once ruled and now loathed, she played the part she had scripted for herself and took to her bed. She'd stormed out of the Justice Department not knowing what they were going to do with her. Another minute there, she couldn't take. Morris, Howard, Ben, we are leaving, *now.* There was this consolation to being a superstar—you knew how to make an exit.

The lawyers discussed among themselves all the way to Los Angeles on Morris's jet while Babette watched her old movies on DVD with the sound down so she could listen to them. None of them came right out and said she was *schtupping* him, but it was obvious from how they talked that there was little doubt in their minds. So humiliating. Yet it was only a taste, a soupçon, of what lay ahead if she was put on the stand.

The next day came the call from Morris, who'd just gotten off the phone with some deputy prosecutor—how many did they have, for God's sake?—to tell her that yes, they were going to call her to testify. It would look too awkward if they didn't. Don't leave the country. Make yourself available. Don't worry, everything will be fine, just tell the truth.

The truth! In the next hour, Babette ate three pints of Ben & Jerry's Celebrity Ripple ice cream. A week in bed, not answering the phone, watching her movies, pints, quarts, gallons of ice cream. Even her silk pajama pants felt tight in the waist.

She watched opening day. Of the billions of human beings who glued their eyeballs to television sets, few watched more intently than Babette Van Anka. Even in extremis to use the bathroom, she held on, bursting, until Judge Dutch called fifteen-minute recesses. The Clintick woman had, thank God, mentioned her only in passing. And Boyce Baylor—oo, a sharp one and no mistaking, and not so bad looking, either, no wonder Lady Bethmac had a jones for him back in law school—didn't even mention her in his tirade against the U.S. government. What was *that* about? Well, all for the good. Maybe this wouldn't be about her after all. For a second, Babette almost felt slighted. Then she decided to celebrate with just one more spoonful of Celebrity Ripple. All right, two spoonfuls.

Chapter 13

Having established the more than adequate credentials of FBI agent Jerry Whepson, DAG Clintick asked him to tell the court what he had observed the morning of September 29.

"There was a great deal of activity on the grounds when myself and Agent Fitch and the members of the FBI crime scene technicians arrived," Agent Whepson began. "The Secret Service especially were in a high state of activity. They were all over the place. A helicopter was up. Dog handlers appeared to be searching the grounds. Uniformed agents, their special response teams, were present in force."

"What would this level of activity suggest to you?"

"That they were looking for someone, or some persons. At this point, all we knew was what we had been told by the Secret Service, that the President had been killed."

"Objection," Boyce said. "Your Honor, it had hardly been established then or even now that the President had been 'killed.' "

This being rather at the root of the whole enchilada, Boyce's objection caused the first sidebar conference—those cozy get-togethers at the bench between attorneys and the judge—of the Trial of the Millennium. Fifteen minutes of furious wrangling over a word. At least it gave the TV commentators time to preen. One remarked that if the trials depicted in the old *Perry Mason* TV dramas had been presented realistically, the show would still be running because Perry's first case would still be going on. Another remarked that Boyce Baylor would not stop at trying to strike references to the President's having been killed. He would insist that there was no actual proof that the President was even dead. The Trial of the Millennium was off and running, like a garden slug galloping across a wide slate patio on a warm July day.

"Proceed, Ms. Clintick."

"Agent Whepson, would you describe the scene when you reached the second floor, the residence of the White House?"

"Again, a great deal of activity. Secret Service. I recognized some of the President's senior staff. Everyone looked, I would say, grim. There were military personnel, quite senior, I could see from the uniforms. It was very tense up there."

"That would be consistent with activity following a presidential assassination?"

"Ob-jection."

Another fifteen minutes of sidebar. Throughout the nation, Americans began to divide into two camps: those who were reassured about their system of justice, and those who thought it was an argument for the Peruvian model, ten minutes in front of a military judge with a hood over his head, the firing squad outside practicing in the courtyard.

In due course, Agent Whepson was allowed to proceed to the President's bedroom.

"I observed the President in bed. He was lying on his back on one side of the bed. His eyes were open, as was his mouth."

"And this led you to conclude?"

"That he was dead. Dr. Pierce, his personal physician, was present. He confirmed to me that the President had been dead for some hours, possibly three or four."

Boyce demanded that the prosecution stipulate—that is, agree—that Dr. Pierce had no qualifications as a coroner. That required twenty minutes of fevered wrangling at the bench.

"Did you observe anything unusual about the President's appearance?"

"You mean, aside from the fact that he was dead?"

"Yes."

"I observed a mark, like a bruise, approximately five centimeters above his right eyebrow."

"Objection. Your honor, this is the United States of America, not"—Boyce said with some distaste—"France."

Judge Dutch sighed. "Sustained, Mr. Baylor."

"What would that be in good old American inches?" Boyce said, implying that the metric system was unpatriotic.

"About two inches." Agent Whepson placed a finger on his own forehead.

"Did the mark appear suspicious to you in any way?"

"Objection."

Another sidebar. Millions of Americans began to wonder if maybe they would just catch the highlights on the evening news.

"You may answer the question, Agent Whepson."

"Since this mark was on the body of a dead president, yes, I definitely viewed it with great interest."

"What else did you observe that alerted your professional instincts?"

"There was a silver object about this size"—he indicated with his hands—"lying on the floor. I did not recognize what it was. It was lying on its side."

"Did you personally touch this object?"

"No. When I determined—I subsequently directed that the crime scene techs, the technicians, examine it using standard procedure."

"That is, using protective latex gloves?"

"That's correct."

"Was the First Lady present?"

"Yes, she was."

"And where exactly was she?"

"She was in the bathroom."

"Did you observe or hear anything that suggested the reason she was in the bathroom?"

"Yes. The sounds I heard coming from the bathroom were consistent with those of a person who was vomiting."

"Throwing up?" Just in case any of the jurors were unclear as to the meaning of *vomit*.

"Did you speak with Mrs. MacMann?"

"After she ceased vomiting? Yes. I identified myself to her and asked her to tell me what had happened."

"And what did she tell you?"

"She said that she had gone to bed at approximately twelve-thirty. There had been a state dinner for the President of Uruguay. She told me that she was woken up by a noise at some point in the night, she did not know when, and had gone back to sleep. She then woke up at six-fifteen, her usual waking time, ordered breakfast in bed. It was when the maid, Ms. Williams, entered with the breakfast that it became clear that the President had been—was dead."

"Did she describe to you the noise that woke her up in the night?"

"She used the word *thump*."

"Did she tell you that she had investigated the source of this thump?"

"I specifically asked her that, and she replied that she had not investigated it. She said she went back to sleep."

"What was Mrs. MacMann's state of mind when you had this discussion?"

"Objection. The question is entirely subjective. Agent Whepson has no competence as a psychologist."

"Overruled."

"Your *Honor*."

"Mr. Baylor. You may answer the question, Agent Whepson."

"I would describe her as calm."

"Was she tearful?"

"Objection. Leading, Your Honor."

"Sustained."

"How did you find Mrs. MacMann, Agent Whepson?"

"She did not seem upset except for the fact of throwing up."

"Objection. Inference. Mrs. MacMann might have eaten something that did not agree with her."

"Sustained."

"Did she express any emotion to you consistent with that of a woman who had just lost her husband?"

"Objection. Agent Whepson was not there in the capacity of grief counselor. Your Honor, I find the prosecution's line here troubling."

"Sustained."

"Did she say anything to you other than her description of the events of the evening and morning?"

"No, she did not."

"What did you then do?"

"I made a determination that we—that is, the FBI—needed to examine the premises thoroughly."

"Why did you make that determination?"

"To see if there was further evidence of foul play."

This prompted a rip-snorting twenty-minute sidebar in which Boyce and Sandy Clintick could be seen hissing at each other like geese. Judge Dutch's glasses kept fogging. He instructed the jury to disregard Agent Whepson's use of the words *further* and *foul play* and adjourned for the day.

The TV commentary that night featured detailed analysis by criminologists, gastroenterologists, and psychologists on the subject of vomiting in general and whether doing it in the presence of law enforcement is a reliable indicator of guilt.

Reporters who had covered Ken MacMann when he was governor discussed the fact that Beth had experienced two difficult pregnancies that ended in miscarriages. Mrs. MacMann had thrown up at a state fair during one of these pregnancies. A video clip of the occasion was shown over and over. She was not otherwise known for having a nervous stomach. If anything, she was known for having an iron constitution. This made Agent Whepson's testimony damning.

Chris Matthews of the show *Hardball* thundered at a guest who said that Beth was "obviously guilty": "What was she supposed to be doing? Sobbing hysterically like Mary Todd Lincoln and pounding on her husband's chest? People throw up when they're upset. Haven't you ever thrown up when you were upset?"

"I never killed my husband," said the guest.

"I used to throw up before the show. Gotta take a break. You're watching *Hardball*."

☆ · ☆ · ☆

Boyce's practice during cross-examinations was to get as physically close to witnesses as he could without sitting on their laps.

Once, in the midst of a particularly withering cross of the owner of a cruise ship that had collided with a tanker carrying liquefied natural gas, Boyce had asked the owner to hold his Styrofoam cup of coffee while he recited to him his conflicting testimony from the court transcript. The man threw the coffee at Boyce's chest, doing himself little good with the jury.

He stood next to the witness box with his right arm resting on it, facing the whole court and the world beyond, smiling pleasantly. The body language said: "And now, my friend, you and I are going to tell these folks what *really* happened that morning, okay?"

The Jeeter printout from yesterday showed that Agent Whepson had scored high with the four white male jurors, so today's performance would be for their benefit. Boyce's voice took on a slight folksy twang. Today he was just a good ol' boy in a $1,400 suit.

"How many years did you say you were with the Bureau, Agent Whepson?"

"Twenty-three."

"Good for you, sir. In that time I imagine you've seen your fair share of action."

The DAG had told Whepson: Watch out for this guy.

"That would depend on your definition of 'fair share.' "

"Of course it would. Of course it would. Good point. How did you happen to be assigned to this case?"

"I was on duty at the D.C. field office at the time. We received a call from FBI headquarters. They had received a call from the Secret Service."

"Saying what, exactly?"

"Objection. Hearsay."

"Your Honor," said Boyce, "we're all just trying to get at the same thing here, the truth."

There was a distinct murmuring from the press section. Judge Dutch glowered.

Boyce continued, "You arrived at the White House with five other FBI agents. What were you expecting to find? A revolution in progress?"

"Objection."

"Withdrawn. You arrived with five agents *plus* an entire FBI crime scene search crew of four agents. How did you know a crime had been committed?"

"The Secret Service informed FBI headquarters that the President had been killed."

"And how did they ascertain that? How did they know that he had been killed?"

"You would have to ask them that."

"I believe we will. I believe we will just do that. So you arrived at the White House already having decided that the President had been murdered by armed revolutionaries—"

"Objection."

"Sustained."

"You had not even arrived at the so-called crime scene and you had already ruled out that this might have been an accident?"

"I was instructed to bring a CSS team."

"I see. You were just following orders. That has a familiar ring to it, doesn't it?"

"Objection! Your *Honor.*"

"Withdrawn. In your testimony you told the court about your experience with the FBI. You've been involved in cases of kidnapping, wire fraud, extortion, mail bombing, organized crime, hate groups. A very impressive résumé. Tell us, how many presidential assassinations have you personally investigated?"

"This would be my first, Mr. Baylor."

"Well, we all have to start somewhere. But then you claim no special competence at evaluating whether a president has been assassinated or died by some other means?"

"Objection."

"Withdrawn. An FBI agent who charges a First Lady of the United States with murdering her husband would probably get a departmental citation—"

"Objection."

"Move along, Counsel."

"Yes, Your Honor. And I apologize if that statement gave offense. Agent Whepson, in your wide experience, have you often interrogated freshly widowed women? Women who, for example, have just woken up in bed with their husbands dead beside them?"

"I've interviewed the wives of bombing victims—"

"I said interrogated, not interviewed."

"I didn't interrogate Mrs. MacMann."

"What were your first words to her? After identifying yourself?"

"I asked her what happened."

"You did not condole her?"

"Condole her?"

"That's right. Telling her, 'I'm sorry about your loss, ma'am.' Or, 'I know this is a difficult time for you, ma'am.' Those are customary sentiments when dealing with a bereaved family member, if I'm not mistaken. Did you express such a sentiment?"

"Mr. Baylor, the President of the United States was lying there—"

"Just answer the question, thank you."

"No, I thought under the circumstances—"

"Thank you. Did Mrs. MacMann ask to have a lawyer present while you, as you put it, interviewed her?"

"No."

"Did she ask to have a lawyer present on any of the subsequent four occasions when you interviewed her?"

"No."

"At no time did she request to have legal counsel present?"

"No."

"Is that unusual?"

"I don't know, Mr. Baylor. As you yourself said, I have no wide experience of presidential assassinations."

The court laughed. Judge Dutch frowned.

"At what point did you inform Mrs. MacMann that she had the right to have legal counsel present during your so-called *interviews*?"

"The second time. After I interviewed Secret Service agent Birnam, and after the FBI lab reported that the fingerprints on the spittoon were hers."

"And how did she reply to you?"

"I believe she said that she didn't need a lawyer."

"Is that all she said?"

"She said that she was not hiding anything."

Boyce went over and took the spittoon from a clerk. It gleamed brightly in the court lights.

"Let's talk about this so-called murder weapon, this fearsome object at the center of the whole world's attention. In your testimony, you said that when you entered the President's bedroom, you did not recognize what this was. And yet you said it was lying on its side. If you didn't know what it was, how did you know it was on its side?"

"Whatever it was, I could tell it was askew."

"I congratulate you, sir, on your fine ability to identify unfamiliar three-dimensional objects that are ninety degrees off-kilter."

"Objection."

"Withdrawn. But you walked into the room and right away knew that this antique receptacle for spit was a lethal weapon?"

"Objection."

Judge Dutch creaked forward in his chair. This is the source of the aura of judges: they have bigger chairs than anyone else. That and the fact that they can sentence people to sit in electrified ones. It's all about chairs.

"Withdrawn. Let's move on. In your testimony you said that Mrs. MacMann told you she was woken up in the middle of the night by a noise. You expressed surprise that she hadn't investigated the source of this noise, is that correct?"

"Normally when people—especially women—are woken up by something, they want to know what made the noise."

"Especially women? Implying that they are the *weaker* species?"

"Objection."

"Your Honor, I was merely seeking to clarify the witness's own re-mark?"

Sidebar.

"In other words, Agent Whepson, Mrs. MacMann should have turned on all the lights, got out of bed, maybe armed herself with a baseball bat to go see if there was a burglar? In the White House."

"Objection."

"Sustained."

"Let me rephrase. You were surprised that Mrs. MacMann, ex-hausted after entertaining half of Latin America in her house, might have just *assumed* that someone else would investigate the cause of this bump, living as she did in the most heavily guarded house on the planet?"

Agent Whepson paused just long enough for Boyce to say, "Never mind, never mind. Let's move on." He was good at creating the illusion of impatience with the molasseslike pace of a trial, of a man in a hurry to get at—what did he call it?—the truth.

"You interviewed Ms. Babette Van Anka, the actress, who had spent the night in the Lincoln Bedroom, down the hall, did you not?"

"I did."

"And what did she tell you?"

"That she had said good night to the President at approximately twelve-thirty and went to sleep."

"Went *right* to sleep?"

Twenty-five hundred miles away, Babette's mouth went dry.

"She told me she had watched television. That she had gone to sleep with the television on."

"Did she tell you that she had heard this thump in the night?"

"She told me that she slept through the night."

"Glad *someone* got a good night's sleep in the White House that night. Just one or two more questions, Agent Whepson. You've been very patient with me. Unlike Ms. Clintick."

"Objection."

"Come, come, Your Honor, I was only attempting to lift our spirits a little."

"You may lift *my* spirits by getting on with it, Mr. Baylor."

"Agent Whepson, at one point in your career you were assigned to the Counterintelligence Division of the FBI, is that correct?"

"Yes, I was."

"Tell the court what they do, would you?"

"The Counterintelligence Division keeps track of foreign intelligence agents working within the United States."

"Spies? That would be foreign spies?"

"That's correct."

"You were in a supervisory capacity there, were you not, in the San Francisco field office?"

"Yes, I was."

"Did an Agent Wiley P. Sinclair work under you?"

"Objection."

Even viewers who didn't know who Wiley P. Sinclair was could tell that this was no standard sidebar conference going on. At one point, Sandy Clintick and Boyce raised their voices so that they could be heard above the shusher, the white noise machine that Judge Dutch turned on during sidebars to prevent eavesdropping.

"This is a key one for the defense," a TV network correspondent whispered to his viewers like a golf commentator during a critical nineteen-foot putt. "Baylor *badly* wants this front and center."

Finally Judge Dutch turned off the shusher. He told the jury that they should not assign any "undue significance" to what they were about to hear.

"Proceed, Mr. Baylor."

"Agent Sinclair worked for you."

"I had twenty-five agents working in that division."

"But did he report to you?"

"Yes, he did."

"And did it turn out that he was selling our secrets to the Chinese government?"

"Yes."

"Hm. That's some counterintelligence operation you had there, Agent Whepson."

"Objection."

"Withdrawn. Did it come as some surprise to you that one of your agents was having a fire sale of our precious national security secrets?"

"It came as a blow to everyone at the Bureau."

"Was the Bureau criticized for lack of diligence in this matter? I understand Mr. Sinclair had been making regular visits to Las Vegas casinos, driving an Italian sports car, going on expensive golf trips."

"There was discussion of that, yes."

"Was anyone at the Bureau fired as a result of this calamity?"

"No."

"Really?"

"Objection. Asked and answered."

"Withdrawn. Did the First Lady, Mrs. MacMann, make any public statements about this affair?"

"I'm not aware of any."

Boyce took a piece of paper off the defense table. It was passed to the bailiff, who passed it to the very sulky-looking DAG, and duly admitted into the record.

"Your Honor, may I beg the court's indulgence and read aloud just a sentence or two from this document?"

Judge Dutch nodded.

"This is from the *Chicago Tribune* of February twenty-seven of last year. Mrs. MacMann was in Chicago making a speech, and this is a news story about that event. There was a press conference afterwards. She took some questions. Here is what it says: 'Mrs. MacMann said that she was "dismayed" by the recent scandal involving FBI agent Wiley Sinclair. "I think there should be some resignations on principle," she said.' End quote." Boyce handed the piece of paper to Agent Whepson. "You never saw those remarks?"

"I had not seen that specific article."

"I congratulate you on that very lawyerly response, Agent Whepson."

"Objection. Harassing the witness."

"Withdrawn. Were you aware of the remarks from any other source?"

"I would say it was certainly known that Mrs. MacMann had issues with the Bureau with respect to the matter."

"And what was the Bureau's feeling about Mrs. MacMann's 'issues' with it?"

"That she was entitled to her opinion. She was naturally concerned. We all were."

"There was no ill will toward her? No sense of 'Who does she think she is? Why doesn't she butt out?' "

"None that I'm personally aware of, no."

Boyce took back the piece of paper.

"No further questions." His three favorite words in all the law.

Chapter 14

*I*t was generally conceded, even by those who remained convinced of Beth's guilt, that the government had not had a good day in court.

Boyce's custom after an especially good day was to hold a "press availability" on the steps of the courthouse.

He stepped out into the blinding glare of the lights, the eager smiles of the media, his number one fans and enablers. Even those who hated him loved him.

"It was a good day for the truth," he began.

Throughout America and the world, food sprayed from mouths, TV sets were cursed at, dinner napkins hurled, channels angrily changed.

He kept his statement brief. The Secret Service, he said, had pronounced it a murder before adducing evidence that it was. The FBI, meanwhile, had it in for Beth because she had dared to criticize them for incompetence. To them, she was just a "busybody wife."

The next day, it was reported that the head of the National Organization for Women had written a "scathing" letter to the members of the Senate Oversight Committee, demanding an investigation of the FBI for its "political persecution" of Beth. Several members of the committee bravely announced to the media that they thought this was a darned good idea. The director of the FBI, a dedicated public servant of impeccable reputation, father of three (girls), devoted husband, now found the media waiting for him on his lawn when he came home from work, demanding to know a) why he had not fired the incompetent

Agent Whepson for the Sinclair affair; b) why the FBI was a hotbed of misogyny; and, for that matter, c) why he had not fired himself?

Deputy Attorney General Sandy Clintick had watched Boyce on television, thumping his chest like an alpha male gorilla. She decided that she too had better get out there on the courthouse steps and do some spinning of her own. She took a deep breath and sallied forth, head held high. She told them that she was "satisfied" with how it was going so far. Agent Whepson had been a "fine and credible" witness. Furthermore, the Federal Bureau of Investigation was above reproach. There was no vendetta against Mrs. MacMann. The government would present compelling evidence in furtherance of its case. Thank you.

Privately, Ms. Clintick was aboil with fury at the FBI for not having reassigned the case to someone other than Agent Whepson once the enormity of it had become clear. But the fact was that it had been Agent Whepson who had been on duty that morning when the call came, and once he began the investigation, that was that, it was his case. Taking it away from him only would have made the Bureau look even more suspect. Boyce Baylor was shameless, but he was also lucky.

But Beth MacMann had killed her husband with that spittoon and lied about it, and she, Sandy Clintick, was going to get her. Not because she had a grudge. President MacMann might have been the husband from hell and might even have had it coming. She wasn't going to get Beth MacMann for that. She was going to get her because she wanted more than anything to wipe the grin off Shameless Baylor's face and shove it up his ass.

As for Beth, she no longer suspected that Boyce was out to lose the case to punish her for pulling a *Casablanca* on him back at law school. On the contrary. She was now racked with guilt for what she'd done to him back then. Sitting there in court watching him eviscerate the government's first witness against her had filled her with remorse. She kept thinking of the look on his face when she'd told him she was marrying Ken.

She and Boyce were having a quiet dinner in a private dining room at the Jefferson before Boyce went back to work to prepare tomorrow's cross-examination of Secret Service agent Birnam.

"Boyce, I—"

That was as far as she got before bursting into tears.

"What's the matter? Hey, it's going fine. We're doing fine."

"It's not *that*." She honked into one of the Jefferson's crisply ironed starched napkins. "Oh, Boyce, I'm so *sorry*."

"Beth. It was an accident."

She looked up from her honked-in napkin. "What was?"

Boyce leaned forward and whispered, "You didn't *mean* to kill him." He sat back. "Anyway, it's not like he was the favorite of all my presidents." He winked.

"What are you talking about?" Beth said, suddenly dry-eyed.

"The number two wife, the Italian, she used to throw things at me all the time. One time she threw this crystal cigar ashtray. From Steuben. Must've weighed five pounds. If she'd connected, I wouldn't be here."

"I didn't *kill* Ken."

Boyce looked at her. This woman could turn on a dime. He'd had clients like this. The guilt built up until it was overwhelming. They'd burst, then before you could hand them a Kleenex, they were over it, back in denial.

"Whatever." He shrugged.

" 'Whatever'?"

"I'm your lawyer. I'm the last person on the planet you have to explain yourself to."

"I was trying to say . . . I never told you sorry. For what I did. Back then."

Boyce said quietly, "There's something I never told you."

"Tell me now."

"When you came to my room that day?"

"Yes?"

"I was going to tell you that I was breaking our engagement."

"What?"

"I'd fallen in love."

Beth stared in confusion.

"There was this . . . guy."

Beth stared. She didn't know what to say.

"He awakened in me something that I didn't know had been there."

"You . . ."

"He'd been in the navy. He was *so* butch."

"Dammit, Boyce. I was trying to apologize."

"Then it turned out he was two-timing me. With this ambitious *bitch.*"

They kissed. First time in a quarter century. Yet it felt oddly familiar.

"Whoa," Boyce said after what must have been five minutes. Thank God no waiter came in. The headlines! "I have to be in court tomorrow."

Beth sighed. "So do I."

Chapter 15

$\mathcal{B}$oyce began his cross-examination of Secret Service agent Woodrow "Woody" Birnam not at his usual station right next to the witness, but from a distance. He stood at his podium by the defense table.

"Can you hear me okay, Agent Birnam?"

"Yes, sir." Agent Birnam was in his mid-thirties and befitting his profession was in excellent physical shape.

"You have a superb record with the Secret Service."

Agent Birnam knew better than to accept Boyce's compliment at face value.

"You're one of the Service's top pistol shots, I see."

"We're all competent with firearms. It's a requirement."

"Don't be modest, now. You're on the competition team that's beaten the FBI team three years running. I imagine that must be a sore point with Agent Whepson."

Laughter. Vlonko noted which jurors joined in.

"You must shoot a great deal to maintain such a level of proficiency."

"Objection. Agent Birnam's marksmanship is irrelevant."

"Your Honor, I guarantee the court that my line of questioning is more relevant than the deputy attorney general's ceaseless objections. She's objecting so many times that I'm beginning to worry about her blood pressure."

"Overruled. But proceed to your point, Counsel."

"I was, Your Honor, I was. How often do you go to the pistol range, Agent Birnam?"

"Pretty regularly."

"Would you please define 'regularly' for the court."

"Twice a week."

"Good for you. Practice makes perfect. I see you fire a .357 magnum six-shot revolver, is that correct?"

"Yes. I also shoot nine-millimeter and occasionally .44 magnum. Also .38 caliber on occasion."

"All these handguns, especially a .357 magnum, these are powerful guns, are they not?"

"They're not small guns."

"A .357 magnum produces one hundred and sixty-five decibels. Am I correct?"

"I wear ear protection."

"I would hope so. That's a heck of a loud sound. Have you worn ear protection every single time you have fired a handgun, Agent Birnam?"

"Objection."

"Your Honor, I am *getting* to my point, if Ms. Clintick will permit."

"It would be hard to say," Agent Birnam said.

"Try, for the court."

"Majority of the time, certainly. Yes."

"Have you ever experienced ringing in your ears, loss of hearing?"

"Objection. Your Honor, this is not a doctor's office. Agent Birnam is perfectly fit. He's passed all his physical tests. This is pointless and harassing."

Judge Dutch rocked twice in his great chair. "Overruled. Answer the question, Agent."

"Nothing significant."

Boyce lowered his voice. "*No* loss of hearing?"

"I'm sorry?"

Even lower: "*No* loss of hearing?"

"Could you repeat the question?"

Boyce raised his voice to a near shout: "*Have you had loss of hearing?*"

"No. Never."

"Hm. Over the course of your lifetime, how many rounds would you say you have fired from the barrel of a handgun?"

"That would be difficult to say."

"Try. Thousands?"

"More."

"Tens of thousands?"

"At least."

"Hundreds?"

"I—"

"A *million*?"

"I don't have an answer to that. A lot."

"Isn't it true, Agent Birnam, that you can sustain significant and lasting ear damage from exposure to a single gunshot?"

"Objection. The witness is not an otolaryngologist."

Clintick was furious. She'd been skunked and she knew it. Boyce had purposefully not filed any pretrial motions having to do with Agent Birnam's ability to hear. He hadn't even told Beth. He hadn't told Beth most of his strategy, for the reason that, knowing Beth, he didn't want to spend half the time arguing with her about how he planned to win this.

"I withdraw the question, Your Honor. Agent Birnam, you were on duty the night of the President's passing—"

"Objection."

"Your Honor, surely this is harassment."

"Overruled."

"Your post was outside the closed door to the second-floor residence, at the head of the grand staircase. According to this chart here"—Boyce pointed to the blowup of the floor plan of the residence—"that would have put you some seventy-five, eighty feet away from the closed door to the President's bedroom—"

"Objection. The court has heard no testimony stating that the door to the President's bedroom was closed."

Sidebar.

"Agent Birnam, leaving aside for the time being whether the door to the President's bedroom was closed, you would have been eighty feet away, on the other side of a door that *you* have said was closed. And yet you claim—"

"Objection."

"Sustained."

"You *state* unequivocally that you heard an argument going on, so far away it might as well have been in another time zone."

"Objection. Your *Honor*."

"Mr. Baylor, I'm warning you."

"I withdraw the figure of speech, Your Honor. Sorry. Force of habit. Agent Birnam, you say you heard this tremendous hullabaloo from nearly a hundred feet away. All the way at the other end of the residence. And what did you hear?"

"The President and Mrs. MacMann. They appeared to be arguing."

"Over domestic or foreign policy?"

Laughter.

"Objection."

Judge Dutch picked up his gavel and aimed the tip of it at Boyce. "That is your last warning, Counselor."

"I ask the court's forgiveness."

Boyce walked toward Agent Birnam. He said in a sincere tone of voice, "Are you certain that it was the President and Mrs. MacMann that you heard?"

"Well, yes."

"How many people were there that night in the residence?"

"Three, counting Ms. Van Anka, the guest."

Boyce paused. He nodded, walked over toward the jury box as if deep in thought. A hush descended on the courtroom. Members of the press nudged each other. *Here we go.* On the other side of the country, Babette Van Anka cowered under her expensive French sheets.

"Let's move on to another area, Agent Birnam. A year ago, the First Lady was quoted in the media to the effect that she felt there were not enough female agents in the Secret Service. . . ."

☆ · ☆ · ☆

The evening news was loud with the sound of .357 magnums being fired and with video footage of Boyce saying to Agent Birnam, "Agent Birnam, with all the money and tremendous effort that the Secret Service devotes to keeping American presidents alive, why couldn't you have spent ten dollars on a decent adhesive bathmat for the President's bathroom?" followed by Ms. Clintick's spluttering objection.

On *Hard Gavel* that night, Alan Crudman was drowning in false modesty.

"Perri, it's not like me to second-guess an attorney of Boyce Baylor's stature. But I have to say, I was amazed that he just dropped the Babette Van Anka angle today. He set up the shot and then just walked away from it. Babette Van Anka is the *key* to defending Beth MacMann. To try to assert that this agent had it in for the First Lady because she'd criticized the Secret Service for not having enough women agents—that just strikes me as throwing *very* long. Look, it's not a secret that the President and Van Anka were—whatever word you want to use to describe them, intimate, best of friends, constant companions. There she was, on the premises the night of the President's death, in the next bedroom down the hall. I do not know why Boyce Baylor isn't making more of this fact."

"Couldn't it be," Perri said, "that if he does make a big deal out of the fact that the President and Van Anka were lovers, that gives Beth MacMann a motive for killing him?"

"Of course it does, but that's *precisely* why a jury like this"—Alan Crudman, defender of J. J. Bronco and other notably guilty defendants of color whom he had gotten off by imputing racist motives to everyone else involved, was always careful to avoid saying "predominantly black jury" when he meant to imply that predominantly black juries had entirely separate agendas and could always be counted on to acquit for tribal reasons—"would respond sympathetically to Beth MacMann."

"Even if she had lied to cover up?"

Crudman shrugged. "Juries like this one live in the real world. Lying to law enforcement officers is just not the worst thing you could do. Plus on this jury you've got middle-aged women who would be predisposed to think that any philandering man who was cheating on his wife in the next bedroom would deserve anything he got. This is a low-hanging fruit. I *don't understand* why Boyce Baylor doesn't want to pick it. Every time Van Anka's name comes up, he wants to move on. You'd think *he* was the one having an affair with her."

☆ · ☆ · ☆

Beth had promised herself that she was not going to watch the evening shows. But with her feelings toward Boyce now rekindled and glowing like fanned embers, she found herself turning on *Hard Gavel,* not for the commentating and second-guessing, but to see what her competition was wearing that night. She had developed a little paranoid theory that the closer she and Boyce got, the tighter Perri's sweaters got.

It was in the midst of checking out Perri's attire that Beth couldn't help but hear Alan Crudman going on about the free pass Boyce was giving Babette Van Anka.

Beth reproached herself for her doubts. Had a lifetime in politics made her this cynical? Or was it just a lifetime with Ken MacMann?

The first infidelity had been with one of her bridesmaids. At least he hadn't dragged her upstairs during the reception, like Sonny Corleone, and thrown her up against the wainscoting. But finding out that your husband has been having it off with one of your bridesmaids, into the bargain, an old friend from boarding school, would put a dent in any new wife's confidence. She even considered leaving Ken. And she was overwhelmed with guilt over how she'd treated Boyce. From what she heard, Boyce had taken it hard. Friends said he was going through some kind of personality change, from nice guy to quiet angry guy. One said, "I hope he doesn't end up one of those people who send mail bombs."

Ken apologized for having an affair with one of her oldest friends. He blamed it on something called post-traumatic stress disorder, the name they were starting to give to Vietnam vets who were acting wiggy. He promised not to do it again. And he was as good as his word, for almost two months. Meanwhile, he appeared to have lost interest in his new wife physically, which is demoralizing six months into a lifetime partnership. And Beth liked sex. She liked sex a *lot*. She started to fantasize about Boyce. It was all so conflicting.

Meanwhile, Ken had made it clear to her that he had a plan, and not just to screw all of her old school friends. He was going to be president, and he was going to do it quickly, whatever it took, so that he could enjoy the experience while he was still young. She wouldn't be seeing much of him.

Friends remarked how changed she was. Beth didn't laugh much anymore.

It was now after 10:30. She knew Boyce went to sleep early. She waited until 10:40. Couldn't help herself.

The voice that answered was already livid at being woken up.

"What *is* it, Beth?"

"I was just listening to"—God, how was this going to sound?—"I was just thinking. I think we need to rethink the Babette Van Anka thing."

"Do you realize," Boyce growled, "how many federal agents are listening in on this conversation? Why don't you just call up the Justice Department and tell them how you think I should defend you?"

"I'm sorry."

"So you keep saying."

"Well, it's *true*. Most men like it when you apologize to them."

"Apologize in the morning, when the G-men aren't listening in. Good night. Good night, boys. Sleep tight, you incompetent bastards."

He hung up.

Beth had to get up out of bed and pace and smoke. She'd started again, a fact that had somehow found its way into the press. To hell with it. Pacing at night without smoking was like a drum majorette parading without a baton.

Was he trying to throw the case? She was attractive, this Perri Pettengill. Why *not* go after Babette Van Anka? What *did* Ken see in her? Never mind. And the husband. Nine miles of bad road. He gave millions to Ken's campaigns—some of it probably in bags—and those Far East associates of his, real charmers. Turned out one of them, for whom Max had wheedled an invitation to a state dinner at the White House, was connected to the Burmese general who protected the poppy business. What interesting friends. To counter the unfavorable publicity, Ken had decided to make campaign finance reform a central theme of his reelection campaign. As the wise man said, You can fool some of the people some of the time, and those are the ones you need to concentrate on.

☆ · ☆ · ☆

"Why not go after Babette Van Anka?" Boyce asked rhetorically over breakfast. He was the temperature of his coffee. Hotter, probably. "You were watching her show again."

"I couldn't sleep."

"Well, watch something else. Something wholesome. Like wrestling. Or one of those reality shows where they chain people together for a week to see if they eat each other."

"They should chain lawyers together."

"That I might watch. Everyone hates lawyers—until you need one."

"Then you really hate them."

Boyce grinned. "Two points."

"Look, I'm not trying to interfere."

"Yes, you are. No wonder you were an unpopular First Lady."

"I wasn't unpopular. I was a transitional First Lady. I was plowing the ground for the ones who'll follow."

"I'd be careful with the ground metaphors. Your husband's fertilizing the lawn at Arlington."

"Charming. Really charming." Beth sipped her coffee. "I didn't sleep."

"I didn't either. My client kept calling me."

"You won't even discuss it with me?"

"All right." Boyce dabbed his mouth with the napkin. "This once I'll discuss it with you. If I go after Babette Van Anka, which I very easily could, it would be shooting fish in a barrel. I could make her look like the whore of Babylon in sixty seconds. And what would that accomplish? One thing. It would give you a motive for killing War God. The jury would reasonably conclude, Sure, she was pissed at him for humping the girlfriend right down the hall. But killing is killing. She coulda waited till morning and divorced him. Only a scheming little putz like Alan Crudman would do something so *obvious* as go after Babette Van Anka. No. I take that back. He's not dumb. He's a putz, but he's a smart little shit. He knows perfectly well that's not the key here. He's just saying it on Perri's show because the majority of the people who watch know fuck-all about trial strategies, and he can get away with saying things like that and look smart on my time. You know something else? For all I know, he may be saying that *precisely* to make you think I'm blowing this case. Did that enter your mind? So any more *questions*?"

"No further questions."

"All right. I'm glad we had this talk. Let's go kick some ass."

Chapter 16

$\mathscr{S}$ophie Williams, the upstairs maid who had pointed out to Beth that her husband was unlikely to be wanting breakfast that morning or indeed any future mornings, had been the subject of furious pretrial motions.

Two months after the fateful day, she sold her story to the *National Perspirer*. It filled four pages inside. The headline on the cover was HE LOOKED PRETTY DEAD TO ME! The subhead promised "Gripping Details of the Stormy MacMann Marriage!"

And delivered them. The *Perspirer* paid $250,000, roughly six times her annual salary. In return, they got a heaping plateful of red meat. Sophie's account was so entertaining that movie producers all over Hollywood and Europe rushed to snap up the rights. It was full of delicious details about Babette's numerous overnight stays in the Lincoln Bedroom. "I sometimes wondered what Mr. Lincoln would have made of all that bouncing and moaning." One night while Babette and the commander in chief were enjoying a soiree of headboard-banging bliss, "Mrs. MacMann was off giving a speech to some family organization about how important marriages are. I felt kind of sorry for her." The First Guest was not, apparently, a favorite of the White House staff. "And I never did care much for Ms. Van Anka's singing or acting."

The so-called mainstream media who publicly affected to disdain the *Perspirer* as a scandal sheet for overweight proles found it all so riveting that they recycled it on their own more respectable front pages, along with the usual grudging attribution and qualifiers.

Babette had to be talked out of suing the *Perspirer* by Nick Naylor and her trio of lawyers. Don't go there, they said. It will only make it worse. Instead she demanded that Max buy the movie rights through one of his dummy Hong Kong companies, in order to ensure that no movie would ever be made. Sophie's new best friend, her agent, had gotten the bidding up to a price that was giving Max indigestion. When it passed $5 million, Max announced that he would not go one dollar, pound sterling, Swiss franc, euro, or yen higher. "Who's gonna want to see this movie, anyway?" This highly insensitive comment triggered a domestic scene of exquisite fury.

The movie rights ended up going for $7.4 million, to a French company and English director, who, according to *Variety,* was planning to ask Babette to play herself. "I see it," he was quoted, "as the television show *West Wing* meets *Murder on the Orient Express.* Washington camp, lots of big stars having tremendous fun. Babette would be marvelous as herself. Who better? I've always wanted to work with her."

Babette menaced Max with the salad tongs, accusing him of, among other failings, insufficient loyalty for not having outbid the French. Nick Naylor, presented with yet another Grab–Van Anka public relations catastrophe, said that at this point Babette might consider accepting the part, to "defuse things." Though certainly not until after the trial. "Naturally, we'd want to see a script first."

At any rate, Sophie Williams was now rich and retired from service in the White House. Sometimes the American dream, like God, works in mysterious ways.

The prosecution wanted Sophie to testify, especially since her account of Babette's previous visits to the White House opened up the can of night crawlers that was the MacMann marriage and established a clear motive for Beth's jealous fatal spittooning of the President.

Boyce fought against having her testify, arguing that she had discredited herself by selling her story to a "lurid, sensation-mongering tabloid" (that, as it happened, he had once defended in a libel case, but never mind). He thus found himself in the position of defending a wronged wife by attempting to suppress evidence of her husband's offenses. If Sophie testified, he'd have to retaliate by making her out as a scheming mercenary who had embellished the truth in order to increase its market value. As Sophie was black, he was not eager to perform a credibilotomy on her in front of a jury consisting of seven African Americans.

So the atmosphere in court this morning was especially charged.

"The United States calls Sophronia Williams."

☆ · ☆ · ☆

"Why," Beth asked in a tight voice, in the car at the end of what had been a very long day in court, "did you keep asking her why I was so unpopular among the staff?"

"I'm trying to establish a conspiracy. Conspiracies need motives."

"You were trying to make me out to be Leona Helmsley. Is this some new cutting-edge defense strategy? Make the jury hate the defendant?"

"We've established that the FBI hated you. When I finish with Agent Birnam, it'll look like he and the entire Secret Service hated you. With Sophie, I was trying to suggest that the staff might have had it in for you, too."

"Suggest? You asked her if I knew the birthdays of her four kids. Do you know the names and birthdays of *your* cleaning lady's kids? And what was all that how much did I spend on Christmas presents for them? And the fifteen minutes you spent on her brother-in-law who's in jail for stabbing someone? I take it you were trying to suggest that I was cold and unfeeling because I didn't try to get him a presidential pardon for stabbing a convenience store clerk. I didn't even know that she had a brother-in-law in jail. It wasn't something she advertised."

"I think we made good progress today."

"You know, Sophie liked me. She all but said so in the *Perspirer* piece. The part about how she felt sorry for me that he was screwing that cow while I was giving a speech to the Promise Keepers about the sanctity of marriage. Why didn't you ask her about that?"

"Gee, why didn't *I* think of that? Then we could have gone on to your motive for killing your husband." Boyce sighed, a deep, lawyerly sigh. "Let me explain this one last time. I want it to look like the entire White House was in league against you. That they went to bed at night dreaming of ways to get even with you."

"What if I'm acquitted, and everyone in the country hates me because I'm supposedly a bitch?"

"You'll get an eight-million-dollar book advance from Tina Brown. Then you can tell everyone how wonderful you really are. Americans love comebacks. It'll be a best-seller. Then you can pay my fee, which is going to be at least eight million."

"Alan Crudman would have been cheaper."

That night Beth smoked half a pack of cigarettes and watched not only *Hard Gavel* but all the shows. The topic on all of them was "How Awful *Is* Beth MacMann?" The *Vanity Fair* correspondent was funny on *Charlie Rose*. "It's a wonder," he said, "we're not all covering a trial for *her* murder." The other guests laughed. Beth's dreams of someday having a political career of her own, running for the Senate or state house back home—so much for all that. Boyce might be winning the case, but he was ruining her reputation in the process.

The phone rang.

"I don't think you're *that* bad." It was Boyce.

"Fuck you." She hung up.

He called back. "Was that your idea of phone sex?"

"Tell me you have a strategy," she said. "Tell me this is going the way you planned it."

"Baby, this is going so well, I'm sitting here doing a crossword puzzle. By the way, what's a four-letter word for woman ending in u-n-t?"

"Aunt."

"Hm. Can I borrow your eraser?"

$\mathcal{B}$oyce did have a plan, and it centered on a single line from Babette's statement to the FBI. He had been careful not to file any pretrial motions having to do with it and not to put on his witness list anyone who might alert the prosecution to this little buried truffle.

Meanwhile, the United States called Captain Cary Grayson. Grayson was the U.S. Navy's top pathologist at Bethesda Naval Hospital, just outside Washington. It was he who had performed the autopsy on President MacMann and who had concluded that the President had died of an epidural hematoma caused by, in the dry, precise language of forensic medicine, blunt-force trauma to the skull. The blow to his forehead had ruptured the middle meningeal artery. Blood had collected between the skull and the dura, the membrane between the skull and the brain, forcing the dura inward. This in turn compressed the cerebral cortex, killing the President.

Captain Grayson was in his late fifties, a trim, graying, bespectacled navy bones of pleasant, professional demeanor, the sort of man you would be thrilled to find at the foot of your hospital bed, checking your chart and issuing crisp commands to the nurses. Into the bargain, he had an impressive chestful of ribbons, including the bright yellow-and-red rectangle denoting service in Vietnam (pharmacist's mate on the aircraft carrier *Independence*). This was, of course, irrelevant to his testimony, but the deputy attorney general, keenly aware that the jury contained two veterans of the Vietnam War, slyly managed to insert a glancing mention of it in her direct examination of Captain Grayson. There was no point in objecting. Boyce could see that all the jurors, not just the vets, were already in love with him. They wanted him at the foot of *their* hospital beds when the time came. Boyce knew from experience that juries tended to love doctors, except for plastic surgeons with practices in Beverly Hills and the 10021 zip code area of Manhattan. Doctors with military decorations—two credibilities in one uniform—they deemed godlike.

Deputy AG Clintick gently walked him through his testimony, reinforcing the fact that the time of death had occurred in the hour and a half following the overheard shouting match. She got him to comment that the President was in fine physical condition, extraordinary, considering his grueling ordeal during the war. Grayson had observed some evidence of coronary heart disease, but nothing serious. Perhaps in a few years, during his second term—objection, sustained—perhaps in four or five years he would have required angioplasty, or the insertion of a stent, but these were now routine procedures. He would have lived to a ripe age. A great loss. A great loss for the nation. Boyce was bursting to object, but you could have heard a pin drop, so he held back.

And then Clintick ambushed Boyce. According to her witness list, the enlarged photographs of the Paul Revere mark on the President's skull were to have been presented by a leading civilian forensic dermatologist. But seeing how mesmerized the jury was by Captain Grayson, the navy's answer to Marcus Welby, M.D., she pulled a fast one and asked that the photographs be introduced so that Grayson could explain them.

During the ensuing sidebar, Boyce protested that Captain Grayson, for all his wonderfulness, was not qualified to discuss epidermal markings that were, as he put it, "more mysterious in origin than the designs supposedly left on the Andes mountains by ancient flying saucers."

A seething Boyce and a placid deputy AG returned to their places. A clerk mounted the three-by-two-foot photographs on an easel. It was the first time they had been shown to the public.

A gasp went through the courtroom. Boyce winced. There was nothing worse for your client than the sound of an entire courtroom having its breath taken away by graphic evidence of your client's alleged handiwork.

The photograph was an enlargement of a five-by-two-centimeter rectangle of presidential forehead.

ƎЯƎVƎЯ

The letters were so clear that they could have been used as an eye chart. *The New Yorker* observed, "They could have been read by Stevie Wonder."

When Boyce had first seen the depressing photographs, he had briefly contemplated an *Exorcist* explanation: that the conspiracy against Beth included even Satan, who had malevolently stamped Paul Revere's mark on the President's skull.

He took a deep breath. Some days you earned that thousand bucks an hour.

Members of the media exchanged smirks. Let Shameless Baylor explain away *this*!

DAG Clintick, at pains to suppress her glee, gently guided Captain Grayson through his description of this damningly conclusive piece of forensic evidence. She had prepared diligently. Did such dermal embossing ever occur naturally on humans? Not like this, Captain Grayson replied. In his wide medical experience, had the captain ever seen or heard of six capital letters naturally occurring on human flesh? No, he couldn't think of any instances offhand. And what would the chances of six reversed Roman letters spelling the name of a Revolutionary War silversmith appearing naturally on human flesh be, say?

Objection. The witness was being asked to indulge in the most extravagant statistical speculation.

Sidebar.

Overruled.

The witness may answer the question.

"Approximately one in fifty-seven billion."

Murmurmurmur.

Objection.

It was a long morning.

When she finished with Captain Grayson, Sandy Clintick flashed Boyce a triumphal smirk.

Boyce rose, walked over to the witness box, and rested his arm companionably on it, as though having a conversation with an old friend.

"Your Honor," he said so casually that he might have been telling the judge that his wife had called and asked him to pick up the dry cleaning on the way home, "the defense stipulates that this mark came from the spittoon."

Sandy Clintick froze. She and scores of Justice Department lawyers had studied every one of Boyce Baylor's cases. In over two decades of aggressive lawyering, he had stipulated exactly twice. Even Judge Dutch, normally as impassive as one of the seventeenth-century Dutch burghers in his collection, raised an eyebrow.

"Only a fool or scoundrel," Boyce continued, "would stand here and waste the jury's time trying to maintain that those letters occurred naturally—or miraculously—on President MacMann's forehead." He was making a speech, but let the deputy AG object while he sounded so sweetly reasonable. "The question is *how* they got there."

"Objection."

"Proceed with your questioning, Counsel."

First Boyce would demonstrate to the jury that he too thought Captain Grayson was the greatest thing to happen to the medical profession since Galen.

He inquired gently into the number of autopsies he had performed. My, my, that *is* a lot. He then dismissed the notion that he thought Captain Grayson was not qualified to comment on the markings simply because he was not a forensic dermatologist. For heaven's sake, was he not the navy's top pathologist? At Bethesda Naval Hospital—custodians of presidential health?

Captain Grayson could only reply as modestly as he could that, yes, his credentials did seem to be in order.

Absolutely, absolutely.

Sandy Clintick thought, *They're having a love fest up there. Any minute he's going to give Grayson a back massage. What the hell is he up to?*

"Captain, in the course of your autopsy, I assume you would examine every square inch of the President's body?"

"Yes."

"Every part?"

"Objection. Asked and answered."

"Did you take tissue samples?"

"Yes."

"Did you take tissue samples from the bottom of his feet?"

"No."

Boyce's face assumed a look of respectful surprise. "I'd have thought that would be routine."

"Objection."

"I'll rephrase. Why didn't you take tissue samples from the soles of his feet?"

"I saw no reason to. I observed the soles of his feet."

"In observing them, did you see traces of soap residue?"

"I did not observe traces of soap residue."

"But without taking tissue samples, can you say, with one hundred percent certainty, that there was no soap residue present?"

Captain Grayson paused. "No, I could not say for certain."

Boyce did not press. Digging up a dead-and-buried U.S. president in Arlington Cemetery is a tall order, and high risk unless you were absolutely certain that his feet were slimy with soap from his last shower.

Just in case, though, DAG Clintick was ready. She had lined up a scientist from Procter & Gamble, makers of the President's favorite shower soap, as well as a physicist from the Jet Propulsion Laboratory. The P&G scientist would testify that the President's bar soap had been specifically designed to leave minimal residue—the result of an expensive lawsuit by a man who had sued the company for $100 million after slipping in the shower. The JPL physicist would demonstrate the unlikelihood—1 in 2.6 trillion—of a slip resulting in the Ǝ Я Ǝ V Ǝ Я imprint on the skull, given the spittoon's normal position in the President's bedroom. Sandy Clintick was not eager to glaze the jury's eyeballs with vectors, g-forces, square roots, and formulas with eight variables, but if it came to that, she was ready.

"Captain," Boyce said, "what effect does death have on human flesh?"

"When rigor mortis sets in, it hardens all the organs and tissue."

"Is it then accurate to say that human skin becomes more impressionable following death? In other words, if something were pressed onto it in the hours *after* death, would an impression be made on the skin?"

"Objection. Captain Grayson is not here in the capacity of expert dermatologist."

Gotcha. Right into the trap.

"Your Honor," Boyce said in a tone of wounded reasonableness, "it was the *prosecution* who presented the captain as expert witness in these matters. I respect and esteem his credentials and accept him as more than qualified to testify on this most basic aspect of forensic medical science."

Several of the jurors actually nodded in agreement. Such moments made Vlonko's heart leap.

"Overruled. You may answer the question, Captain Grayson."

"As rigor mortis sets in, the skin develops pallor consequent to oxygen depletion. Relevant to Mr. Baylor's question, there is a general loss of turgor and elasticity. So, yes, in theory, any indentation or impression would be more likely to persist after death than before."

Bingo.

"So, Captain, if after the President had died, the spittoon were pressed down onto his forehead—"

"Objection!"

"Your Honor, I am merely asking a medical witness if a certain set of circumstances would produce a specific result." He flashed a steely glance at the prosecution table. "And I would point out to the prosecution that I have reserved the right to recall *previous* witnesses."

It was a long and hissy sidebar. How the public yearned to hear what was being said!

Finally Judge Dutch said, "The jury is instructed that the witness is not in a position to state what may or may not have actually taken place."

"Captain Grayson," Boyce continued, "if following the President's death, the spittoon were pressed down onto a bruised area, could that, in your considered medical opinion, have left this vivid impression of Mr. Revere's mark? Like stamping hardening clay?"

"Yes," Captain Grayson said, "that could explain it. Theoretically."

Boyce smiled. "Thank you, sir. No further questions at this time."

Chapter 18

Boyce's cross of Captain Grayson triggered a media hurricane. The front page of the *New York Post* screamed:

SHAMELESS TO GOVT:
YOUDUNIT!

The pixel pundits said that Boyce had just "declared war" on the United States government. Mark Fuhrman, the detective in the O. J. Simpson case, was tracked down by helicopter, shooting elk in Montana, and ferried to a television studio in Bozeman where he could comment on the similarities between the accusation that he had planted the bloody glove in Simpson's backyard and Boyce's allegation that the government bogeymen had embossed the President's skull while he lay cooling.

In fact, Boyce had gotten the inspiration for this grand canard not from the Simpson case, but from the JFK assassination. The harder-element conspiracy theorists back then had asserted that President Kennedy's corpse had been altered in the ambulance on the way from Andrews Air Force Base to Bethesda Naval Hospital, to make it look as though the fatal shots had come from behind. (When any fool *knew* that President Kennedy had been shot from the front, back, and sideways by triangulated firing squads staged by the CIA, FBI, and Mafia.) Boyce kept the source of his inspiration to himself.

Commentators on the legal shows *tsk-tsk*ed that DAG Clintick should have seen it coming. Greta Van Botox, host of *Objection!,* declared, "If you get into the ring with Shameless Baylor, you better be prepared to mud wrestle." Alan Crudman, in his now regular guest slot on *Hard Gavel,* tried to downplay the damage to the government. Privately, he admitted that Boyce Baylor had taken a damaging piece of evidence and nicely jujitsued it to his advantage.

☆ · ☆ · ☆

DAG Clintick called an unusual full-scale press conference to denounce Boyce. "In all my years as a prosecutor," she said, steam hissing from her ears, "I have never witnessed such morally and ethically disgraceful tactics as these. Today Mr. Baylor truly earned his nickname."

With that she turned and walked back into the courthouse, into the basement garage, and into her car and drove back to her office at the Justice Department to command 120 lawyers and investigators to crank up, overnight, a minute-by-minute, second-by-second timeline of the precise whereabouts of every FBI and Secret Service agent, household staff, medical personnel, and body handler on the morning of the President's death.

She knew there was no merit to Boyce's stunning allegation, and that was why it scared her. It was so outrageous, so unbelievable, that one-third of the jury would believe it. People believe unbelievable things because it's self-flattering to think that you are intellectually daring enough to accept what others find preposterous. It's why people believe in UFOs, assassination conspiracies, certain religions, and the possibility that the Boston Red Sox will someday win the World Series.

It had been a dizzying couple of weeks. The DAG called in a highly credentialed plastic surgeon who stated flatly that Boyce's allegation was not medically possible.

Under cross-examination, Boyce removed the plastic surgeon's own skin. The doctor had done a lot of work for the government—transforming the faces of turncoat mobsters and defector spies who needed new identities. By the time Boyce had finished enumerating the crimes of his patients, the doctor made Beverly Hills plastic surgeons seem saintly.

The deputy AG produced more plastic surgeons, dermatologists, skin allergists, and medical examiners to contradict Captain Grayson's assertion. Boyce destroyed them one by one. He made their testimony sound so abstruse, so ambiguous, that no one without a Ph.D. in forensic dermatology could have made sense of it. Boyce's first law of deconstructing scientific evidence was: Make it boring and make it annoying. Vlonko reported that four jurors were now grinding their teeth whenever Clintick stood up to grill another skin doctor. This was progress.

It was chess. Sandy had made a bad move by having Grayson testify about the mark, and Boyce, having seized the advantage, was pressing it, forcing her to move defensively. The media were meanwhile consumed with trying to figure out whom exactly Boyce was planning to finger as the person who'd stamped Paul Revere's name on the President's noggin.

Beth was increasingly consumed with something else.

☆ · ☆ · ☆

"How was your weekend with Perri?" she asked.

"Hm?" Boyce was deep in thought. Today would be an important day in court. Babette Van Anka was taking the stand. Anticipation was high.

What was Beth saying? "Fine. Fine," he said.

"What's she like?"

"Two arms, two legs. Mammal."

"She seems bright enough. For someone who showcases her boobs."

Boyce quietly reveled in Beth's jealousy. What's more, his weekend with Perri in New York had been spent fending off oddly similar questions about Beth. In the midst of a delicious session of welcome-home fellatio, Perri had looked up in midministration and asked, "What's she really like? She seems sympathetic, for a cold-blooded murderer." It took Boyce half an hour to get back to where he had been.

"She speaks very well of you," Boyce said to Beth. "She called you 'sympathetic.' "

"Why don't you ever talk about her?"

"What do you want to know about her?"

"Are you in love with her?"

"Objection. Leading."

"I'll rephrase. How would you describe your feelings for Ms. Pettengill?"

"Amicable, certainly."

"Amorous?"

"That would depend on your definition of amorous."

"The witness is directed to answer the question." Their knees were touching.

The motorcade was pulling up in front of the courthouse.

"Court is adjourned."

"I reserve the right to recall the witness at a future time."

☆ · ☆ · ☆

Nick Naylor nixed going in through the basement entrance. If Beth MacMann was going in the front door, so would Babette.

Babette was not entirely enthusiastic about the idea. Her notion of arriving somewhere consisted of pulling up in a white limousine longer than most aircraft carriers, stepping out onto a red carpet escorted by twelve steroidal immensities with ear radios, then pausing along the way in to be told by a breathless interviewer from *Entertainment Tonight* that she looked "incredible!" and asked whether she was "excited" about her new movie or "really excited."

Shimmying her way through a media gauntlet mob baying at her with questions—"Babette! Babette! How many times did you and Ken do it that night?"—was not her preferred entrance.

Nick had arranged for bodyguards who bore at least a passing resemblance to the human species. He had also quietly arranged for twenty or so (paid) "supporters" to be on hand, waving signs expressing cheery sentiments like WE LOVE YOU, BABETTE! and YOU GO, GIRL! Some specifically hailed her commitment to peace in the Middle East. One even said, SUICIDE BOMBERS FOR BABETTE! All very welcoming and re-assuring. When she took the stand, she would be basking in the warm reflected glow of fan love.

For a woman who spent enough on clothes in a year to dress the population of Liechtenstein, Babette's appearance was decidedly mini-malist. She wore—what else?—a black pantsuit, the uniform of serious modern women. Her copious bosom—nearly unique among Holly-wood breasts for being actually real—was not in evidence. She looked almost flat chested.

But it was the eyeglasses that prompted the most tittering among the press. They were half-glasses, the kind people wear to government hearings so that they look up from incriminating documents and say, "With all due respect, Senator, I draw quite a *different* inference from that." Intellectual accessorizing. Babette's glasses said, "I ruined my eyes on the footnotes of *Foreign Affairs* magazine."

Boyce studied the jury. Many of them were wide-eyed over having a certified Hollywood celebrity in their midst. If the pattern held, it would soon dawn on them that this Hollywood bigshot was here to impress *them*. Then they'd relax almost to the point of cockiness. It would be their one chance in life to have the upper hand with a cele-brity.

"What is your profession, Ms. Van Anka?" the deputy attorney general began.

"I'm an activist in international affairs."

The correspondent from *Vanity Fair* was seen pressing a balled hand-kerchief to his mouth.

Boyce nudged Beth beneath the table.

"What *else* do you do, Ms. Van Anka?" the deputy AG asked.

"I am, in addition, an actor, singer, and recording artist. But at this point in my life I consider myself primarily an advocate. For peace in the Middle East. And the environment."

A collective tubercular sound came from the press section. Eyes rolled like tumblers in slot machines. Judge Dutch glanced sternly.

"You were an overnight guest in the White House on the night of September twenty-eighth and twenty-ninth of last year?"

"Yes."

Babette's attorneys, Morris, Howard, and Ben, had drilled into her the absolute necessity of answering *as briefly as possible*. They were anxious about their client's predilection for lengthy—indeed, interminable—statements. Taciturnity is as rare in Hollywood as fur.

"Had you been an overnight guest in the White House on previous occasions?"

"Yes."

Two one-word answers in a row. Observers marveled. Had Morris, Howard, and Ben installed a shock collar on her?

"How many times?"

"The First Family and I were friends. I stayed there numerous occasions."

Beth scribbled on her legal pad and slid it over to Boyce: "Friend of First <u>Family</u>?"

"How many times, Ms. Van Anka?"

"I couldn't say."

"Couldn't say or won't say?"

"Objection."

"Sustained."

"Ms. Van Anka, this is the official log kept by the White House usher of overnight guests. It shows that you stayed overnight in the White House a total of fifty-six times."

"If that's what it says. I'm honored."

"Would you say that fifty-six times is a lot?"

"That depends on your definition of 'a lot.' "

"On how many of those occasions was your husband also an overnight guest?"

Boyce rose, Galahad defender of the sanctity of the Grab–Van Anka marriage, to express his outrage.

"Your Honor, setting aside for a moment the prosecution's sneering, harassing tone, this question is utterly without relevance."

"Overruled."

After pickaxing away at Babette, the deputy AG established that Mr. Grab "had only been able to join" Babette at the White House on four occasions. Four occasions, out of fifty-six.

"Your husband, then, was with you only seven percent of the time you were there?"

"If that's what it comes out to. Mr. Grab is a busy man. He's frequently away on business."

"What kind of business is he in?"

"The business kind of business."

"Explain that to the court, if you would."

"He finances things. He makes things happen. Wonderful things that benefit humanity."

"What sorts of things?"

"Objection. Your Honor, what possible relevance does it have that Ms. Van Anka's husband is a respected international financier and philanthropist, who has given considerable sums of money to minorities and other charities?"

"Your Honor, I object to counsel's objection."

"Approach," Judge Dutch said, glowering.

Sidebar.

"Ms. Van Anka," the deputy AG continued, finally, "are you familiar with this quote that appeared in the Los Angeles newspaper about you: 'Babette Van Anka, she's so bad you wanna spanka'?"

"Objection. Your Honor, this sacred court of law is no place for scandal-mongers and low gossip."

"Overruled."

Under his breath, Boyce muttered, "All right, then, it *is*."

"I must have missed the paper that day," Babette replied. "I'm busy, too, you know."

"You've never heard this quote before?"

"I heard it."

"And what does it refer to?"

"Not my acting or singing, hopefully."

Laughter.

Nick Naylor thought, *Yesss.* It was his line.

The deputy attorney general smiled. *Okay, toots, you wanna have fun? Let's have fun.*

"Was it your practice, Ms. Van Anka, before spending the night in the White House, to purchase erotic underwear and erotic devices, at a store in Los Angeles called QQ?"

Babette paled. Boyce leapt to his feet.

"Your Honor, this is an outrageous invasion of privacy, and an affront to women everywh—"

Judge Dutch motioned them forward to sidebar number 127.

The mention of QQ sent a palpable thrum through the courtroom. QQ was a boutique that had been started by a woman who before going to jail had operated one of Los Angeles's most elite escort services. After three and a half years of working in the prison laundry, she opened QQ with the backing of those of her former clients whom she had not publicly identified during her trial. It specialized in exotic, upscale lingerie and romantic "excess-ories," as its catalog put it. If Tiffany were taken over by *Hustler* magazine, the result would be QQ. One popular item was the mink-lined crotchless panties ($2,500). A Victorian corset with whalebone stays went for $800. Then there was the set of four sterling silver balls connected by a string with a handle at the end ($3,200).

The TV commentators all waited for someone else to explain to the public what QQ stood for. Judge Dutch groaned inwardly.

The whole world was waiting. In Denver, a pilot delayed pulling back from the gate so that he would not miss hearing on the live radio broadcast what this QQ stood for. Moreover, the passengers approved the delay and heckled a supervisor who came aboard to order the pilot to depart.

At the defense table, Beth thought back to the time when, in an attempt to stimulate her husband's waning interest in her, she had ordered some racy silk thingees from a catalog. She'd put it all on one night, feeling foolish looking at the garter-belted, stockinged, and bustiered reflection in the mirror. Beth MacMann—in a bustier! She'd lit scented candles, dabbed perfume all over, put on romantic music, lain back on the bed, and waited for him to come through the door. And waited. When he'd finally walked in it was past three, and it had been obvious that even he had already had his fill of sex for one night.

Judge Dutch cleared his throat. "Proceed, Ms. Clintick." By now Babette was a jittery wreck. Her intellectual glasses kept sliding off her nose.

"Ms. Van Anka, do you purchase lingerie and sexual-related items at a store in Los Angeles called QQ?"

"I may have. I shop at a lot of stores in Los Angeles."

The deputy AG asked the court to enter into evidence fourteen credit card receipts in Babette's name from "QQ Enterprises, Ltd." One by one, they were projected on the screen mounted in the court-room. The purchases totaled some $23,725. Doubtless, that would impress those on the jury supporting families of four on $30,000.

"These are yours, Ms. Van Anka?"

Babette studied them through her glasses as though they were re-cently unearthed Dead Sea scrolls.

"Apparently."

"Let me draw your attention to the last receipt. What is the date on that?"

"I can't tell."

"Upper left. Would you read that date for the court, please?"

"September twenty-sixth."

"The item listed, would you read it, please?"

"I can't see. These are reading glasses."

"Very well, with the court's permission, I will. 'Mink massage mitt.' Twelve hundred dollars.

"Ms. Van Anka, what does the name of the store where you purchased these items refer to?"

"I wouldn't know that."

"Does it stand for—"

"Objection. Speculation. Speculation of the most prurient—"

"Sustained."

The world would have to wait until that evening, when one unrestrained guest commentator blurted out what everyone at this point already knew. QQ stood for "Quivering Quim," the Victorian term for—never you mind.

Onto the courtroom screen was projected a series of slides. Each vertically filled one-third of the screen. The first was titled "Van Anka Purchases at QQ Boutique, by Date."

The second was titled "B. Van Anka Overnight Stays at White House, by Date."

The third, filling in the last third of the screen, was titled "Nights First Lady E. MacMann Absent from White House, by Date."

The date of each of Babette's fourteen purchases at QQ preceded by one or two days her visits to the White House. The dates of those fourteen—of fifty-six—of her stays in the White House coincided exactly with dates that Beth had been absent.

☆ · ☆ · ☆

"It's a real shame," Boyce said, handing Beth a stiff vodka back in his hotel suite.

"What is?"

"That we were moneyless students when we knew each other. I'd have liked to see you in mink-lined panties. During the sidebar, Judge Dutch gave Clintick hell for going on about the silver balls."

"She seemed pretty wound up."

"She's trying the biggest case of her life. Though at this point, I think her primary objective is to hang me, not you. If that doesn't sound too conceited."

"I wouldn't want a modest lawyer defending me."

"I know we've been over this a hundred times, but you're positive he was banging Babette that night?"

"Boyce, the man was bent over from sexual exertion. I could smell her perfume on him. And when I turned on the light, he did that raccoon thing with the eyes."

"Number three did that once when she came in. I knew."

"It's charming how you've assigned numerical identities to your ex-wives. I've been in love with two men in my life, a serial adulterer and a serial divorcé. Where did I get this karma?"

"When you dumped me. Karma is as karma does. Actually, it wasn't karma at all. It was divine retribution, the wrath of an angry god, for screwing up my life."

"I love it when people of our generation feel sorry for themselves."

"I don't buy into boomer self-loathing. Our generation has accomplished many things."

"Name one."

"Disco, junk bonds, silicone implants, colorized movies, the whole concept of stress as a philosophical justification for self-indulgence. These achievements will tower above minor accomplishments like defeating Hitler, breaking the sound barrier, and inventing a vaccine for polio. Future historians will call *us* the Greatest Generation."

"I think it's why I fell for Ken. He was real."

"What wasn't 'real' about me?"

"I didn't mean it that way."

"It all has to do with your dad. He got a medal in World War Two. Then along comes a chest full of medals from another war and—boom, you're enlisted marching in his parade."

"Maybe. I never felt like spending a hundred grand on psychoanalysis to find out. I'd so much rather spend the money on lawyers."

"Well, it's reassuring that heroes can turn out to be pricks just like the rest of us nonheroes. But that still leaves unresolved the larger question."

134 · Christopher Buckley

"What?"

"How you'd look in mink-lined panties."

☆ · ☆ · ☆

After another day of making Babette Van Anka look like the Slut of the Millennium, Deputy Attorney General Clintick tossed her limp, twitching carcass at Boyce for cross-examination. As Boyce rose to begin, he felt like all the king's horses and all the king's men. Humpty-Dumpty was in a thousand pieces.

Babette warily returned his smile as he approached. By now she knew he was, for whatever reason, on her side, unlike that bitch prosecutor. This Baylor person had said, "Objection!" so many times, he must have carpal tongue syndrome by now. Morris, Howard, and Ben had explained to her why he was being nice: to take away the wife's motive for killing Ken. But they'd warned her: Be careful of him. *Short answers.*

Boyce walked Babette through some preliminaries to reinforce in the minds of jurors that, like many of them, she had grown up poor, that she had in her own, if somewhat overheated, way shown that the American dream worked. He maneuvered the subject around to the movie *They Call Me* General *Powell!* so that Babette could talk about how thrilling it had been to work with the actor Denzel Washington on a biographical movie about Colin Powell. He led her through a tearful account of her role in the movie *Flight 208 Is Delayed,* in which she played an Israeli paratrooper who single-handedly rescues a jumbo jet full of Hasidic schoolchildren from fanatic Palestinian hijackers. It was this experience, she told the court, that had been the epiphany that had prompted her to become a force for peace in the Middle East.

"You and President MacMann were very close, were you not?" Boyce asked, switching topics abruptly.

Babette seemed taken aback by the question.

Boyce added, "I mean, he looked to you frequently for advice on the Middle East, did he not?"

She brightened. "Oh, you don't *know*."

"Do you mean by that, yes?"

"Yes. Yes. All the time, he was calling me."

Eyeballs careened sideways among the press.

"He called you specifically about the Middle East peace process?"

Boyce had learned from his idol Edward Bennett Williams that an ideal cross-examination elicits an unbroken string of yeses. It shows you have total control of the witness.

"Many times. Many, *many* times."

"He relied on you heavily for your input?"

"Yes."

"Objection."

"Your Honor, I understand that the deputy attorney general might be upset because I am questioning the witness without resorting to character assassination, innuendo, and slander, but—"

"Approach."

Boyce endured his sidebar lecture in silence. It was worth it. Later, Vlonko reported that jurors four, five, seven, and thirteen had beamed at Boyce's outburst.

"Ms. Van Anka," he continued, "are people in your position, that is, creative artists of pronounced social conscience, sometimes ridiculed or made to suffer because they dare to speak out against injustice or on behalf of oppressed—"

"Objection!"

"I will rephrase. Ms. Van Anka, have you been attacked for your activism?"

"Constantly."

Boyce shook his head sadly, as if hearing this were all just too painful.

"It must be hard."

"Objection."

"Withdrawn. Is it hard?"

"Very hard. All the time people say terrible things."

"Ms. Van Anka, is it your understanding that powerful forces in the

Middle East were aware of the fact that you had the President's ear and tried to prevent you from advising him?"

"I object. I object strenuously. Your *Honor*."

"Let me rephrase. Did powerful forces in the Middle East try to prevent you from advising the President of the United States on foreign policy?"

"I . . . had the impression . . . yes?"

Boyce nodded. "And did these forces try to accomplish that by spreading rumors that you and the President were lovers?"

Babette nodded. Her chin quivered. She looked into her lap. Then, as if on cue, she burst into tears. *"Yes,"* she sobbed.

Boyce shook his head at the iniquity of it all. "Was this personally painful to you, Ms. Van Anka?"

"You have no idea."

"How did it make you feel, as a woman, that people would say such vile, wicked things—"

"Objection. Your Honor, is defense conducting a cross-examination or a support group session?"

"Ask your question, Counsel."

"How did it make you feel, as a woman?"

"It made me feel"—Babette sniffled—"that for all our progress as a gender, that we still have a long way to go."

"Ms. Van Anka, did you in February of two years ago personally carry a confidential message from President MacMann to the Prime Minister of Israel?"

Babette's eyes widened. Over the years, she had embroidered this nothing of a story into such a heroic tapestry as to make Bayeux blush. She had told dozens of people that the President had asked her to carry a "top secret" message to the Israeli Prime Minister. In fact, the message consisted of, "Tell that bagel-biter his new press secretary has the best honkers in the Fertile Crescent." As Babette told the story, she made it sound as though the President had entrusted her with a plea not to use atomic weapons on Syria.

"Yes"—Babette nodded—"I did. But I can't—"

"Of course I won't ask you to divulge the contents of a highly classi-fied message having to do with national security."

"Objection."

"Withdrawn. Now, Ms. Van Anka, let us turn to a subject that the prosecution seemed to find so personally distasteful. . . ."

Okay, Babs, you're doing great. Now we're going to play connect the dots. His investigators had found the first dot in an interview that Babette had given to one of the women's magazines years ago, just after she had married Max.

"I'm referring to the business of the personal items, the underwear and such from that store in Los Angeles. Did you not give an interview to one of the women's magazines stating"—Boyce glanced disapprov-ingly at the prosecution—"freely and openly and I might add, indeed proudly, that you and Mr. Grab enjoy what one might call a full and loving intimate relationship?"

Babette wasn't entirely sure where this was going, but at this point she would have followed this man up onto an exit ramp of the 405 Free-way.

"Yes. Max and I have a wonderful relationship."

The sound of choking came from the media.

"Thank you for your candor. And did you tell this magazine that you and your husband both believe that the way to sustain a healthy, inti-mate relationship is to"—Boyce smiled benevolently—"keep things in the bedroom *interesting*?"

"Yes." Babette blushed.

"Objection."

"Overruled." Judge Dutch, along with the billion or so people watching, was dying to see where this was going.

"And did you tell the interviewer, without embarrassment—in fact, with evident joy—that your husband enjoys it when you put on sexy underclothing?"

"I did."

"Ms. Van Anka, because of your busy schedules, you and your husband are *apart* much of the time, is that not true?"

"Yes? Yes."

"Does it make you feel close to your absent husband to wear these articles of intimate clothing?"

"Oh, *yes.*"

"Objection."

"Withdrawn. Do you wear these items only when you are with your husband, or sometimes when you are apart?"

"I bring them with me on trips. To remind me of him. When I feel them against my skin, I feel I'm . . . well . . ."

"Thank you. I know these are terribly private matters. When you are apart from your husband, do you ever put on these articles and call him on the phone?"

Connect the dots. Come on, Babs. Babette blushed, smiled, stared into her lap, brushed away a strand of hair. "Sometimes I put on the things so that I can *pretend* that we're together."

Boyce phrased the next question carefully, knowing that there had been no outgoing call to Max from the Lincoln Bedroom on the night of September 28–29.

"Were you planning to make such a call to your husband that night at the White House?" *Just a few more dots and you can go back to saving the Middle East and the caribou.*

"Yes, I was. I . . . that was one of the reasons I retired early."

"But you fell asleep before you could?"

"Yes."

"You retired at twelve-thirty A.M. That would have been only nine-thirty P.M. on the West Coast."

"Right. Max wouldn't be home until later, so I was going to stay up and call him."

"You told the FBI that you got into bed with the television on."

"Yes. I turned on the television. I usually fall asleep."

Now follow me very, very closely here.

"Is there a particular show that you watch late at night?" In media interviews, Babette talked incessantly about her passion for watching public television, where you could always find something "thought-inspiring." (Like the public service announcements for Saab.) Boyce had read every one of these interviews.

"I try to watch"—Babette looked imploringly at Boyce—"you know, substantial shows."

She meant "substantive," but she was trying.

"Public television?"

"Objection! Your *Honor.*"

"I'll rephrase. What sort of television?"

"Public television. Talk shows. Documentaries . . ."

With his back to the jury, Boyce looked directly into her eyes and said very carefully, *"Did you turn on the public television channel that night in your bed?"*

"I . . . yes. I'm sure I . . . yes."

"And you told the FBI that you fell asleep."

"Yes. I was tired. Such an evening. So many Latin dignitaries. They're exhausting. So talkative."

"So you fell asleep, *with the TV on?*"

"Yes."

"You fell asleep with the television on, set to the public TV channel. This was sometime after twelve-thirty A.M.?"

"Yes."

"Your Honor, with the court's permission, I would like to have received in evidence the *TV Guide* listings for the evening and early morning of September twenty-eight to twenty-nine."

A copy of the *TV Guide* from that week was duly entered after a lengthy sidebar initiated by a distinctly unhappy-looking deputy attorney general.

Boyce handed the *TV Guide* to Babette and asked her to read the listings for the early morning of September 29 for WETA, the local public television channel.

Babette put on her intellectual glasses and read, "One A.M. to three A.M., *Who's Afraid of Virginia Woolf?*"

She looked up at Boyce.

No, no. Do not smile at me.

She caught herself.

A murmur went through the courtroom.

"Would you tell the court what *Who's Afraid of Virginia Woolf?* is?" Boyce asked.

"It's a film. A great film. A great American film."

"Would you tell the court what it's about, briefly?"

"It's about two couples in an unhappy marriage. I mean, *really-really* unhappy."

"And what takes place in the movie?"

"Oh, a lot of anger. Shouting. Throwing things. Screaming."

"Shouting, screaming, throwing things?"

"For *starters.*"

"The television in the Lincoln Bedroom is fifteen feet from the bed. Would you have had the volume up so that you could hear?"

"Very up."

"So a movie showing people arguing loudly was playing in the Lincoln Bedroom, not far from where Secret Service agent Birnam was stationed, between one A.M. and three A.M.?"

"Yes."

"Thank you, Ms. Van Anka. No further questions at this time, Your Honor."

Chapter 19

They were calling it "the Timeline of the Millennium."

Normally in criminal trials, timelines—chronological orderings of events—are broken down into minutes. The one Boyce and his team beavered up was in hundredths of seconds. This prompted snide comments among the media that he must have located the White House residence cockpit flight recorder.

Boyce's timeline alleged that an incompetent, vengeful FBI agent Whepson and a resentful, hearing-impaired Secret Service agent Birnam had been alone with the President's cooling corpse for thirty-seven seconds, giving them time to emboss the President's forehead with the Revere hallmark.

Deputy Attorney General Clintick fought like a lynx to have the timeline excluded. She was under increasing pressure following Boyce's astonishing cross-examination of Babette Van Anka.

President Harold Farkley was getting more and more questions about the case, and they were being asked with even less than usual courtesy. One day, after announcing a historic engineering initiative to prevent the Missouri River from overflowing and drenching America's breadbasket, and deploring racial profiling—former secretary of state Colin Powell had again been pulled over by a Virginia State Trooper and spread-eagled across the hood of his car—he was accosted in an unseemly manner by the traveling White House press corps, demanding to know if he had played an "active" role in prosecuting his well-known nemesis, Mrs. MacMann. None, none at all, he averred. His press secretary told him that Bob Woodward, Investigative Reporter of the Previous Millennium, was "making inquiries." Harold Farkley's mouth went dry.

Having lived all his life in the shadow of his own mediocrity, he was determined to defy his karma and win the upcoming nomination. The last thing he needed was a front-page *Washington Post* article ("First in a Series of Articles") with the headline:

SEEKING TO SETTLE OLD SCORE,
FARKLEY ENCOURAGED JUSTICE DEPT.
TO PROSECUTE FIRST LADY

He instructed his press secretary to put out the word—and not quietly—that he had been "skeptical" of the evidence against Beth "all along."

In due course, articles reflecting this new line appeared. The sources were not attributed directly, but there was enough DNA in them to alarm the attorney general. He in turn instructed his press secretary to put out the word—loudly—that he too had had "qualms" about the evidence "from the beginning" but that Deputy Attorney General Clintick had been "avid" to prosecute.

In due course those articles appeared, causing Sandy Clintick to break out in a rash. Whom the gods would destroy, they first make itch.

☆ · ☆ · ☆

On *Hard Gavel,* Alan Crudman's jealousy over Boyce's masterful handling of the case had caused him to evolve into a public second-guesser for the prosecution. It was something of a career reversal for a man who had once boasted that he could have gotten Adolf Hitler acquitted.

In the middle of last night's show, he had gotten carried away in his fever to demonstrate that Agents Whepson and Birnam could not possibly have put on latex gloves, grabbed the spittoon, embossed the presidential forehead, removed the gloves, and replaced the spittoon between 7:33:00 A.M. and 7:33:37 on September 29, while Beth was in the bathroom barfing. Crudman leapt out of his chair to reenact the scenario, lapel microphone still attached, yanking his mike out of its socket and upsetting a water glass.

Perri's attitude toward Boyce had become openly antagonistic. Boyce had stopped coming home on weekends. She couldn't even wheedle anything out of his team as to what was going on behind the scenes. When they did speak, she was unable to get anything out of him. He didn't respond to her cooey little nudgings. His conversation consisted of, "Uh-huh, uh-huh. Listen, gotta go." It was all a bit . . . much. Hadn't Perri nursed him back to emotional health after his disastrous fourth divorce from the socialite mountain climber—what's more, at a time when she should have been concentrating on her own career?

With her producers, she pretended that Boyce was keeping her fed with tidbits. Meanwhile, as she discussed the case on television every night for a larger and larger audience, Perri had become consumed with what, for her, was the larger question of the Trial of the Millennium: Were Boyce and Beth doing it?

☆ · ☆ · ☆

The tricky part in getting Judge Dutch to allow his timeline was that the only person who could attest to Agents Whepson and Birnam's being alone with the corpse was—his client, and of course there was no way he would put her on the stand. One of the triumphs of the American justice system is that the guilty—that is, the accused—does not actually have to defend himself. He can just sit there while lawyers fire spitballs at the accusers and make them out to be the real villains.

☆ · ☆ · ☆

"We go now," said evening news anchorman Peter Jennings, "to our legal correspondent. Jeff, how did it go today?"

"Peter, this was another *bad* day for the prosecution. Mrs. MacMann's lawyer, Boyce Baylor, introduced a timeline of the morning of the President's death that is so minute, so *detailed,* that you have to wonder if this jury, or any jury, would be able to keep it all straight. It tracks the movements of eighteen people in and out of the presidential bedroom over a period of two hours. At the heart of Baylor's argument is a critical thirty-seven-second period when, as he claims, FBI agent Jerrold Whepson and Secret Service agent Woody Birnam were alone with the President's body. He contends that, acting out of personal animosity toward Mrs. MacMann, they stamped his forehead with the Paul Revere silver hallmark on the spittoon so that it would emerge as a murder weapon. The defense contends that the President died in the night as a result of an accidental *fall*. For the past three days, Baylor has *hammered* at Whepson and Birnam *relentlessly*. In the end, they did not categorically *deny* that they were alone with the body while Mrs. MacMann was in the bathroom. I have to say, whatever you think of the argument that this is all some government conspiracy, these were *effective* cross-examinations, especially coming after his *devastating* cross-examination of Babette Van Anka. In the end, the jury may conclude not that Mrs. MacMann is *innocent,* but that she is not, beyond a reasonable doubt, *guilty*. Peter?"

☆ · ☆ · ☆

"I wondered if this was going to happen," said Boyce.

Beth's head rested on his chest. "You knew it would."

They were in bed in a tangle of sheets. Outside, beyond two sets of doors, stood silently fuming Secret Service agents. It was a Friday night, no court tomorrow, and Boyce's war room was quiet.

"How did you get them?" Boyce asked, feeling under the sheets for the silky-furry object. He held it aloft for inspection.

"Aren't they *hideous*? I called a friend in L.A. and had her buy them. Don't worry. She's discreet. It's not the sort of thing I wanted to have reported that I put on my American Express. So now the question is finally resolved."

"Not quite. We know what you look like in crotchless mink panties now. We still don't know what you would have looked like in them back in law school."

"Even more ridiculous than I look in them now."

"I can't believe you wore them in court today. What if you'd had some medical emergency and they'd taken you to the hospital and put you on the table and you're wearing *these*? What a headline!"

Beth snuggled against him. "You were really good."

"You weren't so bad yourself."

"In *court*. Don't flatter yourself."

"Oh. And how was I just now?"

"Mm, adequate."

"Your bill just went up by a million dollars."

"You were amazing. Godlike."

"Ten percent off."

"Just like old times."

It was strange, making love to a once familiar partner after a quarter century. Boyce turned over metaphors in his contented mind. Was it like drinking wine long cellared and ripened? Or was it more like entering a garden in which the vines had matured into—

"The media's saying it's over," Beth said.

"The media isn't the jury. But you heard Vlonko. I don't think I've ever seen him happier."

"Vlonko," said Beth. "Diviner of minds."

"He said jurors six, seven, ten and thirteen were actually nodding when I crossed Birnam."

"Is thirteen the—"

"Homosexual pediatric neurosurgeon of German extraction. You just don't *get* more no-nonsense than that. And *he* was nodding." Boyce sighed happily. "I don't want to jinx it—the gods are watching 24/7—but I *think* we might have this thing nailed. I think they're going to acquit. You never know, but I think you're going to be okay."

Beth reached for her cigarettes and lit one. "I want my life back after this," she said. "Not the old life. My own."

"You're young."

"Ish."

"Sexy."

"Ish."

"Smart."

"How smart was I, to get into this?"

"You were smart enough to hire a good lawyer."

Beth sat up on one elbow and turned to him. She was beaming with excitement. "Boyce, I want to take the stand."

"Huh?"

"I want to testify."

"Is that a cigarette or a joint you're smoking? Are you nuts?"

"No, I want to take the stand."

"I'm not even going to go into that."

"Why?"

"Because it's such an insane notion that it's not even in the realm of thinkability. This was not a particularly easy case. You may have noticed? Just because we're ahead, don't get crazy ideas."

"You've been brilliant. I'm the first to admit that. I know you've worked your heart out on this. But people still think I did it. You heard what they said on TV tonight."

"Who cares what the public thinks? Get yourself a PR guy. Whatsisname, Naylor, the one who does Babette's PR. He could make Saddam Hussein out to be Santa Claus."

"Thank you. That was truly sensitive."

Change the subject, quick!

"I gotta have water. These hotel rooms. My mouth is like the Mojave."

Boyce went in search of water. His mind was reeling. *Astounding. Twenty-five years in politics turns you into a—politician. She's barely off the hook on a murder rap and already she's planning her comeback.* What was she thinking? Well, she wasn't thinking, just like twenty-five years ago when she married War God. The minibar. It would have water. Cool, expensive water from some spring in Finland or Wales, so pure you could wash your contact lens in it.

Boyce got back into bed with an eight-ounce bottle of water that cost $9. He snuggled up against her. Her body was less pliant and responsive than a minute ago.

"Your cross-examinations of the staff," she said, her back to him, "made me out to be a total bitch. Lady Bethmac."

"So what, if it helps you get off a murder rap?"

She turned to face him. "What good does it do me if I get off and everyone still thinks I did it? And that I'm the Joan Crawford of First Ladies?"

"What good does it do you if you *get off*? Apart from not spending the rest of your life in federal prison? Or the death penalty? That's a hard one. I'll have to think about that."

"I need some kind of life after this."

"Boy, you're an easy one to please."

"If I take the stand, I can show them that I not only didn't do it, but that I'm not the First Bitch."

"Listen to me: A jury is probably about to acquit you of murder. Trust me, that is *the* major goal here. It is the *only* goal. Look, acquittal means you didn't do it."

"No, it doesn't. It just means that I got off. I'll be the O. J. Simpson of First Ladies. What am I supposed to do, hang out on public golf courses looking for the real killers?"

"It beats working in the prison laundry for the next forty years. To say nothing of lethal injection."

"What if I want to continue in public life? What if I want to run for public office myself? The Senate."

Boyce stared in the semidark, a pointless dramatic gesture.

"Beth, I know this has been very stressful for you."

"Will you please not speak to me like I'm a mental patient?"

"I won't if you don't act like one. Look, it's not true what F. Scott Fitzgerald said about American lives not having second acts. Look at

Charles Manson—he's got his own Web site. You can do whatever you want after this. My God, the product endorsements alone will be enough to—pay my bill!"

"I have no intention," Beth said icily, "of becoming a product endorser. That's a line of work for overweight British royals and oversexed White House interns."

"How *are* you planning to pay my bill? I suppose we could work something out." He nibbled her ear. "Take it out in trade."

"Stop. According to a study by the American Bar Association, three-quarters of the public thinks that a defendant who doesn't take the stand is either guilty or hiding something."

"For once I agree with three-quarters of the American public. Do you know how many times I've allowed a client to testify in a criminal case? Twice. One was a seventy-eight-year-old Mafia boss in advanced stages of emphysema. I put *him* on the stand so the jury could listen to him wheeze. They felt so sorry for him, they let him go die at home. The second was a Catholic cardinal who'd been accused of unholy communion with an altar boy. Now it was twenty years later and the altar boy had a heroin problem, a crack cocaine problem, and a drinking problem, along with three other unpleasant diseases. So he'd decided to extort from his former parish monsignor, who was now a leading prince of the American church. In this particular case, the cardinal happened to be innocent. A rarity, I know, an actually innocent client. I should have had him stuffed. At any rate, I put him on the stand because how often is it you have an innocent client who dresses in scarlet robes and wears a cross the size of a tire iron around his neck?"

"And?"

"They found him guilty. And you want to take the stand."

Beth stubbed out her cigarette. "All those years with Ken, all those horrible years, I sucked it up, turned the other cheek, looked the other way, worked my ass off. I'm in my forties, I have no money, no visible means of support, other than endorsing antiques you can kill your husband with. I'm a widow—do not interrupt me, please—and everyone thinks I'm an assassin who offed a war hero with a spittoon. This is *not fair.* And I will *not accept it.* And I will *not* walk out of that courtroom into a life of people pointing at me in airports as some historical freak, afraid of turning on the television because Jay Leno and Letterman might be *doing* me in their monologues because nothing else sensational happened that day. Frankly, doing laundry in prison for forty years—or getting hooked up to the death drip—doesn't look half-bad by comparison. If I'd wanted to get off on technicalities, I'd have hired Alan Crudman or Plato Cacheris or some other hotshot. I hired *you* because I need to *win.* Not not-lose. Win. You said I should walk in that first day and look like I'd come to accept their apology? Well, that's how I plan to walk out, like I've accepted *their* apology and now I'm ready to accept the world's."

Boyce considered. "I think we should prepare a statement announcing that you plan to devote the rest of your life to searching for the real killers."

Beth slugged him with the pillow. Hard.

"I'm beginning," said Boyce, "to see how you got that nickname."

Chapter 20

𝒴ou might want to glance at this," Boyce's secretary said a few days later, handing him the Style section of *The Washington Post,* folded over to Lloyd Grove's "Reliable Source" column. "Glance" was code for "Here is something that you are really not going to like."

> The relationship between First Defendant **Beth MacMann** and superlawyer **Boyce "Shameless" Baylor** may be progressing beyond the normal lawyer-client stage. The two were an item in the 1970s when they were students at Georgetown Law, before Lady Bethmac unceremoniously dumped him for the future President. But she may have left the pilot light on. Or they could just be boning up on the next day's court proceedings, in Shameless's $7,500-a-night suite at the Jefferson Hotel.

Grove, the swine. Beth didn't dump him "unceremoniously." And the $7,500 was for three suites, not one.

His mind then turned to the larger issue.

Her Secret Service detail. Of course. They were the only ones who could have known, and they now despised them both. Well, who could blame them? He had accused them of monstrous conspiracy. Still, where was their quiet professionalism? Where was the "Secret" in Secret Service? "Pricks," he muttered.

The irony was that whatever "pilot light" Beth had kept burning for him had been blown out during their argument over her testifying. He probably should not have made the crack about how it was just about this time of morning that her late husband had "committed suicide by spittoon." Beth got out of bed, got dressed, and stormed out of the suite, back to her Cleveland Park Elba. So much for their reunion. It had been fun while it lasted, all three hours of it. This would present an interesting new challenge, not being on speaking terms with your client in the middle of a murder trial.

Warily, Boyce turned on the TV. Instant disaster. On came one of the morning shows. The two hosts were in the middle of a wink-wink fest over it, cracking art-imitating-life jokes about how maybe Beth would get a break on her legal bill. Ha ha ha.

Boyce flipped channels. Swell. There on the screen above the next two hosts was a photo of Beth and Boyce from law school, with the headline LOVE STORY and a caption "Love means never having to say you're guilty."

He began to dial Beth on his cell phone, then thought it better under the circumstances to use a landline. God knows who was listening in.

"I think today," he said, "we might want to use the basement garage entrance to the courthouse."

Beth was in shock, or at least as close to shock as type A personalities allowed themselves to get.

"How did this happen?" she croaked. "Who?"

"Ask your so-called Secret Service detail."

"I did. They denied it."

"Of course they denied it."

"I believe them. But I wouldn't blame them if they had. But these guys are professionals. They don't blab to the press. Even about people who've made up cockamamie stories about how they plant evidence to incriminate First Ladies."

"For the benefit of anyone listening in to this conversation, the former First Lady is obviously hysterical and not possessed of full mental faculties."

"This has to have come from your end."

Boyce thought. "The night desk clerk. When you stormed out of here in the middle of the night. He must have tipped them."

"Give me some credit. I didn't exit through the lobby. We took the elevator to the basement garage. I guess I might as well get used to basements, since I'm going to be spending the rest of my life in them."

"We'll sort it out later. Meanwhile, if anyone asks—and they will—we were working late. It's perfectly plausible."

"On a Friday night?"

"Edward Bennett Williams worked late Friday nights when he was in trial."

"Boyce," she said, "about the other night. I've been thinking."

At least she'd come to her senses about testifying. Thank God.

"I have to take the stand."

"Beth, this is not a good time to discuss this."

"Then when would be a good time? This afternoon?"

"Look, *Vanity Fair* is going to be calling any minute asking us to pose nude in bed for next month's cover. Before we discuss whether you testify, we have some serious damage control to do."

"If you can't find a way to go along with the decision, I accept that."

"What does that mean?"

"It means that I can always add someone to the defense team who would be willing to do a direct on me."

"Team? Your *team* consists of *me.*"

"Boyce, I'm just not negotiable on this."

Time. He needed time. Time to . . . what? . . . crush Valium in her food. That's it. Keep her drugged for the rest of trial. If she nodded off at the defense table, he'd say, You *see* what a strain this poor woman is under?

"Okay. We'll talk about it after court today. Jesus, look at the time. We're going to be late. Have the un–Secret Service drive you in through the basement garage. I'll meet you inside."

"I'm going in the front door, as I have every day."

"Don't say anything to anyone about testifying. Beth?"

She'd hung up.

☆ · ☆ · ☆

Confronted with this fresh hell—as Dorothy Parker put it—Perri had only one way to proceed: full steam ahead. Somewhat nervously, she rehearsed her indignation and dialed Boyce's cell phone, his super-secret cell phone, the one whose number he gave out only to death row wardens entrusted with the temporary care and feeding of his less successful clients.

"Is this *true*?" Perri demanded, dispensing with the usual, "Hi, honey!"

"I'm on my way to court," Boyce said. "Can we talk about this later?"

So it *was* true. As it happened, Perri had been the source of the leak to *The Washington Post*. She had called up Grove and told him that she had walked in on Beth and Boyce in the act. Call it an educated gambit.

"You bastard." Perri faked a stifled sob.

"Look, baby, I'm"   what a morning—"it's got nothing to do with you."

"Obviously not."

"I'll come up this weekend. We'll go to La Grenouille. Champagne, foie gras, that Dover sole with that sauce you like. Grand Marnier soufflé." Just what he needed in the middle of the Trial of the Millennium—a hysterical betrayed girlfriend, with her own television show, costarring Alan Crudman as the Greek chorus.

"You think I can be bought off with a *soufflé*? What do you think I am, some *flight attendant*?"

"Those happen to be the best soufflés in the world."

"Screw the soufflés!"

"Perri honey, I've been under intense pressure here. You have no idea."

My God, he thought, *I sound like Babette Van Anka.*

"You could be disbarred for screwing your client, you know."

"Honey, lawyers screw their clients all the time. And make a good living."

"I'm calling the D.C. Bar Ethics Committee."

"Okay, okay. Listen, I'm pulling up at the courthouse right now. You can probably see me on your TV. Do you see me? That's me. I'm waving. That's for you." He made a kissing sound. "I'll call you the second I'm free. Okay? . . . Okay? . . . Perri?"

She'd hung up. Not yet ten o'clock and already two for two.

☆ · ☆ · ☆

After court that day, they were waiting for him as his car exited the courthouse basement garage. The driver had to stop or he would have crushed a dozen photographers and cameramen. They swarmed around the car, encircling it, scanning the inside with their lenses. Boyce was no stranger to paparazzi, but this was an entirely new level of interest. Now he had insight into what it was to be a Princess Diana. Not wishing to have film footage of his car speeding away from a clamoring, shrieking press become a permanent part of the Boyce Baylor videotape archive, he rolled down the window, smiled, and said, "She's in the trunk." They liked that. They let him go after a few pointless, shouted questions.

Beth had made it abundantly clear, over a strained atmosphere and tuna-fish sandwiches in the soundproof defense room, that she now more than ever planned to take the stand. This led to their most candid discussion about the night of September 28–29.

"If you're committed to going through with this," Boyce said, "then you'd better tell me everything I need to know about what happened. Tell me everything. Including what I really *didn't* want to know."

"All right," Beth said. "He came to bed after screwing that over-the-hill hooker—"

"Stop. Stop right there." Boyce sighed. "You'll recall I spent days doing one of the best cross-examinations of my career—and I don't say that to boast—rehabilitating that 'over-the-hill hooker,' *precisely* so that the jury would conclude that she had *not* been screwing the late President. Which conveniently removed your motive for killing him. And now the first thing you tell me is he was in there doing push-ups with her. Beth, do you understand why this is suicidal?"

"Okay. Ask the question again."

"Would you tell the court what happened on that night?"

"My husband came to bed about two-thirty A.M.—"

"Why so late?"

"I didn't ask."

"Oh, *that's* convincing."

"He's the President of the United States. They get up all the time in the middle of the night to save the world."

"Weren't you curious as to what crisis had him up in the middle of the night?"

"The crisis in his crotch."

"Very good," Boyce said. "We got two questions into a cross-examination before you admitted to killing him. Here are a few more. Did you ever assault your husband? Did he require medical treatment afterwards? Was it your habit to throw heavy objects at him? Did you kill your husband? Did you assassinate the President of the United States?"

"Finished?"

"Not nearly."

"I woke up. It was after two-thirty by the clock. I heard a sound. It was the President, getting into bed. He was frequently up at night, phone calls, emergencies. I didn't think anything of it. I . . . no, that doesn't really work, does it? Okay, you want to know what *really* happened that night?"

"Yes, Mrs. MacMann. Would you tell the jury what *really* happened that night."

"Do you want to hear this?"

"Personally, I'm dying to. But if I were you, I'd stop right there."

"If I tell them what happened, they'll believe me."

"I think you spent too long in politics."

"They'll believe the truth."

"You did whack him with the Revere ware, or didn't you?"

"Not *that* hard."

Boyce buried his face in his hands. "Oh, great."

"I didn't throw it that hard. He barely flinched. Usually he goes down when I throw something at him."

"Be sure to mention that."

"I've hit him much harder before. The time I threw the lamp at him? Four stitches. He had the press secretary say he swallowed a pretzel wrong and passed out and hit his chin on the way down."

"Well, it lets you off the hook. We'll just explain to the jury that he didn't actually die because you bashed him in the skull with a heavy metal object. He died—of something else. His war wounds . . ."

"But that's just it. He did. He had to. Look, he was alive and breathing when he put his head on the pillow. He was smirking."

"You didn't . . . get up in the middle of the night and finish him off? Beth?"

"What do you take me for?"

"I know what killed him."

"What?"

"Gamma rays from outer space."

"I don't know what happened. Maybe she screwed him to death. I don't know, except that I'm not guilty. And I won't have people thinking I am and that you got me off. If you won't help me, I'll find someone who will."

When Boyce got back to the hotel at the end of the day, the police had erected barriers outside. In addition to the mob, he counted six satellite trucks. They were all hoping for a glimpse of at least half of the Fun Couple of the Millennium.

Above he heard a helicopter.

He motioned the driver to go around. His era of basement garages had begun.

Back in his suite, he slumped into a chair and fought the temptation to pour himself a double bourbon.

He went into the bedroom.

The phone rang. Perri.

"I'm putting together tonight's show," she said in a businesslike voice. "Have you got anything for me?"

"There's a rumor." Boyce sighed. "She might be testifying."

"Really? How good a rumor?"

"That's the rumor."

"See you Friday at La Grenouille."

☆ · ☆ · ☆

Boyce thrashed in his bed until around 2:30 A.M. He got up, dressed, and exited the Jefferson in an unaccustomed way—by the outside fire escape.

The ladder deposited him in a back alley that led to the street. As he turned away from the hotel, he saw that a skeleton crew was manning the cameras.

He caught a cab on Connecticut Avenue and gave the driver the cross streets a few blocks away from his ultimate destination.

"Lady Bethmac's stayin' just up the block from here," the driver ventured.

"You think she did it?"

"*Oh* yeah. She killed him with that *bowl*. But that lawyer she got, he'll get her off. Uh-huh. Do you know what he charges?"

"No idea."

"Ten thousand dollars. For one *hour.*"

"He must be good."

"Oh, he *good.* He get the devil off. He and the devil, they get along *just* fine. Got a lot in common. Lot of lawyers in this town just like that." He chuckled. "Don't know if the devil going to have *room* for them all."

He pulled over at the corner of Wisconsin and Newark. Boyce gave him a twenty, along with his business card. The driver inspected it in the light.

"Damn! You him! Can I get your autograph?"

☆ · ☆ · ☆

The last time Boyce had snuck into somewhere had been a girl's dorm back in college days. *Plus ça change.* But that dorm had not been under the protection of the Secret Service, and as Boyce contemplated how to breach the perimeter, it crossed his mind that the director of the Secret Service would gladly pin its highest medal on any agent who shot Boyce Baylor, preferably in the balls.

At the entrance to Rosedale, the estate where Beth was encamped, was a duplication of the vigil back at his hotel. Satellite trucks, vans full of slumbering TV crews. The Secret Service had pulled a car athwart the driveway.

Boyce walked down a darkish street that bordered the six-acre property. There were houses whose backyards abutted the estate. Feeling distinctly criminal, he looked both ways and plunged into one of the backyards. He scaled a low redbrick wall, ruining some meticulously trained clematis vines in the process, and pulled himself over into the forbidden zone.

She was staying in the old yellow farmhouse where George Washington had actually slept once or twice, the home having belonged to his friend and comrade in arms, General Uriah Forrest. Forrest, a wealthy Georgetown merchant, had built the house, three miles up from the river, for his young wife, as a port town was not considered congenial to a lady. Once again the old house was serving as the domicile for a lady for whom the city had proved too much.

As Boyce walked toward the house, he decided that since he had no face mask, grappling hook, or silencer-equipped pistol, there was little point in trying to play James Bond. He would go in like the lawyer he was—threatening to sue everyone in his path.

He got his chance soon enough. He heard the scrotum-tightening sound of a German shepherd saying, in German to his handler: "Please—*bitte!*—please let me just rip out his throat, *then* you can arrest him." This was followed by a commanding human voice saying, "*Freeze!* Put your hands where I can see them! Now!"

It took ten minutes of gradually escalating threats and calls to their superiors before they relented and led him to Beth's door. Three of them stood behind him, scowling, at the ready, in case he turned out to be an assassin wearing a rubber Boyce Baylor face mask.

She came to the door, wiping sleep from her eyes, amazed, clearly, to find him there, but perhaps, he thought, not altogether disappointed.

The Secret Service withdrew. He went in, closed the door.

"I have a solution to our basement garage problem," he said.

She was standing by the mantelpiece, one arm across her chest, smoking. "Oh?"

"I asked you this once before. I'm going to ask you one more time."

"Boyce, I told you—"

"Will you marry me?"

Beth's eyes widened. "At three-thirty A.M.?"

"We could wait until the morning. Judge Dutch could marry us during recess. That would give them something for tomorrow's evening news."

She sat on the couch next to him. "Remember the last time you proposed to me? In the rowboat at Fletcher's Boat House?"

"I remember you said yes. This time, if the answer is yes, I want it in writing."

"Shouldn't we get through this first?"

"We're almost there. As long as you drop this idea of testifying."

"Is that what's behind this?"

"No. I came here to ask you to marry me. I would have brought a ring, but the stores were closed. Look, we lost twenty-five years. I don't want to lose the next twenty-five. We won't have any teeth left. As for the rest of it, I'll give up practicing law, we'll go away. I'll build you a castle, in—wherever you want. I've got lots of money. It's embarrassing how much I've made. We'll be together and not give a shit what anyone thinks. We'll leave it all behind. We'll adopt Korean kids. With Russian kids, you never know what you're getting. Don't think about it. For once, go with your heart. Please. Say yes. Prove Nancy Reagan wrong. *Just say yes.*"

"Yes."

"Oh baby, that's great. That's just terrific."

"After I testify."

Chapter 21

No one believed Perri when, wearing her tightest cashmere sweater on *Hard Gavel,* she hinted that Beth would take the stand *precisely* because it was going so well, in order to rehabilitate herself with the public.

Alan Crudman ridiculed the idea in his most condescending tone, saying that with all due respect, that was nuts, just nuts. No defense attorney worth his salt would allow it. Forget it.

Perri smiled. Let him play her for the dumb blonde. The freckled dweeb would eat his words. Indeed, she felt confident enough to challenge him, right there and then, to a $1,000 bet. Crudman fell for it.

Next morning, while watching the day's proceedings on TV, Perri felt a warm wave of satisfaction wash through her when she saw on the screen a distinctly weary-looking Boyce—had he cut himself shaving?—approach the bench, along with an amazed, eager Deputy Attorney General Clintick. Judge Dutch leaned forward, then seemed to recoil into his black leather throne like an astronaut pinned by the G-force of blastoff. He recovered, leaned forward again, in an attitude, Perri thought, of barely controlled amazement. His face said, "Counsel, are you *quite sure*?" Boyce nodded, as if accepting reluctantly the terms of a plea bargain he had just resoundingly lost. Judge Dutch stroked his chin, waved the lawyers away from his bench like so many flies, and instructed the clerk to remove the jury. Even on television you could hear the excitement rippling through the courtroom. Clerks who had not moved in so long that some viewers were surprised to find they were actually alive and not wax effigies were suddenly all attention, heads flicking this way and that like aroused cobras.

So began the fierce deliberations by a sleepless, frustrated Boyce to try to render his client's entire prior life history inadmissible. His one consolation was that no tape recording existed of a 911 emergency call to the police from the late President, with him saying, "Help! It's my wife! She's attacking me with a spittoon!" So far as he knew.

☆ · ☆ · ☆

President Harold Farkley was in the middle of a meeting with various princes of a Middle Eastern kingdom. He hoped to persuade them to increase their oil production in time to lower prices at the gas pump before the upcoming presidential election. He knew that in return they would ask him to sell them advanced U.S. fighter jets, ostensibly to protect their oil but really to annoy the Israelis. Thus the intractable American position in the Middle East: pleading with Arabs for more oil while providing their enemy with the latest weapons. Another day at the White House.

The chief of staff approached the President's chair from behind and whispered the news into his ear. President Harold Farkley's eyes went vacant in surprise.

"News about the trial?" Prince Blandar inquired.

The President wondered if he should pretend it was something else. "Just a minor development. Nothing, I assure you, as important as meeting with you and Their Royal Highnesses."

One of the other princes asked his cousin to translate.

"His Royal Highness Wazir says that he thinks it was the FBI man, not the Secret Service man, who impressioned the President's forehead."

President Farkley smiled thinly and thanked His Royal Highness for this valuable insight, then tried to steer the conversation back to fossil fuels. One of the other princes began remonstrating heatedly in his native tongue with Prince Wazir. Prince Blandar translated: "His other Royal Highness is expressing to his cousin his belief that the President *fell* onto the silver expectoration receptacle."

He leaned in closer to the President. "What is your own belief, Mr. President?"

Harold Farkley had not been designed by nature for such critical moments. He knew this. He also knew that the right answer might open those lovely oil faucets a crack and float him to victory in November on a soft black cushion.

"Your Highness," he said, "there are times when I think that the United States could learn a thing or two about justice from some of her allies, such as your own kingdom. You certainly don't let lawyers bring your fine country to *its* knees! Ha ha."

Prince Blandar nodded appreciatively. "It is true. A matter such as this would have been taken care of very differently. Several years ago, one of the princesses threatened her husband. It was taken care of the next day. A simple death notice was published the week following. On page seven. End of matter."

"Yes, well, it's certainly been a distraction. I'll be sure to pass along what you said to our attorney general and the secretary of state, who I know is very much looking forward to his upcoming visit with the King. Now about the oil . . ."

☆ · ☆ · ☆

Alan Crudman was in a foul temper the next night on *Hard Gavel* at having been aced out of $1,000 by Perri. He told the viewers Perri had obviously gotten her information from inside sources, whereas *he* had based his judgment on "legal scholarship." She made him write out a check right then and there, to her favorite charity: a home for the emotionally troubled children of divorce lawyers.

Perri glowed that night on TV. Immediately after the show, she got a call from the head of one of the big three networks—who as it happened was himself recently separated from his second wife—telling her how impressed he was, not just by Perri's uncanny acuity, but by her show in general, and how he very much wanted to meet with her at her earliest convenience to discuss a possible relationship. With the network, of course. Was she by any chance free for dinner that night? . . . She was? Why, good, good . . . La Grenouille? Excellent. Everything was so good there. The soufflés!

He'd done his homework.

☆ · ☆ · ☆

Faced with potential disaster, Boyce determined to get it all out on the table in his direct examination. He wouldn't leave anything for DAG Clintick, who was salivating to get her turn at Beth.

"Mrs. MacMann," he said, trying to look thrilled that his client was now finally getting the chance to tell her side of the story, "did you kill your husband?"

"No."

There. See? She's innocent. No further questions.

"Did you and your husband ever fight?"

"Yes. Often."

"Did you ever throw things at your husband?"

"Yes. On at least eight occasions that I can recall. We had a pretty spirited marriage."

"What did you throw at him?"

"Anything I could lay my hands on."

People laughed.

"Such as?"

Beth considered. "I recall . . . a book, a paperweight, a stapler . . . a carton of milk, a shoe—high-heeled—and, oh, the lamp." It sounded like a shopping list.

"Lamp?"

"A desk lamp. It was not a valuable antique, but it did make an impression on him."

More laughter. Judge Dutch glared owlishly.

"Did it require stitches by the White House physician?"

"Yes, it did. Four, I believe. Possibly more. I got him pretty good."

Judge Dutch said that if he heard one more titter, he would order the TV cameras out of the courtroom and clear it of spectators. A billion spectators trembled at the thought.

"Was this incident covered up, for the press?"

"Yes, it was. The press secretary said that Ken—my husband—had swallowed a pretzel and passed out and hit his chin on the way down, nearly killing the dog."

"You say you threw things at the President eight times?"

"While we were living in the White House. I threw things at him on other occasions, before."

"I see. Were these incidents the result of what you might call normal marital stress?"

"Objection."

"Sustained."

"Did you throw things at your husband because he made you angry for a particular reason?"

"Of course. It wasn't just target practice, Mr. Baylor."

Judge Dutch almost laughed himself.

"Did you throw things at him for a *good* reason?"

"Objection."

"Sustained."

"Did you throw these things at him because you felt he had betrayed you?"

Beth paused. "My husband is dead, Mr. Baylor. He's not here to account for himself, so I would just as soon not go into that."

"Objection."

Judge Umin directed the witness to answer the question that had been put to her by her own defense counsel.

"I respectfully decline to answer that, Your Honor."

"I withdraw the question."

"Objection."

Judge Dutch drummed his fingers on the bench. He waved the lawyers up. Boyce was instructed to instruct his client to answer the question.

"Because," Beth said, "I was upset with him."

"Mrs. MacMann, are you a bitch?"

Murmurmurmur.

"I hope not. I've tried not to be. But in politics some people inevitably are not satisfied."

"Are you familiar with the nickname Lady Bethmac?"

"Yes. It's a pun on the awful wife of a king in Shakespeare's play *Macbeth*. She *was* a bitch."

"How did the name Lady Bethmac get attached to you?"

"Let's see. One, I caused a number of people at the White House to be dismissed. Two, the people who were dismissed were not happy about this. Three, newspaper headline writers find it hard to resist a good pun."

"Did you cry at your husband's funeral at Arlington National Cemetery?"

"No, I did not."

"Why?"

"I did my crying that day in private. I have tried, to the extent possible, not to express personal emotions publicly."

"Is that why you never threw anything at your husband in public?"

"I suppose."

"The night he died, did you hear anything unusual?"

"I heard a noise, yes."

"Did you investigate it?"

"No."

"Why?"

"My husband was often up in the middle of the night. He was the President of the United States. It's a 24/7 job."

"The antique silver spittoon made by Paul Revere, why was that in your room?"

"It's handsome, quintessentially American. And my husband liked it. He liked to crumple pieces of paper at night and try to get them in, like a basketball hoop."

"Why were your fingerprints on it?"

"It was in my bedroom, Mr. Baylor. I moved it all the time. People do that with objects in their own bedrooms."

"Just a few more questions, Mrs. MacMann. Why didn't you and the President have children?"

Beth looked at her lap. "It was not for want of trying. I miscarried twice, earlier in our marriage."

"Did you continue to try to have children?"

"Yes. I very much wanted children. I tried very hard."

"After the President's death, you were questioned four separate times by the FBI. According to the 302 forms—that is, the FBI reports of those discussions—you did not once request to have an attorney present. Is that correct?"

"Yes."

"Were you also aware that you were under no legal obligation or compulsion even to speak with the FBI?"

"I was aware of that. I'm a lawyer myself."

"Why did you speak to the FBI?"

"I wanted to tell them what I knew."

"Why didn't you have a lawyer present when you did?"

"I had nothing to hide."

"Even when you became aware that you were a suspect?"

"I still had nothing to hide. Nor do I now. That's why I am testifying."

"Thank you. Your witness, Ms. Clintick."

$\mathcal{B}$eth was in a jubilant mood. They were on their way back to the Jefferson after her testimony. The last time Boyce had seen her this happy was in the 1970s. When they'd walked out of the courthouse minutes ago, the spectators had done something they hadn't before. They'd applauded. Now she was hugging Boyce's arm in the car, nuzzling him, saying, "See?"

He smiled gamely, but his mood didn't match hers. He felt like the Japanese admiral on December 7, 1941, pacing the bridge of the *Akagi,* thinking, *They are going to be so-oo pissed.*

When they reached the war room on Boyce's floor, everyone there applauded. Beth gave a little stage bow and a victory sign.

Boyce wasn't about to ream them out in front of her, but it made him boil. It was a violation of his most sacred rule: *Do not tempt the gods.* And most sacred rule (b): It's not over until the jury foreman says, "Not guilty."

But now here Vlonko came up to them, saying that Jeeter was "off the charts." During Beth's testimony, he reported, most of the jurors had sat there "nodding up and down like those fucking rear dashboard puppies." He reported that Judge Dutch had had his clerk go back to the jury room before the lunch break and tell them to cut it out with the nodding.

"Maybe he'll have to put fucking hoods over them!" Vlonko chortled.

It was good news. Still, this postvictory atmosphere in his war room was making Boyce very nervous. He could hear the gods murmuring, could hear the clanky sound of Vulcan's smithy as he pounded out lightning bolts.

The associate in charge of media monitoring came up, beaming like a July sunflower, to tell Beth breathlessly that the National Association of Former First Ladies had issued a statement supporting her. This *was* significant. The NAFFL was one of the most powerful lobbies in Washington.

There was more: The television commentators were beside themselves over her performance. The associate paused in mideffusion to tell Boyce that he, too, was getting good reviews. Beth went off to watch for herself, leaving Boyce alone in the crowded room with his darkling presentiments.

Phone call for you, Boyce, line five. Judge Dutch's clerk.

The prosecution had just requested—and had been granted—a three-day recess. They needed time to serve subpoenas on several new witnesses.

A string of four-letter words went through Boyce's head.

Who were the witnesses?

The list is being faxed to you right now.

Boyce hung up. Beth emerged from the media room, all excitement. Like Marilyn Monroe returning from her world tour to tell Joe DiMaggio, "You never heard such cheering!" Someone on TV had proposed that as soon as the trial was over, Beth should announce her candidacy—for president!

Boyce, fax for you. Just came in.

He read the names. There were three. Lonetta Sue Scutt. Who was this?

He led Beth into his study and closed the door and showed her the list. She read it. Remarkable how quickly facial muscles could rearrange themselves.

Beth explained about Lonetta Sue Scutt. "Is she going to be a problem?" she asked.

"By the time I'm through with her she'll be so radioactive they won't allow her in tunnels. But tell me about Damon Blowwell. And about Dr. Mark Klatz." He sat down. "Tell me all about them."

"Damon was Ken's political director. Before that, he was his campaign mana—"

"I read the papers, Beth. I know *who* he is. Tell me why he's suddenly a prosecution witness."

Beth considered. "I'm not sure."

"That's helpful."

"I don't know. Damon and I got along all right. I mean, he wasn't . . . well, he didn't really *like* me. But I don't know why he'd be out to get me."

"Why didn't he like you?"

"He and Ken were very close. I was the pain-in-the-ass wife. You know how tribal men can be."

"Did he have any specific reason not to like you?"

"He thinks I killed Ken. That would be his main reason, I'd guess."

"Any other reasons?"

"During the primaries—this was before he stopped drinking and got religion—he was putting out word that one of the wives of the other candidates was a lesbian who was having a hot-and-heavy with her trainer. I told him to cut it out. Came down on him sort of hard. But I mean, it was no big thing."

"He's coming to testify against you. That is a big thing."

Beth considered. "He was in Vietnam."

"Not another war hero."

"Green Berets. I only heard him talk about it once. It was late, we were all stuffed into this little plane. It had been a long day. And he talked about what he did in the war. It was . . . kinda out there. If I'd been the Viet Cong, I wouldn't have wanted to have Damon with his knife crawling into my hootch in the middle of the night."

"Wonderful. We have a hostile Green Beret on our hands. But why is he hostile? We've got three days to find out. I can put my people on it, but it would be helpful if you could give us some direction."

"It's funny."

"What, possibly, could be funny?"

"I'm on trial for assassination. And Damon *was* an assassin. I mean, that was his job. They had a name for it, even. Wet work. He and Ken used to joke about how it was perfect training for politics. But I don't know why he'd be testifying. Sorry."

"Well, when you're not glued to the TV listening to people talk about how you should run for president, try to come up with something."

"Are we feeling hostile?"

"*We* are feeling that *everyone* is being *way* too *overconfident*. Who is Dr. Mark Klatz? Did he advise you which spot on Ken's head to aim for with the spittoon?"

"He's my gynecologist."

"Jesus. And why would your gynecologist be testifying against you?"

"It's just none of their damn business."

"What is 'none of their damn business'? . . . *Be-th?*"

☆ · ☆ · ☆

Deputy Attorney General Clintick put Dr. J. Mark Klatz on the stand first. To Boyce this meant that he was the government's weakest witness. Damon Blowwell she'd scheduled third. That meant his testimony was the most devastating. He had six investigators poring over Damon Blowwell's military records, tax records, credit records, school records. With any luck, it would turn out that he massacred innocent civilians and was an alcoholic wife beater. Beth still swore she had no idea what he had against her.

The deputy AG spent an hour going over Dr. Klatz's impeccable credentials. Boyce already knew how impeccable they were.

He was low-key, in his early sixties, with glasses. His first name was Julius, apparently in honor of the eponymous Roman emperor whose birth gave us the term *C-section*. He had headed up the OB-GYN department at Mount Sinai Hospital. He'd advised the United Nations committee that was trying to get African countries of fundamentalist

Islamic bent to outlaw the practice of cutting off the clitorises of young girls to discourage them from having sex. He wrote newspaper op-ed articles deploring this barbaric form of chastity enforcement. In short— and he was that, too, which somehow enhanced his professional aura— he was the sort of person you would want peering between your legs, going, "Hmm . . ."

Dr. Klatz was manifestly unhappy at being present. He looked as if he would gladly perform a clitoridectomy on the deputy attorney general, without anesthesia.

"When did the defendant first come under your care, Doctor?"

"April of 1983."

"Why did she come under your care?"

"She was recommended."

"Why was she recommended?"

"She had experienced a second miscarriage the previous month. Her physician referred her to me."

"What was your evaluation of her, medically?"

"That's none of your business," the doctor said. "It's none of anyone's business."

Judge Dutch instructed the doctor gently to answer.

Dr. Klatz shook his head. "With all respect to you and the court, you can find me in contempt and put me in jail, but I will not answer that question."

Judge Dutch drummed his fingers and contemplated the dreariness— for everyone concerned—of having the doctor dragged off in handcuffs. He waved up the lawyers.

One of the television networks had hired a lip-reader to decipher what the judge said during the sidebars. They couldn't broadcast a direct translation, of course. But their correspondent certainly seemed to have an uncanny knack for predicting just how Judge Dutch would rule.

The correspondent told his viewers, "My guess is that he will *not* force the issue and will let the prosecution proceed along a parallel line of questioning."

"Dr. Klatz," the prosecution continued, "did you prescribe a regimen of birth control pills for Mrs. MacMann?"

Dr. Klatz looked at Beth. What was the use? They had the prescriptions.

"Yes. You already know that."

"Has Mrs. MacMann remained your patient since April 1983?"

"Yes."

"And has she continued to take birth control pills under your prescription since that time?"

"I have prescribed them. Whether she took them, I can't say."

The deputy AG asked the court to enter into evidence a thick stack of paper, prescriptions dating back two decades and continuing until recently.

☆ · ☆ · ☆

"Tell me the *good* news," Boyce said to his associate who monitored the media.

Beth had gone back to Rosedale for a long bath and, Boyce suspected, good cry.

"The women," the associate said nervously, "are furious. The message they're sending is 'Hands off her body,' 'None of your business,' echoing Klatz's line. The head of the National Organization for Women used the term *vast male conspiracy*. The National Association of Former First Ladies issued a guarded statement standing by her."

"Now the bad news."

"The word *liar* was used twenty-three times during the evening news cycle. CBS used the term *credibility problem*. ABC is teasing tonight's *Nightline* show with the line 'Can we believe her?' Tomorrow's *New York Post* has a story quoting—indirectly—the archbishop of New York saying that if she and the President had had a kid, maybe all this wouldn't have happened."

Boyce groaned and went off to get Vlonko's report.

Vlonko was staring at his computer screen, scowling.

"We got problems with two, four, and eight. Maybe big-time problems."

"Two is the Catholic with four kids?"

"Five fucking kids. And the sister with the Down's baby."

"What about four and eight?" Juror number four taught Sunday school and just loved kids, according to her questionnaire. Juror eight was liable to feel betrayed at hearing that a defendant who'd told the court how desperate she was to have a baby had been popping birth control pills like breath mints for two decades. On weekends, she volunteered at an adoption agency.

"I would say, Boyce, not so fucking good," said Vlonko. "Lips very tight all day. Hardly moving. Hands on laps. This is hostile posture."

The drawback to being a trial attorney was that you couldn't, after a bad day, stun yourself into insensibility with a good stiff drink. The lovely clink of ice, the little cat's feet padding up to the cortex, the furry body rubbing up and down against it like a scratching post.

Not tonight. Tonight would be a long night, spent closely reading articles from medical journals and psychiatric journals about birth control pills as a hormone management tool and on the long-term post-traumatic effects of miscarriage.

Chapter 23

$\mathcal{B}$oyce's cross of Klatz elicited a nearly unbroken string of yeses from the eager-to-help doctor, but it felt like bailing a leaking boat with a too small bucket. He'd have kept Dr. Klatz on the stand longer if he could, just to bathe the jury in his amiable, nonjudgmental, pro-Beth aura.

The prosecution had given Lonetta Sue Scutt a good scrubbing and put her in a dress that managed to cover most of her tattoos. Her hair had been dyed so dark that it had a granular quality, like a wig made from shoe polish and fishing line. For someone who lived in the desert, she had suspiciously pale skin, and decades of two packs a day had cured her vocal cords to sandpaper. She listed her profession as "homemaker" and "exotic dancer."

Aware that her witness did not present the image of Mother Teresa, Clintick kept her direct examination brief.

Had she been in the employ of Governor and Mrs. MacMann? Oh yeah. Had she observed stress in the marriage? Ohh yeah. Had she heard Mrs. MacMann express her intention to—she was quoting here from a statement she had made to the FBI—cut off the governor's penis? Uh-huh. Is that a yes, Ms. Scutt? Oh yeah. And was she fired shortly after overhearing this? Uh-huh, and she threatened me to keep quiet or the state troopers would take care of me. Thank you. Your witness.

Boyce was courtly. He showed Lonetta Sue Scutt no less respect than he would have the Queen of England. Ms. Scutt, are you currently taking any medication? I take a few pills, uh-huh. You have a prescription for OxyContin? That's a powerful painkiller, is it not? Yeah, and I got a powerful pain. What was the cause of the pain, Ms. Scutt? There was this accident. What kind of accident? I got some battery acid powder up my—in the sinuses? Really? How does battery acid powder get into the sinuses, Ms. Scutt? It was an accident, like.

Boyce admitted into evidence the emergency room report from the Morongo Basin Hospital. Lonetta had snorted the battery acid powder. Her cocaine dealer had given it to her. She had paid him for her previous purchase with sex. Along with the sex was included a nasty dose of sexually transmitted disease. The dealer paid her back by substituting granulated battery acid powder for cocaine in her next purchase. It was a miracle she hadn't died.

"Irrelevant!" DAG Clintick cried.

Boyce fired back that she should be ashamed to have called such a witness in the first place. The photo of a foggy-glassed Judge Dutch angrily pointing his finger at them made the cover of *Time*.

"My guess," the lip-reader-assisted network correspondent told his viewers while the judge was wagging his finger and threatening to fine both Boyce and Sandy, "is that Judge Umin may be so *fed up* at this point that he's prepared to sanction both the defense *and* prosecution."

"Ms. Scutt," Boyce continued, "did you telephone the *National Perspirer* and try to sell your story to them for the sum of one million dollars?"

"Why not? Everyone else connected to it is making a fortune."

Lonetta was refreshingly candid.

"Two final questions, Ms. Scutt. Did you tell the *Perspirer* that while serving lunch to Mrs. MacMann and her friend Mrs. Hackersmith, you heard Mrs. MacMann say she was going to cut off the governor's penis?"

"That's what she said."

"And would this be the same gubernatorial organ that you—that you had had in your physical possession before serving lunch to Mrs. Mac-Mann and her friend?"

"Objection!"

Sidebar.

"I will rephrase the question, Ms. Scutt. Were you orally acquainted with the governor?"

"I don't have to answer that. Do I, Judge?"

Before Judge Dutch could answer, Boyce said softly, "I won't keep Ms. Scutt any longer, Your Honor. No further questions. I would like to recall Mrs. MacMann."

Beth took the stand. "Mrs. MacMann, did you threaten in Ms. Scutt's presence to cut off the governor's penis?"

"No, that's inaccurate. I told Mrs. Hackersmith that I was going to cut off his balls."

It took some gaveling to quiet the court.

"Your Honor," Beth said, "I apologize for the language. I could have used a more general anatomical term, but I wanted to quote what I said verbatim."

Judge Dutch, whose glasses were now opaque with vapor, merely grunted. Boyce continued.

"Did you dismiss Ms. Scutt because she overheard you discussing your . . . surgical fantasies vis-à-vis the governor?"

"No," said Beth, looking directly at her accuser. "Ms. Scutt knows very well why she was dismissed."

"Objection."

"Withdrawn, Your Honor. No further questions."

The mood that night in Boyce's war room was somewhat improved. Until Beth said to him quietly, "About what Damon might say? There was this conversation I had at one point with Ken. . . ."

☆ · ☆ · ☆

Damon Jubal Early Blowwell looked as if he might still be in the military and not some K Street political consultant. He was in his mid-fifties, wore his hair trimmed to within a centimeter of his skull, and kept his jaw in a permanent jut. He had suspicious brown eyes, the tight lips of someone anticipating disrespect, and the physique to do something about it. When he smiled, his whole face seemed to suck inward at the center in a fierce pucker that made him look not entirely human. His normal expression was a scowl.

He answered with "Yes, sir" and "No, sir" and bit off the ends of sentences like tobacco plugs. When the clerk swore him in, Blowwell stood rigidly erect and added one last word to his answer: "So help me *God*." Vlonko told Boyce afterward that when Blowwell took the stand, all nine male jurors sat up in their seats.

Boyce had gone back over every public utterance Blowwell had made following the President's death. He had never come right out and accused Beth of murder, but for someone who had been such a faithful family retainer, his coolness toward her had been conspicuously glacial.

Blowwell had gone to work for Ken MacMann the moment that Ken announced he was running for president. He'd been a hard-partying political hack in Alabama. Getting his fellow Vietnam veteran elected president had restored a sense of purpose to his life. He quit drinking and became a born-again Christian. When a former Green Beret with two Bronze Stars finds his way back to the path of righteousness, it's prudent to get out of his way. The citation for his medals was classified. Boyce's Pentagon moles had found out that they were for assassinating eight high-level Viet Cong cadres.

Blowwell had become wealthy since leaving the White House. He now had clients all over the world. But President MacMann's death had been hard on him. Boyce's investigators had found out that he had increased visits to Alcoholics Anonymous to five a week—up from one a week when he worked at the White House. Boyce hoped he would not have to mention that in court, especially since jurors four, seven, and fourteen had relatives who attended AA. He also hoped he wouldn't have to insinuate that Damon's war experiences had left him with, as they say, "issues." Jurors one, three, six, and fifteen had friends or relatives die or be wounded in World War II, Korea, and Vietnam. Boyce really didn't want to have to blow his nose all over a military man's ribbons.

DAG Clintick took her time walking Damon through his background.

"You served *two* tours in Vietnam?"

"Yes, ma'am."

"Was that unusual?"

Boyce knew very well she was just trying to get him to object.

"Probably was not typical."

"Why did you serve two tours in Vietnam?"

"I wanted us to win."

Jurors one, six, and fifteen were nodding.

Boyce thought, *This one is the real article, and he's coming right at us.*

"What did you do in Vietnam, Mr. Blowwell?"

Beth whispered, "Shouldn't you be objecting?"

"Shh."

"My job was to kill the enemy."

"You were Mr. MacMann's campaign manager and, when he became president, his political director at the White House. What did that job entail?"

"Killing the enemy."

The courtroom erupted in laughter. Judge Dutch himself grinned. Boyce thought, *Slick, very slick.*

"Did you and the President have frank discussions?"

"Wouldn't have been much point in having unfrank discussions."

"Of course. You were his confidant, after all." Ms. Clintick smiled. "He trusted you."

"And I trusted *him.*"

"Did President MacMann ever discuss his wife with you?"

"Objection."

Sidebar.

DAG Clintick continued, "Did the President ever confide in you whether he was dissatisfied in his marriage?"

"He did. He told me that he wanted to divorce Mrs. MacMann."

The courtroom stirred.

"Did he say when he wanted to divorce her?"

"Immediately following the reelection."

Judge Dutch had to gavel the courtroom to silence.

"Did he say whether he had made this intention clear to Mrs. MacMann?"

"He told me that he had discussed it with her."

"And what was her reaction?"

"She was not pleased. He said she had called him a name."

"What name?"

"It's a pretty salty term."

Judge Dutch reluctantly gave Blowwell permission to continue.

"She called him a 'cocksucker.' "

Gasps, gaveling. Network censors scrambled, too late, to hit the bleep-out button. Throughout America, mothers cautioned their children that such language was not to be repeated in their households. In Europe, the sound of laughter could be heard through a million windows. In Asia, there was confusion as precise translations were sought. Judge Dutch finally removed his useless glasses.

"So it would be fair to say that Mrs. MacMann was displeased by the President's revelation of his intention."

"I would say yes."

"Did the President say if Mrs. MacMann had said anything further with regard to her intentions?"

"He told me that she was planning to run for public office herself— the governor's office that he had held—after the President was reelected. He said she told him that she would agree to a divorce once she had accomplished that. She told him that the only way she would leave the White House was on her terms."

Murmurmurmurmurmurmur.

"Thank you, Mr. Blowwell. No further questions for the witness at this time, Your Honor."

Boyce was fantasizing: His associate burst through the courtroom doors, breathless, tie askew, bruised, even missing a shoe. He was clutching a U.S. Army dossier designated "Top Secret." Inside was a report that Sergeant Damon Blowwell had been dishonorably discharged for massacring an entire elementary school of peace-loving Vietnamese children, including the school mascot water buffalo, Phong. He had decorated the bar at the noncom officers' club with their little pigtails. Not only that, but—

"Counselor?"

Chapter 24

*W*ell," Boyce said once they were back at the hotel behind closed doors, "your campaign to rehabilitate yourself is coming along nicely."

"Don't start."

"I think I'm doing an admirable job of not starting. You're lucky I don't have a spittoon handy."

"Damon blew that conversation way out of proportion."

"No, darling. What he blew was us. Out of the water."

"You recovered well. I thought your cross brilliant, insinuating that he was a religious fanatic and war criminal."

"We did not 'recover' today. All that was purely for the benefit of juror three."

"Which one is he?"

"She. By now you should know these people better than your own relatives. The lesbian who hated her Baptist military father."

"Oh, her."

"In case everyone else in the jury fell in love with Damon, she's our only hope. My God, what a disaster."

"Damon was spinning. It wasn't untrue, but he made it sound worse than it was."

"Did you call Ken a 'cocksucker'?"

"Yes. And he was."

"When you take the stand again you can tell the jury it was a pet name. My widdle cocksucker. You do realize that Blowwell would not have taken the stand if you hadn't testified? His lawyer told me as much. It was your testimony that finally put his needle into the red and made him come forward with all this."

Boyce took off his tie and hurled it across the room as if ridding himself of a snake that had wrapped itself around his windpipe. "What *is* it with all these war heroes? You can't throw a stone in this case without hitting one. Didn't your husband ever hang out with *normal* people?"

"I think Damon has a problem with female authority."

"He can discuss that on TV with Oprah when he writes his book. Meanwhile, *we* have a problem, with *him.*"

Boyce picked up the phone and buzzed.

"George? Boyce. Did you get anything on him? . . . No VC ears? . . . Are you sure? I'd lay odds there's a My Lai in that man's record somewhere. Have you spoken to *everyone* in his platoon? . . . Well, track him down in goddamn Peru, George, I don't care what it takes. . . . Then *hire* a goddamn helicopter. What about his AA friends? I *know* AA types are fiercely loyal to each other, but we're not dealing with samurai warriors here, George. They're recovering alcoholics. You get 'em alone, you pull out a bottle of hundred-dollar Scotch and hold it under their noses, and I promise, within ten minutes they'll be singing 'Whaddya Do with a Drunken Sailor' and telling you everything you want to know." Boyce hung up.

"What?" he said to Beth, who was looking at him with horror.

"Remind me," she said, "was I in class the day they taught us to suborn recovering alcoholics?"

"Uncivil Procedure 101. My favorite course."

Beth suddenly paled.

"You okay?"

She bolted for the bathroom door. She emerged ten minutes later looking shaky.

"Didn't mean to upset you," Boyce said.

"I've been upset since the seventies."

☆ · ☆ · ☆

"Now you're cookin', George." Boyce hung up.

"Great news," he said to Beth. They were having breakfast, Boyce tucking in heartily to his usual hot oatmeal with wheat germ and mixed berries. Beth bird-nibbled at a muffin and sipped at tea. Her color was still off.

"Guess who beat up an antiwar protester in the seventies for lipping off to him and calling him a baby murderer? Sergeant Blowhard!"

"I'd have done the exact same thing."

"This information was not easy to come by. You could be more enthusiastic about it, you know. Apparently he was tanked when he slugged the guy. That's why he brought it up in AA. This is good. We can use this."

"Oh, Boyce, you didn't pour booze down some poor alcoholic's throat to get this? I just don't think getting recovering drunks drunk is right."

"Don't get ethical me with me, Spittoon Girl."

Beth burst into tears. "I'm sorry," she said. "I just can't seem to get a grip."

"It's okay," Boyce said, helpless as any male confronted with a weeping female, "I'm not going to subpoena a recovering alcoholic."

"You're not?" Beth blew her nose into a stiff Jefferson Hotel napkin.

"Not because I've gone soft," Boyce said. "With the mood the country's in right now, the jury would award Blowwell damages for skinning his knuckles on an antiwar protester."

Beth blew her nose. "Probably right."

He patted Beth's hand. "We'll figure something out."

☆ · ☆ · ☆

"Let's go now to our special legal correspondent, who is outside the courthouse. Jeff, how did it go today?"

"Peter, this was *not* a good day for the defense. Beth MacMann's attorney, Boyce Baylor, filed a motion last week seeking to have Damon Blowwell examined by a court-appointed psychiatrist, in an effort to establish that Blowwell—as the motion put it—has a history of 'vicious sociopathic behavior characterized by extreme violence.' The basis for this is that Mr. Blowwell allegedly hit an antiwar protester back in the seventies. Baylor seized on the incident and tried to have Blowwell's court testimony, considered highly damaging to the former First Lady, thrown out by Judge Umin."

"And how did the judge rule today?"

"Just ten minutes ago, Judge Umin *denied* the motion. Morever, he did so in unusually harsh language, indicating that he is growing rapidly *impatient* with the defense."

"So Mr. Blowwell's testimony stands?"

"Yes. Further, we've just learned that Damon Blowwell has filed a thirty-million-dollar defamation suit against Boyce Baylor. So the atmosphere down here at the U.S. District Court is highly *charged.* Peter?"

☆ · ☆ · ☆

Beth had taken some kind of downward turn that had Boyce at a loss. It was as if she'd lost interest in her own case. In court, she stared straight ahead, a terrible, guilty-looking eye posture—and twice had passed him urgent notes saying she needed a five-minute recess—"NOW!!" The moment they were granted, she flew toward the side door.

Naturally, these quick exits did not go unnoticed. It is difficult to go unnoticed when you are being seen live by over one billion viewers. Commentators remarked that she seemed to be under quite a lot of stress. Asked about this on the steps of the courthouse one day, Boyce was sorely tempted to say, "She's on trial for murdering her husband. Of course she's under 'considerable stress,' you pigeon-brained idiots." Instead he remarked that the reason for her downcast countenance was that, as former First Lady of the land, it tugged at her heartstrings to see the country she so loved torn apart by this tragedy.

But as one pundit put it, the country was not being torn apart. If anything, it was rapidly approaching unanimity on the matter of her guilt.

☆ · ☆ · ☆

"Boyce?"

"What?" He was in a foul mood. Judge Dutch had denied yet another motion, his case was going down in flames, and the night before on Perri's show, Alan Crudman had declared that Boyce Baylor had made a "tragic error" in putting Beth on the stand. He knew very well Boyce had tried everything short of locking Beth in a closet to keep her from taking the stand.

"There's something I need to tell you."

He'd been afraid of this. It had happened before. And it always happened right about now: The client would break down, *just* as Boyce was about to go in and give his closing argument, and blubber all over his legal pad that—sob, gasp—they *were* guilty. Thank you. Thank you for sharing that with me as I prepare to go in and tell the jury that they are about to make a terrible mistake.

He said, "Beth, you could really help me right now by—"

"I'm pregnant."

They were in the car going to court. He could hear the courtroom rumbling from this atomic news, the media gasping with pleasure—a whole new layer of scandal!—the shocked, drawn faces of the jurors, spectators clamoring, Judge Dutch, eyeglasses fogged, gaveling, gaveling, ordering the bailiffs to clear the courtroom. He saw headlines, the evening news, heard the titter of his colleagues. He saw it in all its dire and awful vividness.

"That's so . . . great," he squeaked.

He was seized with joy. He'd never heard such good news. He'd never wanted children by any of his wives, sensing as he had that none of the marriages was likely to last. And now the only woman he had ever really loved had just announced that she was pregnant by him! Admittedly, the timing could have been better—twenty-five years later and in the middle of her trial for murdering the President of the United States. Otherwise it was wonderful news.

He detached himself from her long enough to ask, "But—you were on the pill."

"I went off them about the time we went to trial. I was getting headaches and the doctor said to stop for a while while he monitored my estrogen. I never got around to going back on. It wasn't as though I were likely to get pregnant, right? I thought you might have guessed. All those trips to the bathroom."

"A lot of clients have to use the bathroom in a hurry. Nerves. I was focused on the case."

The case!

He saw himself standing next to Beth in front of Judge Dutch. For the sentencing. Judge Dutch was wearing contacts so his glasses wouldn't fog. Beth's belly was huge with child. She was wearing maternity clothes. They held hands, not proper in court, strictly speaking, but they couldn't help it. Judge Dutch's voice kept catching in his throat. "In light of your condition, Mrs. MacMann, the United States will not avail itself of the sentence of death which would normally be imposed in such a grievous, indeed, heinous case. But because you have been found guilty of one of the most serious crimes there is—if not *the* most serious—it is the judgment of this court that you serve the balance of your life in prison, without possibility of parole."

He heard the gasps, the sobs. He turned, saw the tears streaming down Beth's cheeks as she stood there for the last time in her life wearing nonprison clothes. Saw the marshals approaching with steel manacles and leg chains. Heard Judge Dutch straining to control his own emotions as he concluded that this terrible tragedy had claimed more than the life of the President of the United States—it had forever blemished the honor of the United States and, perhaps most tragically of all, had robbed an unborn child of its mother, who would be only a person in an orange uniform on the other side of thick glass. Case closed, and may God have mercy on us all.

Down came the gavel. Beth was led away.

"No!" he cried.

"Boyce? You okay?"

☆ · ☆ · ☆

He filed motion after motion. "Loco motions," they were dubbed by *American Lawyer* magazine. He moved to dismiss on the grounds that Beth's Secret Service detail was spying on her and passing the information along to the prosecution. Judge Dutch tossed it in the judicial wastebasket. Boyce moved for a mistrial on the grounds that one of the jurors had just dozed off for five minutes during a stretch of stultifyingly dull testimony by an expert in acoustics. Into the wastebasket. He moved for a mistrial because the second cousin of juror fourteen signed a contract for a book titled *Second Cousin of Juror 14: My Story*. Wastebasket. Three for three.

Boyce dispatched his most unethical investigator—a former U.S. intelligence agent who had had to resign after being caught selling Stinger antiaircraft missiles to the Serbs—to Vietnam with a suitcase of hundred-dollar bills with which to bribe an entire hamlet of Mekong Delta peasants into suddenly recalling that Sergeant Damon Blowwell had wantonly massacred half its population one night—just for the heck of it. The scheme fizzled when the investigator got as far as Bangkok, where he exchanged the $100,000 for heroin and caught a flight for Amsterdam, where he exchanged the heroin for $500,000 of ecstasy, which he secreted in large wheels of Gouda bound for Atlanta. It would have been awkward for Boyce to pursue him through the courts, so he let it go, charging the $100,000 to one of his corporate clients as a week's worth of "photocopying and messenger services."

Judge Dutch dismissed each of Boyce's motions with mounting choler and vexation, at one point warning him icily that if he received one more of these appalling roadblocks, he would call down upon Boyce's head "the lesser angels of my nature."

Boyce's furious motion filing was to buy a few weeks for Beth to get over her morning sickness before the deputy AG got her on the stand for cross-examination. That was going to be bad enough without Beth having to be excused every five minutes to dash to the bathroom. As a rule, juries are not impressed if you have to throw up every time a difficult question is posed.

Judge Dutch was getting suspicious of Beth's frequent calls of nature. His clerk had told Boyce that the judge was considering having her medically examined. That was to be avoided at all costs. Meanwhile, Boyce put it out to the press that Beth had been temporarily inconvenienced by a nasty "tummy bug." In moments of daydreaming, he found himself calling his child by the nickname Tummybug.

Chapter 25

*U*nited States calls Elizabeth MacMann."

How subtle, Boyce thought, of Clintick to drop Beth's maiden middle name, Tyler, which Beth had always made such a point of using. It would start Beth's cross-exam on a note of annoyance.

He slid his legal pad across the defense table toward Beth.

She's wearing panty hose underneath

She gave him a smile that said, "I'll be okay."

The television commentators went into their TV golf tournament whisper.

"Elizabeth MacMann is rising . . . walking around the defense table . . . walking now toward the witness box . . . climbing up into the witness box . . . Barbara, how would you describe her outfit?"

"It's a pantsuit, of course. Black. We know that much. We do not know *who* the designer is. It looks like a cross between Ann Taylor and Carolina Herrera. . . ."

"Judge Umin now reminding Mrs. MacMann that she is still under oath."

"She's made a point, generally, of wearing clothes by American designers. . . ."

"Sitting down, now . . ."

"You'll notice she is *not* wearing the pearl necklace that she wore when she took the stand previously."

"What do we read into that?"

"I'm not sure. It was given to her by her late husband. So you could read all sorts of things into it. Or not."

"Deputy Attorney General Sandra Clintick, approaching the witness stand. What's she wearing, Barbara?"

"We do have that information. Saks Fifth Avenue double-breasted jacket with skirt and off-white crepe de chine blouse—"

"I have to interrupt you—here we go."

"Mrs. MacMann," DAG Clintick began, "you testified earlier that there—I'm quoting from the transcript—may have been more than eight occasions when you violently attacked your husband. Is that correct?"

"No, it's not. I said I might have thrown something at him. I did not characterize it as a violent attack."

"You do not consider throwing objects at or striking people acts of violence?"

Boyce winced. It was a textbook instance of why a defendant should never take the stand.

"I would not consider, for instance, throwing your shoe at your husband in a moment of domestic stress a quote violent attack. I would consider that pretty fairly standard husband maintenance."

There was laughter in the courtroom, though none, Vlonko pointed out later, came from the jury box.

"Would you consider throwing a heavy metal object at his skull a violent attack?"

"Objection. Conjecture."

Overruled.

"Yes," Beth said. "I certainly would. I'd consider it not only violent but unlawful and punishable at law."

"As First Lady, you spoke out against domestic violence."

"Yes, I did. On numerous occasions."

"Do you consider that hypocritical?"

"Objection."

Overruled.

"No, Ms. Clintick. I distinguish between marital spats and domestic violence."

"Even when these so-called marital spats result in contusions, lacerations, bruising, and stitches?"

"My husband was a six-foot-three former naval officer and outweighed me by more than seventy pounds, Ms. Clintick. He was perfectly capable of defending himself from the likes of me."

"Even at night, in the dark, while he slept?"

"Objection."

Sustained.

"You're asking hypothetical questions, Ms. Clintick," Beth said. "I'll answer directly: I did not hit my husband with that spittoon in the dark, as he slept."

"Was he awake when you hit him?"

"Objection. Asked and answered."

Overruled.

"I did not hit him."

"Did you throw the spittoon at him?"

"Objection, Your Honor. Asked and answered. Ms. Clintick's line of questioning constitutes harassment."

Overruled.

"I've answered that question, Ms. Clintick," Beth said tightly.

"Answer directly. Did you throw the spittoon at him?"

"I told the FBI agents that I did not."

DAG Clintick looked over toward the jury and apparently liked what she saw.

"Mrs. MacMann, as a college student, you played softball?"

Boyce knew this one was coming. The horror, the horror . . .

"I did."

"What position did you play on the team?"

"I was the pitcher."

"So your aim would be pretty good, wouldn't it?"

"With a softball, decades ago."

"You pitched four no-hitters in the season your senior year."

"The batters weren't that good. No disrespect to Smith College intended."

Clintick's alma mater, as it happened.

"In your testimony, after admitting that you had violently attacked your husband on numerous occasions, when you were asked why you did that, you replied that since your husband was dead, you were not going to say. Is that correct?"

"Yes, it is."

"Whom are you trying to protect, Mrs. MacMann? Your dead husband or yourself?"

"Objection."

Overruled.

"I am trying, Ms. Clintick, to defend myself against a charge of murder. But I will not do that by dragging down a man to whom I was married for twenty-five years and"—Beth sighed somewhat—"who is considered by the country a hero."

"Did your husband cheat on you?"

"That's none of your business, Ms. Clintick."

"Your Honor?"

After a sidebar, Judge Dutch instructed Beth to answer the question.

"You would have to define 'cheat' for me."

"Did he sleep with other women while he was married to you?"

"I very much doubt that."

An explosion of laughter.

"Mrs. MacMann, were you aware that your husband engaged in sex with other women?"

U.S. marshals were poised to serve subpoenas on half a dozen of Beth's friends to whom she had confided her problems over the years. If they denied that Beth had told them about it all, they would open themselves up to charges of perjury. Beth knew this. She had nowhere to go.

"I prefer not to be aware of some things," Beth said.

"Is the name Amber Swenson familiar to you, Mrs. MacMann?"

"Yes."

"Rita Ferreira?"

"Yes."

"Violet Bronson?"

"Yes."

"Jo Anne Casardo?"

"*Yes.*"

"Tammy Royko?"

"Uh-hum."

"Is that a yes, Mrs. MacMann?"

"Yes."

"Cass Macklehose?"

"Yes."

"Serena Whitmore?"

"Yes."

"Objection. Your Honor, is the prosecution going to read the *entire* phone book?"

"With the court's indulgence, there are only twelve more names on this list."

Throughout the country, phones rang. The next day, the headline ALL THE PRESIDENT'S WOMEN appeared in three hundred newspapers. DAG Clintick came under heavy fire from the women's groups. Lawsuits were threatened, none filed. Ms. Clintick's team had done their homework diligently.

As this honor roll was called, Boyce forced his features into a blank expression. Clintick moved in for the kill.

"Is the name Babette Van Anka familiar to you?"

"Of course it is," Beth snapped.

"No further questions at this time, Your Honor. Reserve the right to recall the defendant at a future time."

"How bad?" Boyce asked Vlonko as they stared at the numbers on the screen.

"Fucking bad."

☆ · ☆ · ☆

"Beth, honey?" They were lying together on top of the bed in Boyce's suite, staring at the ceiling, holding hands. "There's something I need to tell you."

"Can't we just not think of anything right now?"

"Now is not a good time for not thinking of anything."

"That's so Washington," Beth said. " 'Now is not the time for partisanship.' 'Now is not the time for politics as usual.' Please."

"I have to be your lawyer for a moment."

Beth sighed.

"The case," he said, "as you may be aware, is not . . . is, well, it's not . . ." He was so unused to giving his clients bad news that he was at a loss.

"We're going down," Beth said. "In flames."

"We're not going up. We're not really even going sideways. Eliminating those directions leaves down."

"I'm so sorry, Boyce. I screwed everything up. I'm *so* sorry."

"Now is not the time for self-recrimination."

"After I'm convicted—would that be the time?"

"Let's look at it from a purely tactical point of view. If it comes out that you're pregnant, and that's a question of when rather than if, the jury is going to feel very jerked around. You say on the stand that more than anything you wanted to have a baby. Then your OB/GYN says that you've been on the pill. Then you get pregnant in the middle of your murder trial. It's not an ideal situation."

"What *is* it with these hormones? All I can do is burst into tears."

"Now is not the time to burst into tears. Right now I need you sharp and hard. I need you pre-sorry, pre-pregnant. I need Lady Bethmac."

Beth wiped her tears defiantly. "All right. Screw sorry."

"That's my girl. Ready?"

"Ready."

"Okay. Whatever happens, just go with it."

"What are you talking about?"

"You didn't know anything about it. Understand?"

"Boyce, I need you to defend me, not get into trouble."

"Baby, trust me. I *am* defending you."

They were quiet awhile.

"I don't know what you have in mind. But one of us has to not be in prison to raise this child."

Boyce said nothing.

"Whatever it is, don't. I'm asking you."

Chapter 26

 he people you knew.

To get the people you knew took time. Boyce begged a day's recess under the pretext of needing time to locate a "vital" defense witness, an utterly irrelevant maid who had once done part-time cleaning for the MacManns.

Boyce used the cell phone listed to "B & B Seafood." It was his fishy phone, the one for very sensitive conversations.

He reached Felicio on *his* cell phone, which was listed under God knew whose name, probably someone dead and the less you knew about it the better. You never knew where Felicio was at any given moment. Boyce could hear Peruvian-sounding flute music in the background. On a previous call, he had heard explosions.

"I need you," Boyce said. *"Ahora."*

The upside of knowing the people you knew was that they were grateful to you. Latino clients were grateful to the point of embarrassment. They named their children after you, offered to kill your enemies. Even inconsequential ones.

Twelve years before, Boyce had kept Felicio from spending the rest of his life in a U.S. federal prison for trying to steal one thousand pounds of C-4 explosive from a military base. The government claimed Felicio was planning to use it to blow up the local U.S. embassy, in retaliation for ending its support for Felicio's rebel group. Felicio's defense—admittedly bold—was that he was going to use it to blow up the infrastructure of the corrupt dictatorship.

Boyce took the case pro bono to show his contempt for the U.S. government's "war" on drugs that in the course of twenty years had put one-third of the black population in jail while reducing the availability of drugs by a factor of roughly zero. By the time he was finished, the jurors were ready to enlist in Felicio's rebel army and not only overthrow the corrupt dictator, but also storm the U.S. embassy. Every year since, Boyce had gotten a Christmas card from Felicio, who was now chief of security for a chain of Central and Latin American hotels.

Felicio was overcome with emotion at being asked for help by his old savior. *¡Cómo no, patrón!* He would be in Washington on the next flight. No—he would come by private plane! He would be there before dawn! Boyce said that dawn would be early enough. He gave Felicio a general idea of the area in which his assistance was being sought, so that he could bring along whatever specialists he needed.

The breakfast was arranged at a hotel in Tysons Corner in Virginia, a half hour from Washington. Boyce booked the room himself. Felicio was waiting for him when he walked in.

☆ · ☆ · ☆

Boyce's next call was to Sandy Clintick. She was surprised to get it. She didn't bother to conceal her feelings. Boyce told her he wanted to meet with her. In private.

Fine, she said. Come to my office. Boyce politely declined the opportunity to be ambushed by photographers, slipping into a side door at the Justice Department. He counterproposed the Metropolitan Club. He arranged for a private dining room. Seven o'clock? See you then.

Sandy Clintick was shown in. Boyce extended his hand. She simply nodded and sat down. Her body language said, "So?"

"I might," he said, "be able to talk my client into agreeing to an involuntary manslaughter charge. But I would insist on two and a half years. Max. House arrest."

Sandy Clintick stared at Boyce. Finally a smile appeared, not the kind that bathes you in warmth.

"When I took this case," she said, "I tried to go into it as I would any other. Do the job, don't make it personal, walk away. I was actually looking forward to going to trial against you. I've observed you over the years with interest. Sometimes with admiration. Then I finally met you. And, do you know, I've almost forgotten that you have a client. To be honest—something you may have a hard time relating to—at this point I don't care about your client. But I do care about you. And I'm going to beat you."

She paused.

"You've given me insight, Mr. Baylor. And I'm grateful to you. You've restored my belief in evil. So the answer is—go to hell. I am going to convict your client. Just for the pleasure of making you lose."

"Fair enough." Boyce grinned. The rule never failed: Forgive your enemies. It makes them madder than hell.

" 'Fair enough'?" Deputy Attorney General Clintick laughed, amazed. "It doesn't bother you to be called evil?"

"I've been called worse."

She shook her head.

"If this conversation leaks," Boyce said, "I'll know where it came from."

"I have *so* many better things to do. Including," she said, rising, "being here."

☆ · ☆ · ☆

MACMANN DEFENSE REPORTEDLY SEEKING DEAL

"What's this? What the hell is this?"

Beth held *The Washington Post.* She read aloud: " 'Sources within the Justice Department say that MacMann attorney Boyce Baylor initiated contact to explore the possibility of a reduced charge, from first-degree murder to involuntary manslaughter. According to them, Baylor was rebuffed.' " Beth looked up. "Is this *true*?"

"Do I look like the sort of lawyer who would go hat in hand to some hack prosecutor, to beg? Give me some credit."

"No no no. None of that. Answer the *question.*"

"This puts us in an excellent position. PR-wise. We'll crucify her for this. Deliberate leaking. Trial by media. It's scandalous. We might even succeed in getting her thrown off the case."

Beth took his hand and placed it over her belly. "Swear. On this."

"It was just a friendly little chat."

"Dammit, Boyce!"

"Oh," Boyce said dismissively, "I just wanted to give her a chance to vent before closing arguments. It's like milking a rattlesnake. Leaves 'em with a little less venom."

"You should have *asked* me."

"I asked you," Boyce said, "not to take the stand."

"So she wants blood?"

"The good news is it's mine she wants."

"So that's it? That's the ball game?"

Boyce sat beside her. "Look on the bright side. You have a brilliant attorney, the best in the country, and . . ." He sighed. "All right, it's not an ideal situation. But don't you give up. Things can change. You never know what's going to happen in a case like this."

" 'Case like this'? You've tried a 'case like this' before?"

"Oh, dozens."

"Boyce!"

"What?"

"It kicked!"

Boyce felt. "Sure it wasn't gas?"

"It wasn't *gas.* I felt it."

"Do they kick at this point? We should get a book."

"It kicked."

"Maybe it was objecting."

"Boyce, this baby is going to be born in a prison."

"It's going to be all right." He put his hand on her belly. "Swear."

☆ · ☆ · ☆

Juror number fifteen emerged from his shower in his room at the Capitol Suites Hotel and moistly walked barefoot across the carpet toward the one object that had given him pleasure in the last five months, the television. The U.S. Marshals Service had installed some sort of block—one of the jurors had nicknamed it the J-chip—so that the televisions in their rooms could not receive normal programming, only documentaries, cartoons, sports, and movies. The Home Cooking Channel, Self-Discovery Channel, Celebrity History Channel, Police Chase Channel, and the Self-Abuse Channel.

He had had no news of the outside world in almost half a year. The country might be at war. The stock market might have crashed. Maybe they'd cured AIDS and landed on Mars. Maybe aliens had landed and taken over. Who knew? They didn't get newspapers or magazines, unless the marshals went through them first with scissors and cut out the references to the case.

He took off his damp towel and gave his delicates a good scratching. The only other nice thing about this incarceration, which had now lasted longer than a typical prison sentence for mass murder, was that you could stand buck naked in a room and give your balls a good fondling without the wife or kids walking in on you.

Nads firmly in hand, he picked up the remote control with his free hand and hit the power button. He looked over at the desk mirror. He'd gained fifteen pounds eating the crap they served. He was sourly contemplating the protuberance of his waistline when he heard an unfamiliar sound—a news report coming from the television. He turned and watched. There before him was one of those guys, the whatya-callem, commentators. He recognized him from the O. J. Simpson trial, the boyish-looking one with the glasses.

"Peter," the man was saying, "Boyce Baylor has *denied* the report that he sought a plea bargain with Deputy Attorney General Sandra Clintick. But this story *refuses* to die. Independent sources have confirmed, to me directly, that Baylor and Clintick *were* seen entering the Metropolitan Club several days ago, just *moments* apart. . . ."

Juror number fifteen thought, *Hell is* this?

☆ · ☆ · ☆

Juror number seven's thoughts were similar. She had been crocheting while watching the Biography Channel but had decided fifteen minutes into it that she was just not that interested in Marie Osmond. How did these people qualify for "biographies," anyway? What was the world coming to?

She had been flicking through the channels in search of the Home Cooking Network when all of a sudden she came on the public television channel. How had that come on? It was the *news* show, the one with that nice man from Oklahoma, Mr. MacLehrer. And heavens, here he was discussing the trial, with a young historian with a hairpiece. What on earth? How was it they were getting television news all of a sudden? She watched, fascinated. So that Boyce Baylor had tried to arrange a plea bargain, eh? Well, he certainly should, the way it was going, and if I were you, Mr. Big Shot Defense Attorney, I wouldn't drive too hard a bargain. Why he ever put that woman on the stand, she'd never understand.

☆ · ☆ · ☆

Juror number nine listened to the news about the trial for half a minute before changing back to the Sports Channel. The Lakers were playing the Knicks.

Chapter 27

*B*oyce was in his hotel television studio doing an interview with the *Today* show, denouncing Deputy Attorney General Sandra Clintick for "shamelessly" leaking "false and injurious" information to the media when they moved in. They arrested him in midinterview on live television. It made for what is otherwise the most misused phrase in the English language: "must-see TV."

As he was handcuffed by the FBI agents and read his rights, with some five million viewers watching, the show's producers could only offer a silent prayer of thanksgiving to the television god for this amazing benison, the first live arrest of a lawyer on network TV.

The director of the FBI denied that the timing was intended to humiliate Boyce Baylor. The agents were simply following procedure. Of course no one believed this, much less the director of the FBI, but the media was so grateful to him for providing them with such a spectacular moment that they didn't press.

Boyce knew what was happening before the viewers did, since he knew the meaning of, "You're under arrest for violation of 18 U.S. Code 371." It took the producers a few minutes to clarify that the legalese stood for "conspiracy to tamper with a federal jury." Within a few more minutes, they rousted their legal correspondent out of bed— he apologized profusely for not having been watching—to inform them that the standard penalty for conviction of such a crime was five years in a federal prison, plus certain and permanent disbarment.

Boyce noticed as they rode down in the Jefferson's elevators that the FBI agents—there were four of them instead of the usual two, presumably in case he decided to shoot it out—were grinning. How sweet this moment must be for them.

"You're having a good day, aren't you?" he said, his tone not unfriendly.

"And it's not even coffee break yet," one replied, beaming back at him.

In the car on the way to FBI headquarters, Boyce considered clinically, *So this is what it feels like, riding in the back, handcuffed.* What empathy he would now have with his clients. Assuming he ever had any more clients.

How had they known? Had they tapped his fishy phone?

Felicio's plane? God knows whose plane it was. Felicio had some colorful friends. Maybe customs had noted the tail number and tracked it. Were Felicio and Ramon in custody?

More to the point—had the plan worked? Had the jurors been polluted? If so, Judge Dutch would have no choice but to order a mistrial. And in a new trial, Beth would not repeat the mistake of taking the stand. All she would have to do was follow the script of the first trial up to that disastrous point, and then she, and Tummybug, would be all right. Now they could visit him in jail. *Look! That's Daddy behind the glass! He can't hear us! Wave!*

They were pulling up in front of the FBI Building. There must have been two hundred of them, yelping, baying.

"I see you called ahead."

"Since you like going in front doors so much."

They were putting him through the full perp walk so that the moment could be recorded for all posterity, in all its ingloriousness.

He heard the first question shouted at him. "Boyce—who're ya gonna call?"

It was an interesting question. Whom does Boyce Baylor call when *he* needs a lawyer?

He ran a few names through his mind. Whoever he called automatically became the top law dog of the land.

No. Boyce was not yet ready to pass the baton of greatness. He was *still* the greatest. Though admittedly, if you were being hustled off in handcuffs, your number one status might be open to question.

When he went through the door, every agent in headquarters was there in the lobby to watch. They were all smiling. Then they all burst into applause.

"Thank you!" Boyce shouted. "Great to be here."

After the mug shot and fingerprinting, he posed for pictures with the arresting agents. Might as well be a good sport about it.

It was a mere special agent in charge who did the interrogation. Boyce was disappointed. He'd been expecting at least a deputy director. Clearly, they were determined to pretend it was "just another case."

He smiled at the SAIC and his deputy. "Oh, fellas, fellas. You don't really think I'm going to talk to you, do you?"

☆ · ☆ · ☆

Judge Dutch was not a happy camper. He interviewed the jurors separately, in his chambers. In addition to being unhappy about his jury being tampered with, he was troubled by something else: the FBI's handling of it. Something was not right. Only moments after juror number seven had reported to the U.S. marshals that her television reception had undergone a miraculous improvement in reception, the FBI had swooped into the hotel in force—thirty agents, rushing into the jurors' rooms, yanking out the cords of TV sets, taking statements, isolating jurors.

In other words—they *knew*. Then why, for God's sake, hadn't they moved in sooner, to prevent it? Judge Dutch would have words with the director.

Meanwhile, he would now interview juror number fifteen. So far, only four jurors had admitted to having seen coverage on their television sets. Number nine was ambiguous. He "thought" he might have seen "something." The judge could not penetrate beyond this, other than to get a play-by-play recap of the Knicks–Lakers game. Jury of peers. God save us.

Judge Dutch had initially impaneled a jury of eighteen, giving him twelve plus six alternates. He would have to dismiss these four, leaving him with two alternates. At this point, he could only pray that of the remaining jurors to interview, no more than two had seen anything. Otherwise it would be the Mistrial of the Millennium. The prospect made Judge Dutch consider, in this order, shooting himself, giving up the law, drinking an entire bottle of gin. Option three might lead, pleasantly enough, to accomplishing options one and two.

He nodded gravely at his clerk to bring in juror fifteen.

☆ · ☆ · ☆

Boyce asked simply, "What's your evidence?"

Wide grins. One of the agents walked over to a VHS and pressed play. A TV monitor anchored to the ceiling produced an image: Boyce, Felicio, and Felicio's technical man in the Tysons Corner hotel room. The quality of FBI surveillance tape had much improved since the grainy days of the DeLorean and Mayor Marion Barry busts. These days it was all so digital. Boyce listened to himself saying, "There will be a very big story on the TV news tomorrow night. That's what I want them to see. Can it be done by then?"

Felicio conferred with his guy.

"*Sí, patrón.* No problem."

The FBI man pressed stop. "Want popcorn?"

"You know," Boyce said, "if I didn't know better, I'd swear that was me."

The agent in charge chuckled. "So it was you who leaked the story about the plea bargain? That's slick, Counselor. You ask the deputy AG for a meeting just so you'd have something worth leaking."

The other agents nodded approvingly. "That's good."

"You want to make a call, or watch the second reel?"

"Have you arrested the other two people in that video?" Boyce asked.

"You mean the ones you'd swear were Felicio Andaluz and Ramon Martinez, if you didn't know better? You'll probably run into them at your arraignment. They said to say *hola.* They've been very helpful. Told us all about your phone call."

Something wrong here. Felicio had been tortured by some of the best interrogators south of the border, where forcibly extracting information was as old a profession as gold mining. This too often involved removing gold (fillings). So Felicio wouldn't have warbled for these gringos. His pain threshold *began* at crushed knuckles. What was the worst these palefaces could do to him? Threaten to take away his cigarettes?

So if they knew about Boyce's call to Felicio, which they apparently did, they had to know *on their own.*

Had they tapped his fish phone? That was a wiretap he could fight.

Still, what a mess. He needed to call Beth. She'd have heard by now. Mongol farmers in their yurts would have heard the news by now.

"Boyce! Is this true?"

"Did I ask you that?"

"Are you all right?"

"I'll be out of here in an hour."

"Wouldn't bet on that, Counselor."

"As soon as I post bail."

"Who was that?"

"Agent Dokins, my new best friend. I'm surrounded by my fan club here." He cupped the phone. "Yo, J. Edgar, you going to claim I'm a flight risk?"

The agents grinned.

Boyce sighed. "They're being pricks about this, naturally. Make that two hours. Beth?"

"Yes?"

"You understand what this means? Don't say anything. You didn't know anything about this, so you'll be fine. You can tell them the truth about this. You didn't know. Everything's going to be fine now. Do you understand?"

"Boyce, you're calling from FBI headquarters after being arrested for jury tampering. By what definition is this 'fine'?"

"Just tell Babcock to bring a fresh shirt, the Turnbull and Asser, with the burgundy tie. Along with the bail. I'm not going to walk out of here in the same shirt."

☆ · ☆ · ☆

Boyce emerged from the J. Edgar Hoover Building four and a half hours later, looking natty and upbeat for someone facing five years plus professional extinction. They tried to route him out the side door, but he insisted on going out the way he came. More or less every television camera in North America was there to record the moment.

"I have a short statement," he said above the roar of shutters. "After that I'm going to my office to check the U.S. Constitution to see where it says that the government has the right to harass and jail lawyers in the middle of trials. It would appear that the government is so afraid of losing this case—which they never should have brought in the first place—that they'll stop at nothing. Now they have stooped so low that the backbone of the law may be permanently bent. Thank you. See you all in court."

☆ · ☆ · ☆

He could tell she'd spent the better part of the morning crying.

"You ought not to cry so much. It makes you puffy."

"Why did you do this?"

"This is no time for that. What it is time for, however, is a drink."

He ordered a Bloody Mary from room service. He flumped onto the sofa and loosened his burgundy tie.

"How'd I look on TV?"

"It was an improvement on the *Today* show. At least you weren't arrested in the middle of it." Beth sat opposite him. "I won't ask if it's true."

"Thank you."

"Is it true?"

"What's true is that Judge Dutch will have no choice but to order a mistrial. Which means you get to start over. I won't be defending you this time. But whoever does will be a better attorney than I was, because they will not allow you to testify."

Beth looked pale. "You sacrificed yourself for me?"

"I can't have my child born in prison, for God's sake."

"How did they catch you?"

"Our attorney-client relationship is about to change. Maybe the less we discuss this, the better."

He looked at the phone. "I better get on the blower. Felicio's going to need a lawyer. I need a lawyer. You need a lawyer." He chuckled. "Another great day for the profession. Everyone needs a lawyer. Maybe we could get a bulk rate at one of those firms that advertise on late night TV."

"You're awfully calm about all this."

"I wonder if they give you a court-appointed attorney when you get to the Pearly Gates? I never thought of that. What a practice that would be."

Chapter 28

Judge Dutch issued his ruling after judicious deliberation. Determined—indeed, obsessed—with not being overturned on appeal, he checked in with his old mentor on the Supreme Court, as well as with a few other solons of the bench. Then he did what judges alone can do: he ruled.

There would be no mistrial.

The result of his interrogations had produced a total of six jurors who had watched trial coverage on their hotel television sets. These would be dismissed as alternates. This left him with twelve jurors. These twelve were now isolated on a military base under twenty-four-hour guard by U.S. Army Special Forces troops. There were no television sets in their rooms. They were transported to and from U.S. District Court in a military convoy, like al-Qaeda prisoners in Cuba. Some pundits declared this slightly melodramatic, but at this point Judge Dutch no longer cared what anyone—much less the media—said. His sole goal in life was to get a verdict. If the jurors had to be housed in subterranean vaults in the New Mexico desert—fine. He began to drop dark hints that he would remove the cameras from his courtroom. Instantly the media clammed up.

He read his ruling in court. The jury was not present. He avoided looking at Boyce. Then he got to the part in his ruling stating that Boyce would not be permitted to continue as counsel. He looked him straight in the eye.

"Objection. Your Honor, may I approach?"

"No."

Judge Dutch continued reading. Defense counsel had been arraigned on charges of conspiracy to tamper with a federal jury. He also faced disbarment proceedings by the Ethics Committee of the District of Columbia Bar. Pending disposition of those cases, it would be "grossly inappropriate" and morally intolerable for Mr. Baylor to remain as counsel. Though of course he was innocent until proven guilty.

He granted Mrs. MacMann a week's delay so she could arrange for new legal representation. He gave Boyce one final, disgusted look. Boyce thought he was going to pronounce sentence of death: *And may God Almighty have mercy upon your soul.*

☆ · ☆ · ☆

It was a glum little party they made back at the Jefferson. Chairs were drawn up in a circle. Boyce, Beth, and half a dozen of the best legal minds in the country chewed over how exactly to proceed. Beth's phone had started ringing minutes after the news of Boyce's arrest, lawyers salivating to represent her, no matter that chances of winning at this point were slim to nil. Beth MacMann was going down. On the bright side, it was possible that she and Boyce might end up doing their time in the same facility. Wouldn't that be cozy? Thank God no one yet knew she was pregnant.

Three television monitors were on with the sound off. As the lawyers talked, Boyce's eyes kept wandering to the screens. There was Perri on *Hard Gavel,* looking scrumptious. Crudman was on with her. Curious as Boyce was, he couldn't bring himself to turn up the volume. Death by hanging, lethal injection, or burning at the stake he could take, but not the condescension of Alan Crudman.

Some commentators insisted that Beth had put Boyce up to the jury tampering. Others said, No no no, this has all *his* fingerprints on it. Did he not get that terrorist Felicio Andaluz off twelve years ago for trying to blow up the U.S. embassy in Encantado? How do you think he got his nickname, anyway?

Boyce glanced at another screen.

POLL: OPINION OF BAYLOR

POSITIVE: 3%

NEGATIVE: 96%

At least 1 percent was still undecided.

The third monitor was showing old footage of a younger Boyce and Felicio during Felicio's trial. It was always strange, Boyce thought, seeing your youthful pixelgänger on TV looking back at you, thinner, hairier, inevitably wearing a wider tie. How strange and self-mocking it must be for movie stars to watch their early flicks in the winter of their lives. Felicio looked like a right-wing version of Che Guevara— revolutionary, but clean, with haircut and new shirt.

Boyce had called Linc Caplan at Skadden, Arps to ask him to take on Felicio and Ramon's defense and to send him the bills. Oh, the bills. What sweeter justice could there be for a lawyer than to find himself on the billing end of his brethren? Boyce's own income stream, that mighty green Amazon that had been flowing toward him for so many lush years, would soon be no more than a dried and cracked arroyo.

Then he saw on one of the monitors—the video of himself and Felicio and Ramon in the hotel room! As the others continued to talk, Boyce plucked the remote off the table and turned up the volume, just in time to hear himself giving Felicio the deadline for polluting the jury.

It stopped conversation in the room. As indeed, around the nation.

The FBI videotape ended and was replaced with the image of Perri. It was *she* who had shown the tape! Perfidy, thy name is Pettengill. Boyce was stunned.

Everyone in the room was staring at him.

"Isn't someone," he said, "going to say something contemptuous about the FBI leaking its evidence to the media? Or were you waiting for me to go first?"

"It's outrageous."

"Goddamit, where do they get off?"

"A new low."

"Who the fuck—pardon me, Mrs. MacMann—do those cocksuckers think they are?"

"Thank you," Boyce said. "That was collegial of you."

"Would you excuse Boyce and me for a moment?" Beth said.

When they were alone, she said, "So that's why you went to Clintick. So there would be something newsworthy on TV the next day for your friends to beam into the jury's hotel rooms?"

"We shouldn't be discussing this."

"They would have found out it was you. Sooner or later."

"By then you'd have been in the middle of a new trial."

"So I've ruined your life twice."

" 'History repeats itself, first time as tragedy, second as farce.' "

"You realize our child is going to hate us."

"So do most lawyers' kids."

☆ · ☆ · ☆

The nice thing about being a judge—aside from the big chair—was that they had to come to you.

Sitting in front of him in his dark and woody chambers hung with four-hundred-year-old still lifes and portraits of fish and merchants was the director of the Federal Bureau of Investigation. The director's evident nervousness was deeply satisfying to Judge Dutch.

We'll get to the broadcast of this video in a moment, the judge began. Though it's not my case and I have no jurisdiction, I'm very, very curious to know how a show called *Hard Gavel,* hosted by Baylor's former girlfriend, came into possession of it.

The director began to answer evasively. The judge held up a hand, a gesture combining serenity and absolute power. Continue in that manner, the gesture said, and by this hand thou shalt know the true meaning of woe.

What I desire to hear from you first, Judge Dutch continued, running his fingertips along the edge of the blade of a letter opener that had once belonged to Supreme Court justice Potter Stewart, is the following: Your agents videotaped Boyce Baylor and those jalapeño hoodlums in a hotel conspiring to tamper with a jury. My jury. *Why, then, did you permit them to go forward and pollute the jury?* And while we're at it, why was I not informed?

The director mumbled out some boilerplate about procedure. Seeing Judge Dutch's normally placid face staring back at him like an Assyrian lion, he stopped.

We needed, he said, to catch them in the act.

Who . . . needed?

The Bureau.

Judge Dutch had indulged in violent expostulation only once before, after learning that an art dealer in Amsterdam was trying to sell him a still life of a dead flounder and two lemons, allegedly by De Grootie, but in fact by one of De Grootie's pupils, Flemm Vander Flemm.

It's no small thing to alter the metabolic rate of the director of the FBI, yet Judge Dutch succeeded. He would demand a Senate investigation. For *starters.*

Now, he continued, while we are on the subject of the Bureau's possibly criminal misconduct—Judge Dutch bit down on the final syllable as if it were a crisp breadstick—*how did that videotape leak?* Or was it that FBI evidence tapes had become the latest thing in reality TV?

We're looking into that. Be assured, Judge, we are looking into it.

Do. Look *deeply* into it. And inform me of your findings. Before I hear about it on television.

Yes, Your Honor.

Chapter 29

*W*hen you're hot, you're hot. When you're not, the hotel management shows up at the door with your bill. Ten months of three suites came to—after discount—$1,845,322, including room service. With a velvety clearing of his adenoids, the manager asked that Boyce vacate "at the earliest convenience." The "media situation," he explained, had become "disruptive to the other guests."

Simultaneously, Sandy Clintick moved to have Beth placed in custody as a "flight risk."

How Beth was planning to skip the country while under the "protection" of a dozen Secret Service agents was not clear. But feelings were running so high against her and Boyce that the polls showed most Americans in favor of putting her behind at least some kind of bars. For Boyce they favored hanging, preferably before he could be tried and after lengthy torture, *peine dure et forte.* It was all a glorious excuse for a national splurge of lawyer bashing.

"It's incidents such as these," Alan Crudman wrote in an op-ed article for *The Boston Globe*, "that weaken Americans' faith in their legal system."

"I thought I'd already hit bottom," Boyce said to Beth, "but being looked down on by Alan Crudman gives new definition to bottom."

"He called me this morning," Beth said. "He wants to take the case. He wants to file a motion."

"Pass the hemlock. I'm listening."

"Mistrial for reasons of ineffective assistance of counsel. He thinks Dutch would go for it. Even if you don't get a mistrial, it's very solid grounds for a reversal after conviction."

Boyce chuckled darkly. "I'd sooner swallow leeches than spend ten minutes with Alan Crudman. But he's a helluva lawyer. You should consider it. Look at the scumbags he's gotten off."

Beth looked at him.

"Sorry. Didn't mean it that way. I meant, go for it."

"I told him to go screw himself."

"Beth, it's hard enough paying Alan Crudman a compliment. Don't make me work at it."

"I'm not going to ruin your life three times."

"I wouldn't feel it. You develop a callus after the second time. Look, it's not a bad idea he's got there. You can file an affidavit along with the motion saying that I *forced* you to take the stand against all your better instincts. You had no idea I was conspiring to tamper with the jury. And my getting thrown off the case has completely compromised your defense. You should be given the opportunity to start over. These are all perfectly good arguments for a mistrial. Dutch will have to go for it. He's painted himself into a corner. The Supreme Court would back him up in a second. You've got to do it. You have to do it for—"

"I don't want to hear that I have to do it for the Tummybug."

"Well, you do, Beth. Even if you don't want to hear it."

"I'm not going to. So forget it. We'll find some other way."

"At what point in your life did you decide that stubbornness was one of the cardinal virtues?"

"When at age eleven I saw that the world was ruled by men."

"Fine. Condemn our child to life in the prison playground."

"Maybe it would be better not to *have* the child."

They were silent.

"That's a terrible thing to say," Boyce said.

"I know. I didn't mean it. I was just trying to hurt you. I'm sorry." Beth considered her belly. "I'm going to start showing soon."

"What a media feast that's going to be. They ought to be paying us an entertainment fee. Think of the content we're providing."

Beth put her hands to her stomach. "*This* is content." She smiled.

☆ · ☆ · ☆

"We go now to our legal correspondent."

"Peter, *another* tumultuous day in the MacMann case. We have just learned that Beth MacMann will take over her *own* defense. Mrs. MacMann *is* a lawyer, after all—it was at law school that she *met* Boyce Baylor and the late President—though she has never *practiced*. This is a highly unusual development. It's hard, if not impossible, to think of someone taking over their own defense in a murder trial at this late stage, but then just about everything about this case has been unusual."

"What will Boyce Baylor's role be? Will he have one?"

"His *role*, Peter, will consist of defending *himself* on the very serious charge of jury tampering. At the moment, we understand, he is occupied with moving *out* of the Jefferson Hotel, where he maintained his so-called war room. We've learned further that he is *suing* the Jefferson for wrongful eviction. . . ."

☆ · ☆ · ☆

The government had seized his bank accounts, so Boyce found what are politely called alternate arrangements across the river in Rosslyn, Washington's unbohemian left bank, a suburban sprawl of glassy highrises where most of the pedestrians work for various defense agencies and the cabdrivers come from countries badly disappointed by U.S. foreign policy.

It wasn't so bad, though living without the room service took some getting used to. The papers ran photographs of the outside of the motel juxtaposed with photos of the previous one, under the caption "How the mighty have fallen." The relative modesty of his new surroundings even gave him a bit of *nostalgie de la boue,* reminding him of his early days of defending corrupt union officials, mobsters, and—lowest of the low—providers of illegal soft money. He became a local celebrity at the Szechuan Sizzle Chinese restaurant around from his motel. The owner paid him the highest compliment a Chinese restaurateur can bestow: he didn't charge for the soup.

Boyce listened with one ear to the machinations of his legal team, who were busy filing motions and preparing a defense in the face of dismal and overwhelming evidence. But try as he might, Boyce had no interest in his own case. He did not relish the idea of spending five years in prison, surrounded by victims of inferior lawyering. All he could think about was Beth and Tummybug.

Judge Dutch had stopped short of placing Beth in custody, but just for good measure he had ordered that she be placed under a kind of house arrest. Marshals were ordered in to "protect" the house in Cleveland Park where she was staying. So she now had two rings of federal protection around her, her Secret Service detail on the inside and bulky men in windbreakers on the outside. At night, over a phone line that they were fairly sure was tapped, Beth and Boyce joked darkly about the tunnel the two of them were digging.

In the mornings, Boyce would show up in a taxicab, with at least two vans full of television camera crews following, and ride with her in her now even longer motorcade to the courtroom. She would get out at the front entrance. He sat in the car with the contemptuous Secret Service agents, watching the proceedings on a portable television set. During breaks, Beth would return to the car, parked in the courthouse basement, to get his comments and notes. As the TV correspondent would say, it was an unusual arrangement.

Beth had called to the stand the White House curator, F. Dickerson Twumb. The idea was to show that she so revered eighteenth-century American silverware that she never would have used it to crush the skull of her husband. It somewhat left open the suggestion that she'd have been happy to use some other less precious blunt object.

"Well," Beth said, entering the car with her folders and legal pads, followed by the faithful Vlonko.

"I'm uneasy with this witness," Boyce said. "He doesn't seem to like you very much, frankly."

"You have to understand about curators. They think it's *their* White House, and they regard all First Ladies—with the exception of Jackie Kennedy—as menopausal busybodies whose idea of decor is an Ethan Allen showroom. When we got to the White House, I had the temerity to suggest to him that I found Albert Bierstadt's landscapes boring, and he went into a snit from which he has apparently not yet recovered."

"Great witness for the defense." Boyce snorted.

"He did say I was particular about the silver."

"Vlonko?"

Vlonko shook his head. "Jury's not so fucking happy today. Not happy yesterday, either. Or the day before. Maybe they don't like army food."

"All right," Boyce said. "You go back in there and you grab this guy by his bow tie and get him the hell off the stand. Who's your next witness?"

"I want to recall Secret Service agent Birnam."

"Why?"

"I want to put it to him, 'If you think I was such a threat to the President, then why didn't you rush into the bedroom and shoot me?' "

Boyce shrugged. "Why not." He glanced furtively at Vlonko. Vlonko's look said it all.

☆ · ☆ · ☆

Boyce was having a morose, solitary dinner of Chairman Mao chicken and crispy shredded beef at the Szechuan Sizzle before going back to his room. His eyes strayed to the television monitor over the bar. The sound was off, with the closed captioning on. On the screen he saw the flashing lights. The captioning scrolled:

CAPT. CARY GRAYSON, WHO PERFORMED THE AUTOPSY ON PRESIDENT KENNETH MACMANN, IS IN CRITICAL CONDITION FOLLOWING AN AC-CIDENT ON THE GEORGE WASHINGTON PARKWAY. HIS CAR WENT OFF

THE ROAD AND HIT A TREE. HE WAS TAKEN TO NEARBY BETHESDA NAVAL HOSPITAL AND UNDERWENT SURGERY...POLICE SAY THERE MAY BE EVIDENCE THAT HE WAS INTOXICATED...

Intoxicated? Grayson? He called Beth on his cell phone. It didn't matter if the feds listened in, though his attorney, Judd Best, had been assured by the U.S. District Attorney's Office that there were no outstanding eavesdropping warrants on him.

"Were you planning on recalling Dr. Grayson?"

"No. Why?"

"He's in surgery and may not come out of it. Car crash."

"Poor man."

"Well, the poor man may have been drunk at the wheel when he went off the road into the tree."

"Grayson?"

"Turn on the news."

On the other end, Boyce heard the sound of the channel he was watching silently at the bar.

"Jeez," Beth said.

Boyce looked around to see if any reporters were listening in. He said into his cell phone, "Not to be morbid about it, but tomorrow morning I want you to go to Dutch and say, 'Look, I was planning to call this guy again and *now* look.' He'll ask you what you wanted to hear from Grayson. I'll think of something. Toxicology, whatever. But you'll say it's *crucial,* and without his testimony we—you—are being deprived of *vital* evidence. Wait."

"What?"

"I just thought of something. Pure genius!"

"Well?"

Boyce looked around again. "No, not on the phone. Tomorrow, on the way to court."

☆ · ☆ · ☆

"Well?" she said next day as they were riding to court.

Boyce lowered his voice. "Wouldn't they love to hear this in the front seat up there." He whispered, "We—you—tell Dutch that you were going to recall Grayson to testify in greater detail about that suspicious postdeath imprinting of the Revere mark on Ken's forehead. *But they got to him before you could.*"

"Who got to him?"

"They—the Secret Service. *They ran him off the road.*"

Beth looked at him. "Boyce, honey, I know this has been an awful strain on you."

"Dutch'll hit the ceiling. But it doesn't matter. You bring it up in the closing arguments. Look—seventy-five percent of the American people *still* think that JFK was killed by his own people. Trust me, at least one juror will think, *Hmmmm.* And all you need is one juror."

"It's nuts."

"Of course it's nuts."

"I don't know if I have it in me." Beth sighed and sat back in the seat. "What I'd really like to do is go into that courtroom today and say, 'Here, here's what happened. Here's the truth of it.' "

"Beth, how many times do I have to tell you. The truth has no *place* in a court of law."

"I know, I know. But my belly is swelling, my tits won't fit in the bra anymore, they want to put me away. I'm tired."

☆ · ☆ · ☆

Boyce spent a busy morning calling his shrinking group of media friendlies, trying to convince them that Dr. Grayson's mishap on the George Washington Parkway was no accident.

"Who," he said darkly, "had the motive? Who had the means?"

"You're saying the Secret *Service* tried to kill him?"

"I know. Hard to believe, isn't it? But that's what they said about Vince Foster."

"Boyce, Grayson was drunk. He was tanked."

"Exactly. And who had the means to plant the booze on him?"

"Oh, come on."

"If you don't want it, fine. I gotta go, that's *Newsweek* on the other line."

"No no no. Hold on. Do you *know* this, or are you guessing?"

"Did Woodward know?" Boyce said. "Did Bernstein know?"

☆ · ☆ · ☆

It's an axiom of journalism that if you can get one paper to print a rumor, all the others will rush in to print it on the grounds that someone else did. It was for the best that poor Dr. Grayson was still in a postoperative coma after undergoing seven hours of brain surgery. By noon the next day, it was being speculated, mostly on the Internet, that his accident was no accident.

The Secret Service was being besieged by calls wanting to know if they had run him off the road—to keep him from testifying that the Revere mark *had* been planted by them. The day after that, the *Times, Post,* and half a dozen other pillars of journalistic reputability were running items headlined:

SINISTER MOTIVES ALLEGED IN GRAYSON CRASH

The Secret Service directed inquiries to Bethesda Naval Hospital, where an embarrassed doctor stood before the podium at a press conference to say that Dr. Grayson's blood alcohol level upon arrival at the emergency room was—clearing of throat—"slightly elevated above the legal limit."

How elevated?

Clearing of the throat. "Point one nine."

God in heaven, the man was stinking! Plastered! Navy drunk! Oh, what do you do with a drunken sailor, so *ear-lie* in the *mor-ning*?

Another navy doctor, this one with more ribbons than Christmas morning on his white chest, was trotted out to say that Captain Grayson was a man of impeccable reputation who was not only the navy's top pathologist, but had served his country valorously in war. Naturally, the President's death and his involvement, his testimony, had been a strain. There was no excuse for what had happened, but no one had been harmed but Dr. Grayson, and so while we all pray for his recovery, let us bear in mind that he surely is as human as the rest of us.

The media, sensing that moral outrage and opprobrium might be out of place, ceased baying for the time being and set up a death watch outside Bethesda Naval.

Chapter 30

*B*ut *why* was he drunk? Why was this white-gowned, medal-wearing paragon of military and medical virtue driving blotto into trees?

Boyce hid from his media pursuivants in the Szechuan Sizzle, poring over the transcript of Grayson's testimony, over the toxicology reports from the President's autopsy, over everything pertaining to the doctor. No clues to this seemingly out-of-character behavior presented themselves. At the trial, the doctor himself had been an exemplar of professional calm in every way. Reviewing the tapes, Boyce saw that his expression had been serene and unruffled. Following his testimony, the women's magazines had been full of his pictures. *People* magazine had declared him one of its "50 Most Reassuring Men in America," an event that according to reports had given everyone at Bethesda Naval a good chuckle, no one more so than Dr. Grayson.

Meanwhile, Judge Dutch had reacted volcanically to the media reports about the Secret Service allegedly pouring whiskey into Dr. Grayson and then driving him off the road into the maple tree. He knew exactly where this canard had begun to quack. In retaliation, he gave orders that no vehicle carrying Boyce Baylor could enter even the basement garage of the courthouse. It turned out that this was, in fact, beyond even his august sovereignty. Judge Dutch's glasses now fogged at the merest mention of Boyce Baylor. The joke began to circulate around the courthouse clerks that the next car to veer drunkenly off the George Washington Parkway would be Judge Dutch's Volvo.

But at least the Trial of the Millennium was coming to a close.

For Beth, however, there was little light at the end of this long tunnel. Las Vegas bookmakers were laying thirty-to-one odds on conviction. And ominously, some commentators were remarking that her physique seemed to be changing, almost as if she were, well, pregnant.

☆ · ☆ · ☆

One evening a few minutes past ten o'clock after returning from working at Rosedale with Beth on her concluding argument, Boyce sat in his usual booth at the Sizzle, nursing a glass of inferior brandy and staring halfheartedly at a motion he was filing in his own case. As he worked, a fortune cookie was placed in front of him.

He looked up to tell the waiter that he did not want a fortune cookie, only to see the back of someone disappearing briskly toward the restaurant's front door. Odd.

He looked at the fortune cookie. Its fortune protruded from the sugar clam lips.

He extracted the piece of paper cautiously, as if it might be the fuse to a bomb. In the kingdom of the tricky, the paranoid man still has all his fingers.

It was in handwriting.

> *Confucius say public phone Colonial and Nash soon
> ring with interesting tiding. 10:15 pm. WPS.*

Boyce threw a twenty on the table and walked out of the Sizzle. There are no emptier streets at night than those of Rosslyn, Virginia. He walked the two blocks to the intersection of Colonial and Nash. It was dark and out of the way, just the place to kill someone. Not that anything that exciting ever happened in Rosslyn.

Calm down, he told himself. But he was nervous.

He answered on the first ring.

The voice on the other end was cheerful, like that of someone who wanted you to try their long-distance service, at significant savings.

"I always said, if I'd stuck around for my trial, you're the man I'da hired, Counselor."

Boyce had never heard Wiley P. Sinclair's voice, so he had no way of knowing if this was really Wiley P. Sinclair, former FBI counterintelligence officer, betrayer of his country, agent of Chinese intelligence, code name Confucius. All of this he knew from the public record.

"Tell me something," Boyce replied, "that would convince me that I'm really talking to Confucius."

Chuckle. "You mean, like a PIN?"

Wiley P. Sinclair was the FBI's Most Wanted fugitive. He had made a jackass of them (not an especially daunting task). It was said that he was still working for the Chinese. His double agenting had, among other things, helped them get the Olympics and a nifty new U.S.-designed nuclear-tipped torpedo for their submarine fleet.

On visits to Beijing, U.S. presidents and secretaries of state would demand that China turn Wiley over to them. The Chinese would blink through the cigarette smoke and say that they had no knowledge of this Wiley P. Sincrair and then suggest that if there were such a person, he must be working for the imperialist lackeys in Taiwan. And that would be the end of the Wiley P. Sinclair portion of the agenda for that visit.

And now Boyce was—or might be—speaking to him from a pay phone in Dullsville.

"I figured," Wiley said, "that you might want some bona fides. They're in your room waiting for you. Bit of a step down from the Jefferson, isn't it?"

"Why are we speaking?"

"It's complicated, Counselor."

"Trust me. I can handle it."

"Combination of reasons. You've given the bastards one hell of a run for their money. I like your style. Okay, I could tell you I'm doing this just to help, but you'd figure out that's bullcrap. So I'll level with you. My current employers would be very pleased if this information came out. And you're perfectly placed to be the one to bring it out. So here's the 411."

"The what?"

"The information." Wiley P. Sinclair laughed. "Counselor, I'm surprised. I keep up better with the English slang living in Pandaland than you do."

☆ · ☆ · ☆

Boyce didn't dare say it out loud to Beth in the car the next morning, just in case it was bugged. He wrote down the substance of what Wiley had told him.

Beth read, looked up sharply at Boyce. He took the paper back, tore it up, and put the pieces in his pocket.

"How can you be sure it was he?" Beth asked.

"When I got back to my hotel room, there was an envelope under the door. It was the PIN to his old ATM machine. I had someone in my office check his FBI file. It was in there. No one else would know that."

"Except for the FBI. They could be setting you up."

"I considered that," Boyce said. "But why would they bother at this point? I'm going down in flames as it is. Why pour gasoline on me now?"

"To make you burn brighter."

"Maybe. But what if it was him?"

"He."

"This is a gift, Beth."

"He's a traitor to his country."

Boyce was reminded that Beth had been First Lady of the United States. "Is this the time to be splitting ethical hairs?"

"It's not a hair, Boyce. The man is evil."

"Precisely. He and I are on the same bandwidth."

"It's wrong."

"So the Chinese got the Olympics. So they got a torpedo. Is this the end of the world?"

"He protected all their agents in California who were stealing secrets from Silicon Valley."

"No one's saying the man's a saint."

"This is like trying to explain vegetarianism to a shark."

"So why bother? This is not the time for ethical hand-wringing. Save it for your book."

"Just *why* does this fugitive traitor want to help me? I'm asking out of curiosity, not for ethical reasons, if that makes you feel any better."

Boyce decided to leave out the part about how Wiley was doing this for Chinese intelligence.

"Because he genuinely believes you're innocent. And feels that this is a way of doing at least something good. To make up for past misdeeds. Would you deny a fellow human being the chance to atone?"

"The only person on the planet who believes I'm innocent is a former FBI agent who sold out his country to finance his gambling addiction. What a fan club."

"Now is not the time to be choosy."

☆ · ☆ · ☆

Judge Dutch listened without comment, his glasses misting to opacity. Deputy Attorney General Sandra Clintick listened in silence with an expression that needled from contempt to incredulity and outrage.

Beth concluded, "I wanted to inform you both of this privately. I know this comes late. I also realize that there are ramifications, since it involves sensitive issues of national security. But there it is, and I intend to pursue it."

"This information," Judge Dutch said, "where did it come from?"

Beth cleared her throat. "From Wiley P. Sinclair."

"Objection!" Sandy Clintick snapped.

"We're not in court, Ms. Clintick," Judge Dutch observed. "You're free to express yourself in nonjudicial language." He turned back to Beth. "But I have to say, Ms. MacMann, I'm not impressed by this. Not a bit."

"I would rather myself that it had come from some other source, Your Honor."

"This is disgraceful, Your Honor," Clintick said. "Disgraceful and desperate."

The judge rocked in his chair. "Mrs. MacMann, if this turns out to be without foundation and you are ultimately found guilty, I will . . . weigh this at the time of sentencing. Do you understand the implications?"

Beth nodded. "Yes, Your Honor."

"What if this witness—assuming I even allow you to call him—denies it? As he well might? What then?"

"Your Honor," Beth said, "surely you don't expect me to discuss matters of legal strategy in front of the prosecution?"

Beth and Sandy Clintick left the judge's chambers together. Alone in his outer office, Clintick turned to Beth.

"When are you due?"

"June."

Clintick smiled icily. "There's nothing you two wouldn't stop at, is there?"

"It was an accident."

"Oh, right."

"You think this was part of the overall defense strategy?"

"Why not? It's actually a smart move. Makes it harder for the judge to hand down a death sentence, doesn't it?"

Beth returned the gelid smile. "Is that why you haven't mentioned it in public?"

"I'm hoping to get a verdict and sentence *before* you show up in a maternity dress."

"I'll try not to hold you up."

☆ · ☆ · ☆

Wiley P. Sinclair, being skilled in the arts of evasion, counterevasion, and even counter-counterevasion, had left Boyce with a means of contacting him, involving bright orange stickers and a stop sign on Glebe Road. A few hours later, Boyce was at a pay phone in Old Town, Alexandria. Wiley P. Sinclair laughed when Boyce told him what he wanted.

"Now doesn't *that* take the cake," Wiley said. When he was finished being charmed by the idea, he said, "You know the three cardinal rules, right? Don't eat at a place called Mom's, don't draw to an inside straight, don't go to bed with someone who's got more problems than you do. Here's a fourth: Don't try to outfox someone named Wiley."

"I wouldn't presume to try to set a trap for you," Boyce said. "But we need this document. Otherwise they're just going to deny it, and where does that leave us? Who're we going to call then?"

"No way, Counselor."

"Do you want this to happen, or not?"

"Are you saying it's a deal breaker?"

"Yeah."

There was a long pause. Then Wiley P. Sinclair chuckled.

"Oh, are they going to be hot for my ass again. Red hot. I'm going to have to relocate so deep in Pandaland that I may end up discovering a whole new *species* of bear. But okay. You're my kind of lawyer, Counselor. You do whatever you gotta do for your client. Say, I just gotta ask—she did it, right?"

"That's on a need-to-know basis."

"I can't wait to see their faces when she waves this thing in court. You a betting man, Counselor?"

"Not in your league."

"Do you know they had two hundred agents in Vegas looking for me? I was there, and they missed me! What a buncha numb-nuts. I went in *drag*!" Wiley laughed. "Lay you three to two that Judge Dutch is gonna burst a nose artery when she shows up in court with this."

Wiley insisted on making the arrangements. Boyce counted the laws that he, Boyce, was breaking in doing this. He stopped at six.

Chapter 31

Two days later, Beth and Sandy Clintick were back in Judge Dutch's chambers.

"I will ask you a last time not to use again the word *bullshit,* Ms. Clintick," Judge Dutch said. "We're not in court, but neither are we in a bar."

"Then I'll use the word *travesty,*" Clintick said, fuming. "This is a travesty. And you are permitting it."

"I haven't permitted anything as of yet, Ms. Clintick. But I won't permit *that* sort of language. Anywhere."

"She comes in here"—Clintick pointed at Beth, who was quietly enjoying her fury—"with an affidavit, by a fugitive *traitor* . . ."

"I've made no determination yet as to the affidavit, Ms. Clintick," he said, then cast a disdainful glance at Beth. "Other than to acknowledge that it exists."

He picked up the piece of paper imprinted with the notary public's seal. "I take it," he said, "that this notary had no idea who Wiley P. Sinclair is."

"That would be correct, Your Honor. Mr. Sinclair—or so I was informed by Mr. Baylor, who supervised the notarizing and witnessing—was asked for two forms of identification, which he provided. A driver's license, apparently still valid, and a Social Security card."

Judge Dutch sniffed. "This is appalling, Mrs. MacMann."

Beth shrugged. "I admit it's untidy, Judge. But Mr. Sinclair's legal ability to make an affidavit is unaffected by his status as a fugitive."

"We appear," Judge Dutch said with a sigh, "for the time being to have hopscotched beyond the issue of his criminality. Mr. Baylor will have to bear the burden of that matter. Since he is the one who"—he looked at her unbelievingly—"had the unlawful contact with our fugitive, Mr. Sinclair. Of course, Mr. Baylor can always claim that there was some duress, or that he was unable to effect the arrest of Mr. Sinclair."

Beth wondered—was he prompting her?

"At any rate," he continued, leaning forward, "we must now confront this Log Cabin business."

☆ · ☆ · ☆

"Defense calls Roscoe Farquant."

Oh, the stir, the buzz, the rumbling, the craning of heads and shifting of glutei in Judge Umin's courtroom. Boyce, feeling more than ever like a mole in his backseat hole in the bowels of the courthouse basement garage, would have given a testicle and three Supreme Court decisions to be there in person.

It had—naturally—leaked to the media that Beth was going to call the head of the National Security Agency, the only agency left in Washington that really had any secrets worth knowing. Her subpoena had created a sensation. NSA lawyers said he would not honor the subpoena. Judge Dutch replied that in that case he would have General Farquant arrested. The NSA relented. Nothing so concentrates the mind as the prospect of handcuffs.

No one knew what exactly she planned to ask him. The pixel pundits frothed over with speculation.

Farquant was, as most NSA chiefs tended to be, a former military person. He looked it: trim, peach fuzz hair, glasses, eyes beady with the big-big secrets. He looked like a man who wouldn't tell God something on the grounds that God was not cleared to know.

"General Farquant," Beth said, addressing him in a courtly, respectful manner, "I won't waste your time or the court's establishing your credentials, which are beyond question. You are the director of the National Security Agency, and have been for the last five and a half years. That agency collects electronic information on behalf of the U.S. government. Is that an accurate description of its role?"

"It is a very general description of the agency's function," he replied.

"Does the code name Operation Log Cabin mean anything to you?"

Nothing so excites a Washington audience as introducing the term *code name* in a public setting. Invariably, what follows is evidence that the government has, once again, been up to something disastrously ill advised, or at least very, very naughty.

General Farquant stared unblinkingly at Beth, the court, the nation, the world beyond. The only sign that a white phosphorous grenade had just gone off in his stomach was a slight lateral twitch of the eyeballs.

"I'm not in a position to comment on that."

Boyce bellowed out loud with delight, startling the Secret Service agent in the driver's seat. Yes! The crew-cut SOB hadn't denied it outright!

"Was Operation Log Cabin put into effect some eighteen months ago?"

"I'm not in a position to comment."

"Of course. General Farquant, was Operation Log Cabin a covert surveillance program, mounted by the National Security Agency, whereby electronic eavesdropping devices were placed in the Lincoln Bedroom at the White House? So that your agency could monitor the conversations?"

A giant sucking sound could be heard in the courtroom.

"I am not in a position to comment on that." For all his sangfroid, General Farquant was beginning to resemble the frog placed in the pot of water that is slowly brought to a boil.

"Objection," said Sandy Clintick. "The witness has answered the question to the best of his ability."

"He most certainly has not," said Beth.

Judge Dutch thoughtfully tapped his cheek with a finger. "Overruled."

Beth continued. "Was the purpose of Operation Log Cabin—which presumably was so named after the fact that Abraham Lincoln grew up in a log cabin—"

"Objection. Conjecture."

"Oh, honestly," Beth said.

"Sustained."

"Was the purpose of Operation Log Cabin to obtain information on persons who were guests of President MacMann and the First Lady?"

"I'm not in a position to comment."

"On the night of September twenty-eighth, year before last, Ms. Babette Van Anka, the actress and activist, was a guest in the Lincoln Bedroom. Was such a device implanted in her cell phone or other personal effects by an agent or agents working for NSA?"

"I'm not in a position to comment."

"Thank you, General Farquant," Beth said pleasantly. "You've been most forthcoming."

Boyce slammed his fist against the window and bellowed, "Yee-hah!"

"Sir," said the Secret Service agent in the front seat, "do you *mind*?"

☆ · ☆ · ☆

The President summoned his chief of staff.

"This Log Cabin thing, what the hell?"

"Do you want to know, sir?"

"No, I don't. But goddammit, Henderson."

"Yes, sir, I agree completely."

"Get me distance on this. I want miles of distance between this and me."

"I—we—all understand that, sir. We are at the moment working on that."

"When did it—no, I don't want to know. Get me—who's in charge of this, this bucket of night crawlers?"

"No one at NSA seems to be stepping forward to claim credit for it, sir. We're—"

"Heads. I want heads, Henderson. Heads lined up like golf balls, in the Rose Garden."

"Understood."

"I leave for Europe tomorrow. Sweet Jesus. I'm going to be with the heads of seven countries—plus the Queen. The Queen, Henderson! Of England! Did any of them stay in the Lincoln Bedroom during the MacBeth administration?"

"Heads of state typically stay in Blair House or the Queen's Bedroom, as you know, sir." Henderson cleared his throat. "However, the Queen of England did, in fact, stay in the Lincoln Bedroom on one occasion. She had expressed interest in it. Apparently she is a fan of Lincoln's. So the MacManns put her there. I have the date here. . . ."

The President's face drained of color. "I'm spending the night at Windsor Castle. As her guest."

"Sir, I think we can make it clear that this Operation Log Cabin was in no way sanctioned by *this* White House. For all we know, it wasn't even sanctioned by the last White House."

"Well, let's get *that* message out and cranking, and fast."

"Yes, sir. Right away."

"Henderson."

"Sir?"

"What were they after, for God's sake?"

☆ · ☆ · ☆

It was probably just as well that Babette Van Anka was not driving herself to the studio to record her annual message of peace for the coming Easter-Passover holidays or she might have driven off the road and into a royal palm. She had given up watching the trial weeks ago, on the grounds that it was not good for her skin. Now her cell phone rang, the first eight bars of the sound track from *Fabulous, Fabulous Me,* the movie that had cemented her status as a star. Before she managed to say hello, she heard the sound of Max, calling her a cow in every language that he and his ancestors had spoken, with a few Far Eastern languages thrown in for good measure. He then related the substance of that morning's testimony. And hung up.

Babette played the scene as she might in a movie. She rolled down the window and hurled her cell phone out of the car, in case it too was bugged. Fortunately, this being Los Angeles, there were no pedestrians to injure.

She told Massimo, her driver, to take her to LAX instead of the recording studio.

"Which airline, madame?"

"*Any* airline! International!"

She cursed Max for swinishly not sending the plane to get her. He had brusquely informed her, between epithets, that he needed it himself to remove himself even farther from U.S. justice.

Money. She would need money. As a star, she rarely carried any, since other people paid. Her secretaries took care of the occasional pecuniary necessities, supplying her with ironed banknotes. She looked in her purse. There were a few crisp, folded one-hundred-dollar notes. More would be needed. But she could hardly present herself at the bank. She didn't even know which bank handled the Grab–Van Anka cash. Then she remembered the television commercials showing people inserting cards in machines and getting cash. Triumphantly, she produced a credit card from the purse and directed Massimo to stop at a machine.

She leapt out and inserted the card. After several minutes she raced back to the car.

"It keeps asking for a personal identification number," she shrieked at the hapless Massimo. "What the *fuck* is a personal identification number?"

Massimo explained, earning himself a cuff on his chest. "How am *I* supposed to know it? Call someone! No—don't! Into the car. Into the *car*! Drive! Just *drive*!"

At the international departures terminal, she frantically scanned the names of the airlines and ordered Massimo to stop when she saw one that seemed more foreign than the others.

She hurried in after divesting Massimo of his pocket money. Heads turned at the spectacle of America's most notorious film star. The morning's trial testimony had played over all the television monitors at the airport, so everyone was up-to-date.

She went directly to the "Emperor Class" check-in counter. A businessman, presumably an emperor, was being assisted. Babette placed a peremptory elbow on the counter. The man turned to tell the pushy broad to cool her heels. When he saw who it was, his mouth gaped.

"I require a seat," she informed the check-in agent, a lovely young woman dressed in a silk sari from her native land. "I require the *entire* first class section. Here—" She dumped half a dozen credit cards on the counter.

"I'm afraid, Ms. Van Anka, that we are completely booked in emperor class."

"You'll have to move them to business class. I'll pay for their seats. I have a scene I have to rehearse, and I need absolute privacy."

"So charter a jet," said the man she'd elbowed aside.

"I regret very much, Ms. Van Anka, but I cannot move other passengers. But there is one seat available in business class."

Babette threw up her hands. "All right, all *right*. I was just trying to *help* you. Give me the seat."

"May I see your passport, please?"

"I don't *carry* a passport."

"You need a passport to enter the country."

"Don't be absurd," Babette said. She pointed to her face. "*This* is my passport."

Glances were exchanged behind check-in. A more senior agent was summoned, a quintessence of competence and courtesy in a blazer with numerous little medallions on his lapel betokening years of competent handling of crises small and large. But on the matter of a passport, he was gently unmovable.

It was at this point that Babette, who had, to be sure, been under a strain these many past months, finally and irretrievably lost it.

She stormed off to a series of first class check-in counters of international carriers, demanding a seat, if not the entire section. Alas, the passport requirement was the deal breaker at each one. Her remonstrations drew a crowd. Her choices of words eventually caused security to be alerted.

The famous photograph of her being half carried away—she had tried to bite the Wackenhut security man—by half a dozen personnel, like some Seattle protester, was soon over the wires and onto the front pages, accompanied by the news that Max was, apparently, well on his way into somewhat deeper exile in the Far East, aboard his own plane, the first class section of which was all his own.

Chapter 32

As Babette was being subdued by Wackenhut and the LAPD, Beth was moving to subpoena the Log Cabin tapes. This was a complicated legal maneuver, inasmuch as the National Security Agency had not acknowledged that they existed.

Allowing the Wiley P. Sinclair affidavit had become a radioactive decision. Protesters now gathered outside the courthouse carrying signs calling for Judge Dutch's impeachment. The right wing was especially in dire need of mollification.

When the director of the FBI was observed one morning entering the judge's chambers, one of the television networks promptly reported that the judge was being arrested for treason and that the highest law enforcement officer in the land was personally doing the arresting. The FBI quickly issued a statement saying that the director had merely wanted to "confer" with Judge Umin.

Boyce made himself more available to the press than a politician running in the New Hampshire primary. However, since the latest polls showed that over 80 percent of the American people now viewed him not only as "loathsome" but also as "worse than a traitor" to his country for having colluded with the fugitive Wiley P. Sinclair, he did most of the interviews à la Deep Throat, in basement garages, parking lots, and public parks. Every day he had to move from motel to motel to avoid a stakeout by the media. His face was now so recognizable that if he presented himself in public, people snarled and hurled objects at him. He wore dark glasses inside buildings. He went to a disguise shop and bought himself a mustache. During one TV interview, he forgot to take off the mustache—the producer mischievously did not point it out—which got his face replastered across the next day's front pages with snide captions.

The theme of Boyce's media drumbeat was that the President of the United States must "come clean" with the American people about the bugging of the White House. If he did not act, then Congress must surely step in.

"How do you feel," ABC News asked Boyce as they stood in a remote section of Fort Marcy Park overlooking the Potomac River, "about the fact that the majority of the American people say they despise you?"

"So do the majority of my ex-wives," Boyce said. "But that doesn't change the matter that the government is in possession of evidence that will exonerate my client."

The President of the United States, Harold Farkley, spent his week in Europe being photographed with a series of unsmiling foreign heads of state. Buckingham Palace expressed its displeasure over the putative taping of the Queen and the Duke of Edinburgh during their White House stay by refusing to be photographed shaking hands with him. The President of France declared that he would never set foot in the White House again, "in the event there is a microphone in my soup." The Prime Minister of Japan suggested that the head of the NSA should cut off his little finger by way of apology. Foreign newspapers ran cartoons showing Abraham Lincoln hiding under a bed wearing headphones, listening in on the pillow chat above. In truth, President Harold Farkley's foreign tour could not have been called a success.

Meanwhile, the 672 other people whom the MacManns had over the years invited to spend the night in the Lincoln Bedroom by way of thanking them for having donated millions in "hard" money to their campaign and political party were enduring their own individual autosda-fé at the hands of a gleeful media. They were all being tracked down and asked how they "felt" about having been bugged. The answer was generally, "Not great."

Assuming that they *had* been bugged. The National Security Agency was in high hunker-down mode, refusing all comment. This corporate muteness, however, was rapidly exhausting the national patience. The various congressional oversight committees were being forced by public opinion and a salivating media to *tsk-tsk* and demand—demand!—the truth. Moreover, protesters were beginning to show up at the agency's main gate in Fort Meade, Maryland, outside Washington, with furious signage saying, RELEASE THE TAPES and FARQUANT IS BIG BROTHER. The pixel pundits generally agreed that government hadn't been this much fun since the early 1970s.

☆ · ☆ · ☆

"Sir?"

"What, Henderson?"

"Frigby is outside, with the latest polls."

"I don't have time. What do they say?"

"I thought you might want to hear directly from Frigby, sir," said the chief of staff, who knew from experience never to be the bearer of bad tidings when you can let someone else do it.

Frigby, reluctantly granted access, gave it to the President straight. A majority of Americans blamed him personally for Operation Log Cabin, despite the fact that he had not authorized it or been president when it was put into effect.

"How can this be, Frigby?" he pleaded.

The chief of staff looked away. Harold Farkley's pain was too much to watch.

"Sir," said Frigby, "the majority of the American people can be pretty obtuse, when you come right down to it."

"What are you saying?"

"You need to get rid of this issue, sir."

"Goddammit, Frigby. Goddammit, Henderson."

"Yes, sir."

☆ · ☆ · ☆

"What I'm about to tell you must go no further than this room," Roscoe Farquant said to Judge Dutch. It was 10:30 at night. They were alone, having both entered the vacant chambers of another judge, one half hour apart, by separate doors.

"I can keep a secret, General," Judge Dutch said a bit stiffly. "The FBI agents who vetted me for this position will attest to that."

"Let's leave the FBI out of this," said General Farquant. "First you should have some background."

When he had finished, Judge Dutch's glasses had completely misted over.

"General," he finally said, "you've thrown a monkey wrench the size of the Washington Monument into my trial."

"NSA's charter is strictly collective. We are not an investigative agency. You can see why it made no sense—more to the point, why we were unable, from the standpoint of national security—to come forward with any of this."

"Whatever," said Judge Dutch, who liked every now and then to show his command of current English slang. "But this impeaches the testimony of one of the leading witnesses in the trial."

"Notwithstanding, this was a highly classified intelligence-gathering operation. Until it was compromised by Mr. Sinclair."

"How did he know about it?"

"Presumably from his employers in Beijing."

"How did *they* know?"

"That question raises a multiplicity of modalities. Obviously, Log Cabin was compromised. At any rate, by alerting Mr. Baylor to its existence, Mr. Sinclair has effectively rendered any intelligence we gained from Log Cabin useless. That, obviously, was his objective, to protect Mr. Grab."

"But you told me you didn't get anything on Grab."

General Farquant sighed. "No, we did not. Our conclusion ultimately was that Mr. Grab does not discuss his dealings with Indonesian middlemen for Chinese intelligence with his wife."

"Grab got the Indonesian oil contracts, President MacMann got covert contributions to his reelection campaign from the Chinese military? Laundered through Grab's offshore corporations. Is that it?"

"Essentially. That being the case, you can perhaps see why electronic surveillance of Mr. Grab was warranted."

"Why didn't you just plant the bugs on him directly, at his home?"

"I would rather not go into that, Judge. It's highly sensitive."

"I'm highly insensitive. Go into it. I insist."

"The NSA is not allowed to spy on American citizens within the United States. We found a loophole."

"Go on."

"The White House is a federal facility. You do not need a court order to conduct surveillance within a federal facility. If the bug happens to leave the federal facility, we have no control over that. If you follow."

"That's some loophole. So you bugged not only the Lincoln Bedroom, but the personal effects of the people staying in it, so that when they left, you could continue to listen in."

General Farquant nodded. "Cell phones, PalmPilots, laptops."

"Why not just rely on the FBI and CIA to take care of it?"

"After the Wiley P. Sinclair incident, the Aldrich Ames incident, the Hanssen incident, our faith in the integrity of the CIA's and FBI's ability to keep secrets was, you will appreciate, minimized. And if you can't trust the CIA and FBI, who can you trust?"

"The NSA, apparently," Judge Dutch said somewhat tartly. "But if you were only after Max Grab, why did you tape six hundred and seventy-two other people?"

"Judge, I came here to convey to you privately that if a subpoena by the defendant were narrowed to one particular tape, that of September twenty-eight, then NSA might not contest the subpoena. Otherwise . . ."

"The NSA might just declare that no such tapes exist. And burn them all. Is that it? And that's the end of it?"

"I'm not in a position to comment on that."

☆ · ☆ · ☆

"Boyce!" Beth was speaking on a cell phone given her by a Washington girlfriend, out of view of the Secret Service. She had dialed a pay phone in Arlington, just within the outer limits of the radius within which Boyce was permitted to travel pending the disposition of his own criminal case. "They just called. Dutch is going to allow the subpoena, provided we limit it to the one tape."

"That's great news. But . . ."

"What?"

"Don't you want to hear what's on those *other* six hundred and seventy-two tapes?"

"Not right now."

"I want to be there in court when they play it. I'll wear a disguise. I'm getting good at them."

"Just stay in the car. For God's sake, Boyce."

"Your SS men want to shoot me. The looks they give me."

"Hold on. Oh jeez, it just came over the news."

"What?"

"Babette. Guess who's representing her?"

"Not—"

"Alan Crudman."

☆ · ☆ · ☆

Alan Crudman was notorious within the legal fraternity for billing his clients not only for his legal services, but for going on television to talk about them. Typically, he would talk about them for five minutes and then devote the rest of his airtime to plugging his latest book, each of which was, "in all modesty, my best."

Within hours of being hired by Max Grab—now said to be "in seclu-

sion" in either Macao or Kuala Lumpur—to represent Babette, Crudman's publisher announced that his book on the case, provisionally titled *Tape Rape: The Framing of Babette Van Anka,* would be in stores two
weeks after the trial ended.

The night before he accompanied Babette to court, Alan Crudman
managed to appear on all three television networks, plus half a dozen
cable shows, for an estimated $17,500 aggregate of billable hours.

However, despite successfully squeezing himself into the final round
of the Trial of the Millennium, he faced the nightmarish fact that ultimately it was not *about* Alan Crudman.

Eighty percent of the American public might detest Boyce, but they
loved watching him. After months of listening to Alan Crudman drone
endlessly on television about how he would have handled it all, no one,
really, was in the mood for much more of his self-glorifying yadda-
yadda. Judge Dutch certainly wasn't.

"If it please the court"—Crudman rose—"we ask for a delay in order
to file a motion to suppress this so-called evidence."

"Denied."

"But Your Honor—"

"Sit down, Mr. Crudman."

A ripple of laughter went through the press section.

"With all respect, I will be heard," Crudman said hotly.

"Mr. Crudman, this is not *Hard Gavel.* But I will," Judge Dutch said,
raising his own hammer of authority in a distinctly minatory way, "use
this if you remain standing one more second."

Crudman sat, flushing redder than a boiled ham. He whispered to a
pallid Babette, "I'll crush him on appeal."

This remark was caught by the network lip-reader and duly re-
layed to the viewing public, along with the obligatory preface that the
correspondent was just guessing at what Crudman was saying to his
client.

☆ · ☆ · ☆

NSA tape number 4322-LC was duly entered into evidence. A special master of evidence had been appointed by the court to take custody of it once the NSA had handed it over.

Judge Dutch warned those who were "participating" in the proceedings via television that the tape they were about to hear contained material of an *adult* nature. This had the effect of causing every teenager in America flipping through TV channels to stop right here.

"You may start the tape," Judge Umin instructed the clerk of the court.

☆ · ☆ · ☆

"Oh, baby, baby, baby, *Mr. President . . .*"

Heads turned toward Babette, slumped forward in her seat. There was speculation that she had, in fact, died.

The media section was in extremis. When they heard the sound of a violently creaking boxspring mattress along with repeated thumps— evidently the sound of a head, either Babette's or the President's, smacking against the venerable Lincoln headboard—several of them temporarily lost control. They saved themselves from expulsion by masking their laughter as tubercular coughing fits.

Presently a prolonged "Unh" was heard on the tape.

A groan of male exhaustion, then forced purring: "Nothing wrong with *you!*" Then, "Would you like me to . . . ?" Followed by a female gasp of surprise and the sound of something suspiciously genital being plunged into water and ice cubes. Then an apparently valedictory grunt and the sound of a door opening and closing.

The judge ordered the clerk to stop the tape.

There was silence in the courtroom.

Crudman rose in his seat. "We challenge the authenticity of this tape and move to have it stricken from the record. This is obviously an attempt, *by* the government and, if I may, *by* this court to impugn the testimony of Ms. Van Anka."

The consensus of the pixel pundits that night on TV was that Crudman, confronted with this steaming evidence, had decided to try to shift the attention back to his own glorious self by provoking Judge Dutch to find him in contempt. However, Judge Dutch did not rise to this bait, instructing him simply, once again, to sit down and shut up— using, of course, rather more dignified language.

Chapter 33

Crudman responded to this indignity by going on network TV that night and hinting that the judge was "anti-Semitic." It was an odd assertion, given that Judge Dutch was himself a member of the tribe. Confronted with this inconvenient fact, Crudman shot back that the judge was a "self-hating Semite." It was the general consensus that the only Semite toward whom Judge Dutch might be anti was Alan Crudman, but this was no serious charge, since it put him squarely in the mainstream of American public opinion.

It was not a quiet tableau outside Babette's hotel, the Elegant, a few blocks away from her previous home away from home, the White House. Several hundred cameramen had assembled, it was suggested, so that they would be on hand when Babette leapt out her seventh-story window. In his television interviews that night, Boyce said she really should have stayed at the Jefferson, where the management was so notably hospitable toward participants in the trial.

The scene inside Babette's suite at the Elegant was no less tumultuous. Her entourage now consisted of Crudman and his team of half a dozen lawyers and investigators doing what they could to gird Babette's loins against an almost certain criminal indictment for perjury; her nutritionist; trainer; yoga instructor; doctor armed with hypodermics and state-of-the-art beta-blockers; her publicist, Nick Naylor, now upping his own daily dosage of Prozac; and three of her most stalwart sycophants, flown in from Los Angeles to remind her how fabu-

lous she looked and what a great movie this was all going to make—
taking care not to say, "After you get out of prison, darling."

☆ · ☆ · ☆

Boyce and Beth lay on the floor of her Cleveland Park aerie. They
could hear the hum of the media satellite trucks parked outside the
gates. Boyce's own traveling press stakeout team had followed him
here, but at this point so what.

Boyce was going over court transcripts. Beth filled out legal pad after
legal pad with questions for her impending cross-examination of Babette.

"I like to think that I'm a reasonably compassionate person," Beth
said. "But to be honest, I'm looking forward to crucifying her."

Boyce held up the transcript of the tape recording. "Where she says,
'Nothing wrong with *you*.' Here, line twenty-five. Tell me what you
know about that."

"It's the sort of thing women tell men to make them feel good.
Hasn't anyone ever told you that?"

"As a matter of fact, no."

Beth patted him on the rear. "They will."

" 'They'? You mean the attractive large men with tattoos I'm going to
meet in prison?"

A look of pain came over her. "Boyce. It's not *funny*."

"I'm not laughing. All right, let's take it one trial at a time. We have
two problems. First, we were the ones who made Babette out to be
the chaste and faithful Mrs. Grab and patroness of peace in the Middle East. We were the ones who gave her an alibi, that she was in bed
with curlers watching Elizabeth Taylor on TV screaming at Richard
Burton. *Now* you're going to be telling her, You lying slut, you were in
there *schtupping* my husband. That hangs her on a hook. But it doesn't
get you off yours. Because now you really have a motive for killing
him."

"It's a problem."

"So let's look at this 'Nothing wrong with *you*.' What's going on here?"

"She's flattering him on his performance."

"Beth, the man sounded like he was dying."

"All men sound like they're dying when they make love."

"And all women sound like they're pretending to die? Putting aside the sexual politics for a moment. Okay, they're banging away, someone's head is bashing against the headboard—which, by the way, you will contend was *his* head, which *completely* compromises the Revere bruise. Excellent. So they're screwing away . . . he sounds like he's about to collapse . . . she's going 'Oh, baby, baby, *Mr. President*'—a little kinky, by the way—and they finish. *Unhhhh.* Now she flatters him on his performance. He doesn't respond. Then there's this gasp coming from her. Here, line thirty-four, almost like he's coming after her again for more, which isn't likely since he sounds like he's about to have a heart attack . . . and that sound of ice and water. Is he drinking? Did he have booze on his breath when he got back to the room?"

"I don't know. I didn't kiss him. He wasn't a boozer, though. There's always a carafe of ice water on the nightstand when guests are staying."

"Did he usually drink water after banging you?"

Beth sighed. "I can't remember. It's been a while."

"Well, *try.*"

Beth thought. "Sure. Everyone does. You're thirsty after a good lay, I seem to recall."

Boyce replayed the tape in his mind. "It's not the sound of drinking. There's no gulping. There's ice tinkling and an 'ah' sound. It's the sound of something being *immersed.*"

"His . . . ?"

"What a gentleman."

"We're not dealing with a gentleman. An officer, maybe, but no gentleman."

"Back when you and War God were enjoying full marital relations, was his normal postcoital behavior to get up and immerse his hot dog in the water jug?"

"Not that I can recall."

"So why's he doing it here?"

"Maybe it was sore," Beth said with a trace of jealousy. "Maybe it was chafed. From friction."

"Well, tomorrow when she's on the stand, I want you to home in on the ice water. No matter how awkward it gets. Why did the President dip his willy in your water, Ms. Van Anka? Why? Why?"

"I can hardly wait," Beth said without relish.

"Stay on that until you get an answer. Replay that part of the tape until she crumples. That's *key.*"

☆ · ☆ · ☆

"Defense calls Babette Van Anka."

Babette took the stand dressed in a black pantsuit and Jackie O dark glasses, which she was asked to remove.

Judge Dutch directed that she be administered the oath. Babette said that she needed to confer with her attorney, Mr. Crudman. Judge Dutch waved Crudman forward. Crudman, a wee man, had to stand on his tippy-toes before the bench. Judge Dutch shook his head and then waved the unwanted counsel back to his corner.

The judge informed Babette that despite the fact that she was still under oath from her previous testimony, "a new oath is in order."

According to the ratings released afterward, Beth versus Babette was the most widely watched part of the Trial of the Millennium. Over one and a half billion human beings tuned in. Once again, airline pilots called in sick, elective surgeries were postponed. Even the launching of America's newest aircraft carrier, the *Tom Clancy,* was postponed, spurious technical reasons being alleged. No one wanted to miss *this.*

Nor did Boyce, but that morning did not find him in his customary observer post, in Beth's Secret Service car in the courthouse basement, being glowered at by fuming agents in the front seat.

☆ · ☆ · ☆

Bethesda Naval Hospital is a venerable, bleached-white stone presence off Wisconsin Avenue, just beyond the northern border of the District of Columbia. It is here that Marine One, the presidential helicopter, brings presidents for their annual checkups, so that their most intimate medical details can be shared with the entire world. It was after one of these visits in the late 1970s that navy doctors vouchsafed that the President of the United States was afflicted with grave hemorrhoids. The capable doctors of the United States Navy are the custodians of the health of their commanders in chief.

The people Boyce knew included those who knew about professional-quality disguise and professional-quality fake IDs. So this morning, as an estimated 178 million Americans sat glued to the television watching the two Amazons of the Trial of the Millennium have at each other, Boyce Baylor, wearing glasses, wig, and mustache and dressed in the uniform of a vice admiral in the U.S. Navy Medical Corps, strode confidently through the main gate, presented his badge to the marine guard, and proceeded on his way. He found a men's room, where in the toilet stall he removed from his briefcase a clipboard, white hospital gown, and stethoscope. He checked himself in the mirror. The most reviled man in America now looked like the most respectable. It gave him a thrill to see his new identity. Boyce saluted himself smartly, took a deep breath, and went out the door.

He'd defended enough doctors accused of gross malpractice to know his way around basic medical lingo, but just to be safe, he had crammed himself with some trauma and coma-related buzzwords like "fixed and dilated" and "Babinski reflex."

He presented himself at the nurses' station and politely but crisply asked for Dr. Grayson's room.

When the nurse, a lieutenant, looked up and saw three admiral's stars, she pointed the distinguished-looking man on his way with a respectful, "*Sir.*" Boyce nodded pleasantly.

There was a marine guard outside his room, but marines are trained from day one to salute admirals so vigorously that they nearly concuss themselves.

"Sir!"

"As you were, marine," Boyce growled with what he deemed appropriate hierarchical condescension. He wondered if he should have barked, "Straighten that gig-line, Corporal!"

Dr. Grayson was sitting up at a forty-five-degree angle, with the usual tubes running in and out of him. Life-support machines hummed and clicked.

A nurse, red haired, pretty, was in attendance.

"Admiral?" she said, obviously surprised at seeing this unfamiliar face.

"As you were, Nurse. Admiral Quigley, from Cinclantnavmedcom." It sounded official, anyway. He added, "Norfolk."

The nurse's eyes widened at the augustness of the syllables.

"Yes, sir."

"CNO asked me to look in on Captain Grayson."

"Yes, sir."

"How's he's doing?"

Boyce knew from the item in the paper three days earlier that Captain Grayson had come out of his postcrash coma.

"Sir, his vitals have stabilized. The Medrol appears to have turned around the cerebral edema."

"Hm," Boyce grunted, apparently satisfied. "Usually does. How did he do on the Babinski?"

"No evidence of brain damage, sir."

Boyce leaned closer to her to whisper. She smelled lovely. "How is he doing *psychologically*?"

"He appears depressed, sir."

"Um." Boyce nodded knowingly. "Would you excuse us?"

"Sir." She left. Boyce approached the bedside.

"Well, good morning, Captain," Boyce greeted him heartily. "You're looking fit for sea duty."

Captain Grayson did not answer. The only sea duty he looked ready for was burial. It wasn't the damage from the car wreck. Boyce could see that. The man might be healing, but he was still broken inside. The eyes were lifeless with pain.

"You're not watching the big trial, Captain? Mrs. MacMann is cross-examining the actress Ms. Van Anka."

Captain Grayson turned and looked at Boyce. The eyelids fluttered. The eyes studied Boyce's face carefully. They moved to the admiral stars on his epaulets, then back to Boyce's face. They narrowed suspectingly.

"You know who I am, don't you, Captain?"

A placid look came across the captain's face. It was as though, standing on the bridge of a ship after a fierce engagement, he had just received the news that the damage from a torpedo had been repaired and that the ship might now not sink after all.

"Sorry about the uniform," Boyce said. "It was the only way to get past the marines. I know how much this uniform means to you. I think I know how much President MacMann's service in the navy means to you."

Pain flickered back into the eyes.

"Shall we watch, Captain? Shall we watch the trial together?"

Captain Grayson looked stricken and, for a moment, lifeless.

Please, Boyce thought, *don't let the machines start beeping.*

Finally Captain Grayson nodded. Boyce rose and turned on the TV monitor.

Chapter 34

*M*s. Van Anka, I'd like to draw your attention to the testimony you have already given this court and to this jury," Beth added for good measure. "Would you at this point care to modify, or change, that testimony?"

Babette looked mournfully toward her attorney. Her entourage was seated with the spectators, beaming encouragement at her, slipping her thumbs-up gestures, but at this point it would have taken an entire Hollywood Bowl full of supporters to cheer up Babette. She asked the judge if she could confer with her counsel. Judge Dutch wearily waved Crudman, Beth, and Deputy AG Clintick forward for a sidebar.

"Ms. Van Anka," Crudman said, "is willing to modify her prior testimony, which occurred at a time of severe emotional distress, on the condition that she receives total immunity from any future prosecution for perjury."

Judge Dutch leaned back in his chair. Beth and Sandy looked at each other. Of late, the deputy AG's attitude toward Beth had softened.

The judge leaned forward and whispered to Crudman, "No way in hell, Counsel."

The network correspondent translated for his viewers, "My guess is that Judge Umin will *decline* any petition from Van Anka's defense attorney to immunize her prior testimony."

Beth suppressed a smile at Crudman's humiliation as he went to the witness box to give Babette the unhappy news. He added that the judge would rue the day. He would be crushed on appeal! Meanwhile, go with plan B.

Beth now resumed her cross-examination. "Is that your voice on the tape, Ms. Van Anka? Along with the President's?"

"Sounds a bit like me. But I couldn't say."

This brought a gale-force expulsion of air from the lungs of the spectators. Judge Dutch did not gavel silence. He seemed too occupied trying to maintain his own composure.

Beth, too, was having a hard time. "I see. Any guesses as to *who* it might be?"

DAG Clintick did not object. She was looking down at her table, trying to retain her composure.

"I couldn't say," Babette said. She smiled bravely. "I have many imitators."

Crudman winced. The idiot—he'd told her, Give them nothing! Keep your answers *to the minimum!*

"Imitators?" Beth said.

"I'm a well-known actress. My voice is widely known. Some people try to sound like me."

"The woman on this tape isn't you, but is trying to sound like you? Is that what you're saying?"

"I don't know *what's* going on in that tape."

"Ms. Van Anka," Beth said sympathetically, "the authenticity of that tape has been certified by a special master of evidence appointed *by* this court as having been recorded in the early morning hours of September twenty-ninth, during which time it is a documented fact, as recorded by the chief usher of the White House, *and* the Secret Service, that you were a guest in the Lincoln Bedroom, where this tape *was* recorded. Now are you telling the court, the jury, that that's *not* you?"

It was all too much. Here Babette Van Anka's training as an actor overtook her instinct for self-preservation. If she was going down, by God, it would be a going-down worthy of Bette Davis or Joan Crawford or Gloria Swanson.

"Yes, it's me! Of course it's *me*! I loved him! Unlike you! Who murdered him!"

Crudman bolted to his feet. "Your Honor, my client is not herself. Move to strike her remarks—"

It took several minutes to restore order. "Ms. Van Anka," Judge Dutch said sternly, "another outburst like that and I will find you in contempt of court."

"Oh," Babette moaned. "You don't *know.* . . ."

"You will answer defense counsel's questions directly, to the best of your ability. Without commentary. Is that *understood*?"

"This is a perversion of justice," declared Alan Crudman. Indeed, that became the title of the first of his three books on the case.

"You are out of order, Mr. Crudman. And I have run out of warnings to you. The clerk of the court is instructed to remove Mr. Crudman."

Crudman was removed. Outside the courthouse, he told the media that he now knew what it was like to be a "Jew in Hitler's Germany" and vowed to "pursue justice all the way to the Supreme Court." The Supreme Court, one reporter pointed out, was really only a few blocks away.

Inside the courtroom, after a ten-minute recess, Judge Dutch told Babette that the rest of her cross-examination could be postponed until she had engaged other legal counsel.

Beth rose. "Your Honor, in that case I move that Ms. Van Anka be placed in custody as a flight risk. Her husband, Mr. Grab, is currently being sought by federal authorities and is at large abroad. The Attorney General's Office has indicated that they will seek an indictment of her for false testimony. It is therefore our contention that she may attempt to flee."

Murmuring. Sidebar. The judge leaned back in his chair, turned to Babette. "Ms. Van Anka, the court finds that given the circumstances, you present a flight risk. You may either continue your testimony here today, without legal counsel. Or you may continue it later. However, in the meantime, I will order that you be held at the federal detention center pending that testimony."

"Jail?" gasped Babette.

"Detention."

"No. No, no no no no. I want to testify. Now. Right away."

"Very well. You may proceed, Mrs. MacMann."

"Ms. Van Anka," said Beth, "you admit, then, that that *is* your voice on the tape."

"Yes. I said so, didn't I?"

"So you did. I don't wish to make this any more difficult for you than I know it must be. . . ."

"You have *no* idea. No one has *any* idea how hard this is."

"I'm sure it is," Beth said, taking a breath. "It would appear, to judge from the tape, that you and the President were engaged in . . ."

"Pressing the flesh," whispered a reporter.

". . . in sex. Is that a fair inference?"

"We made *love*. You wouldn't know about that."

"Ms. Van Anka," said Judge Dutch, "I will not warn you again."

"What? What did I say?"

"Was the President," Beth continued, "all right?"

"He was fantastic."

"On the tape he sounds . . . Forgive me, I'm not sure quite how to put this, he sounds very . . . Let me put it this way: Did you observe him . . ."

"I did more than observe him, honey."

"Indeed. Was he physically all right? On the tape he sounds tired."

"Of course he was tired. He'd just been to the moon and back."

"It's a long trip." Beth nodded. "So physically, he performed, um, well?"

"I said, he was great."

"Even after a long evening? At his age?"

"Maybe he was inspired."

"Let me draw your attention to the transcript. . . ." Babette was provided with one. "Here on page seven eighty-three, line thirty-five. Your Honor, I ask that this portion of the tape be played for the court."

The sounds of Babette's gasp and the tinkling of ice cubes, followed by a short male *"Ahhh,"* were heard.

"What was happening at this point, precisely, Ms. Van Anka?"

"He . . . needed . . . he was . . . he was thirsty. He was having some water."

"That doesn't sound like someone drinking. It sounds like something being immersed in water."

Babette was silent.

"Ms. Van Anka?"

"What?"

"Was he drinking?"

"I said that already."

"We can call in forensic acoustic experts to advise the court to reconstruct what that sound is."

"He had a hard-on, all right? He had a hard-on and he was going back to your room—where he was worried that you might kill him, which you did. He dipped his business in the ice water to make it relax. All right?"

Judge Dutch had to gavel the courtroom back to something resembling order. Babette's entourage was warned that if they did not stop making those sounds, they would be removed.

"And did his . . . business relax, Ms. Van Anka?"

"What do you want from me?"

"The truth. That's all."

"No, it didn't. He had to sort of . . . stuff it into his trousers."

"The President was in his late fifties. It had been a very long evening at this point, entertaining a head of state, many guests, then entertaining, I guess, you, in a vigorous physical manner. The time was now after two A.M. And yet even after exhausting lovemaking," she added, "if indeed it could be called that, are you telling the court that he *still* maintained an erection?"

"A monster."

"That's unusual."

"How would you know?"

"Ms. Van Anka," said Judge Dutch, "my patience is at an end. One more comment like that and I will find you in contempt, and you will spend the weekend in detention. Is that clear?"

"Yes. *Yes,*" Babette moaned.

"Ms. Van Anka," Beth continued, "did the President have any pharmaceutical assistance that night, to your knowledge, that would have enabled him to maintain such a . . . heroic erection, even after sex?"

"I . . ."

"Yes?"

"He had some Viagra."

Murmurmurmurmurmur.

"Viagra, the prescription medicine that enables men to achieve and maintain erections. Is that what you mean?"

"*Of course.*"

"The President took Viagra?"

"Sort of. In a way."

"How do you mean, exactly?"

"Oh, God. It's . . ." Babette looked over imploringly at the judge. "It's *private.*"

"This is a murder trial, Ms. Van Anka," said the judge. "You are legally and morally obliged to provide such evidence as you are aware of. Which you should have done the *first* time you testified."

"All right all right. The President and I had . . . been intimate before. And on the last several occasions he had been unable to perform. I mean, as a man." She sighed heavily. "You know what that does to a man's ego. I wanted him to be happy and fulfilled. He was the President of the United States. If a president isn't fulfilled, then the world is at risk. I didn't want him to . . . I didn't want to say to him, 'Here, take this.' So I ground up a few pills into powder and mixed it with some moisturizing cream and applied it to my . . . self. So that it would, you know, act . . . topically. Like ointment."

"You created a Viagra ointment and applied it to your private parts?"

"What's *private* anymore?"

"And this topical ointment, apparently, got into the President's system?"

"Hard as the Rock of Gibraltar."

Beth said, "No further questions for the witness at this time."

Chapter 35

So," said Beth back at Rosedale, "was it good for you, too?"

"Not bad," Boyce said. "Not bad at all. You might just make a good trial attorney in five or six years."

"We're still not off the hook. So he was hopped up on Viagra. Funny that didn't make it into the autopsy report."

"Maybe the doctors were concerned about the dignity of the orifice."

"It still leaves me waiting for him, lurking behind the door, holding the spittoon."

"Someone else was impressed with your cross-examination. In fact, deeply moved."

"Alan Crudman? O. J. Simpson? I give up."

"Captain Cary Grayson."

"How do you know that?"

"I spent the morning with him."

"You saw Grayson?"

"Oh, I saw Grayson. Captain Grayson and I bonded today."

"How'd you get in to see him?"

"Never mind. But he's ready to be deposed. And since he looks like he's about to die any second, I suggest you get on the phone to Judge Dutch right now and set it up. Right away."

☆ · ☆ · ☆

Judge Dutch gave the necessary instructions. Within an hour and a half, he, Beth, Sandy Clintick, two clerks, a stenographer, court video and sound technicians, and a notary public were roaring up Wisconsin Avenue in a U.S. marshals motorcade to Bethesda Naval Hospital. This naturally attracted the attention of the media, who joined in with their own motorcades, attaching themselves serially. By the time the procession reached Bethesda Naval, the motorcade was fifty-four vehicles long—longer even than a normal presidential motorcade. It's in the *Guinness Book of World Records,* under "Longest Motorcade."

In the rush, no one thought to notify the main gate of Bethesda Naval that the mother of all motorcades was about to roar through. When the marines saw this imperial millipede approaching, flashing more lights than most airports, they assumed that it must be none other than the President of the United States, gravely wounded. They called inside with this information, causing such alarm that every trauma surgeon in the building—naturally wanting to succor their commander in chief—rushed to the emergency entrance. When the door of the lead limousine opened and out stepped the leading participants in the trial, the doctors stared at one another in disappointment and confusion.

The admiral in charge of Bethesda Naval didn't quite know whom to call. For a moment, it occurred to him to summon the marines in force. But Judge Dutch was the face of maximum authority in the land, and when the judge informed the admiral that he had official business, there was little the admiral could do but say, This way, sir.

Captain Grayson had to be wheeled into a larger room to accommodate the juridical crowd.

It was just as well that they had arrived when they did, for the captain died of his injuries that morning at 4:30 A.M., a few hours after his deposition was concluded, of causes not yet detectable by medical science.

☆ · ☆ · ☆

The tape was played the next day, in court.

Beth: Captain Grayson, you performed the autopsy on President MacMann the morning of September 29. Your prior testimony to the court was that he died of an epidural hematoma resulting from blunt-force trauma to the head. Do you wish now, under oath, to retract that testimony?

Capt. Grayson: Yes, I do.

Would you then tell the court how the President's death came about?

There was no epidural hematoma. I did observe evidence for trauma. An apparent contusion, with modest ecchymosis, but no laceration. But this was not the cause of death.

What did the President die of, Captain?

He died of lethal cardiac arrhythmia.

In other words, his heart failed?

Yes. Most likely ventricular fibrillation due to a progressive fall in blood pressure, associated with an excessive dose of medication. His heart stopped.

Were you able to determine why his heart stopped?

The President had mild coronary heart disease. But this was not what killed him. Toxicology reported a high concentration in the blood of sildenafil citrate.

Is that the chemical name for the prescription drug Viagra? The one used to help men achieve and maintain erection?

Yes.

Are you then saying that the President died as a result of an overdose of Viagra? Is this possible?

In someone with coronary heart disease, Viagra in high concentrations can be fatal. The President received a lethal dose of it.

How much of it was there in his blood?

The equivalent of approximately 300 milligrams. The pills come in 50-milligram tablets. Six tablets' worth.

What conclusion, then, did you draw from these observations?

I concluded that the President had expired following or during an act of coitus.

Did you falsify the autopsy report, including the toxicology report?

Yes, I did.

Why, Captain?

The President was one of the most decorated veterans of the U.S. Navy. He served his country in war with distinction and with valor. I could not let history record that he had died in such a way.

So you blamed his death on the bruise?

Yes.

Did you intend, in so doing, to implicate the First Lady of the United States in a murder case?

No. No. I never intended that. I regret that truly. That was—no. No.

I understand, Captain.

At the time of the autopsy, I knew only that the President had been found in his bedroom. My intention was that it be blamed on an accident. A fall in the night, in the bathroom. An accident.

After the First Lady was subsequently charged with murder, why didn't you come forward?

I wanted to. But I could not make myself do it. I was still protecting my commander in chief. I was certain . . .

Certain of what, Captain?

I was certain that Mr. Baylor would get you off. He gets everyone off. I'm sorry, Mrs. MacMann. I'm so very sorry.

I understand, Captain.

Forgive me, Mrs. MacMann.

I do, Captain.

At this point in the videotape, Beth asks Deputy Attorney General Clintick if she wants to question the captain. Sandy Clintick is seen declining with a shake of her head.

Chapter 36

The front page of the *New York Post* showed a picture of a weepy Babette below a headline that could not have been larger had the news been that a meteor was about to crash into the earth and end human life:

SHEDUNIT!

On TV, pixel pundits tripped over one another trying to respin their earlier proclamations of Beth's certain guilt.

"There was something about Van Anka's previous testimony that never sat right with me," declared *Time*'s reporter.

"I was never comfortable with the rush to convict Beth MacMann," said *The Washington Post*'s man.

Beth's phone began to ring again, now from agents and movie producers and publishers.

"Tina Brown just called. I might be able to pay your bill after all," Beth told Boyce.

Her elation was interrupted by the news that Alan Crudman had filed a motion to quash Dr. Grayson's deathbed deposition on the grounds that his medication, which included morphine, rendered it unreliable. There were precedents for such a motion, though Vlonko, still in court charting the minute-by-minute reactions of the jury, reported that Dr. Grayson's deposition had been "fucking dynamite," leaving most of the female jurors in tears. Even if Judge Dutch did throw out the Grayson deposition, the jury might still go with its emotions.

"We could still lose this thing," he said. "We're gonna have to dig him up, Beth."

"I would really, really, rather not."

The President had been buried at Arlington Cemetery as a hero, with the highest honors a nation could bestow. The caisson bearing his body had been drawn by horses across Memorial Bridge to the solemn *tum-tum* of drums, followed by the traditional riderless horse, with reversed boots in the stirrups. At the graveside there had been a twenty-one-gun salute, an overhead flyby of a squadron of navy jet fighters in "missing man" formation, the echo of "Taps." Was it good politics for his widow and her criminally indicted lover-lawyer to send in a backhoe to dig him up to see whether he had lethal levels of Viagra in his veins?

"On the other hand," Beth said, "I'm glad they didn't embalm him, in case we do need to go back in for another toxicology. I can't believe I'm talking this way about my husband. My whole life has turned into an out-of-body experience."

"Your whole life"—Boyce patted her belly— "is right here."

"Feel."

"He wants to know whether we've got his ticket on the Lisbon plane."

"Tell him Daddy's working on it."

☆ · ☆ · ☆

Babette looked eerily composed as she took the witness stand. Either she was sedated or the raised stakes had concentrated her mind. She was past hysterics now and into icy defiance. She was facing criminal indictment, not only for perjury but also for assassinating the President of the United States with an overdose of erection medicine. Most legal commentators agreed, at least, that she wouldn't be charged with first-degree murder. Negligent homicide? Wrongful assassination, with an explanation? There were no precedents.

"We are," said Edgar Burton Twimm on the *Charlie Rose* television show, "navigating in muddy water, in fog, at night, without a compass."

Beth had with her a laptop computer with a wireless Internet connection. At the other end of the connection was Boyce, still barred by an angry Judge Dutch from the courtroom. He was in a hotel room not far away, watching the proceedings on television, with his own laptop, connected to a high-speed computer line. He was able to communicate with Beth in print, on the screen, in real time.

He saw Beth on the TV, preparing to stand and begin her examination. He typed, YOU GO, GIRL.

She rose and went to the podium, bringing the unfolded laptop with her.

Boyce typed, CONTROL THE WITNESS.

"Ms. Van Anka," Beth began in a friendly way, "you are familiar with the substance of Captain Grayson's deposition?"

"The man was out of his skull on morphine," Babette said. "He didn't know what he was saying."

Alan Crudman preened by way of indicating to all that this was his ingenious line, not Babette's.

"Objection. Witness is not in a position to make a medical evaluation as to the reliability of the deposition."

Heads turned in surprise. It was Sandy Clintick. Whose side was she on, anyway? The consensus among the pixel punditariat was that with Boyce Baylor removed, the deputy AG now lacked an opponent "really worth hating."

"Sustained," said the judge. "You will confine yourself to answering the question put to you directly, Ms. Van Anka."

Beth continued, "You heard what Captain Grayson said in his deposition?"

"I *heard*."

"You told the court that you applied Viagra, mixed with moisturizer, to your . . . to the . . . to the relevant area. Is that correct?"

"Yes."

"How much Viagra did you use?"

"What do I look like, Lee Harvey Oswald? I wanted the man to be happy. Not dead. "

Boyce typed, NOT FOR YOU TO DETERMINE. PS YOUR LAST MOVIE SUCKED.

"That's not for you to determine, Ms. Van Anka. That's a question that can only be resolved by a medical authority."

"A medical authority who falsifies autopsy reports and gives deposition when's he doped to the gills? Please. I wouldn't entrust an ingrown toenail to the man. May he rest in peace."

"Objection."

"Sustained. Ms. Van Anka, you are to answer the questions."

"*This* is why my people left Europe."

"One more comment and I will find you in contempt."

Boyce typed, JUMP IN—NOW!! IT'S THEIR STRATEGY, TO FORCE A MISTRIAL. CONTEMPT→HOSTILE JURY→ DISMISSAL.→LET'S WIN **THIS** ONE NOT WAIT FOR THE NEXT.

"Babette," Beth said.

Babette started at Beth's use of her first name.

"Sorry. Ms. Van Anka. We—I—only want to find out how much Viagra you used that night. That's all. Under oath, please, just tell the court how many pills you crushed up and mixed in with the cream."

"You mean, honestly?"

The courtroom exploded with laughter. Alas, the irony was lost on Babette, who had lived for too long in a community where insincerity was the norm.

"Honestly." Beth smiled.

"Three. The fifty-milligram ones. I just wanted the man to be able to perform, not hold up the tent."

"Three pills? The blue ones?"

"Like this." Babette formed a diamond shape with her thumbs and forefingers. "You know, you can split them in two, but I figure, why?"

"I see your point."

Suddenly the two women were like old friends, chatting away knowledgeably about how much Viagra their partners required.

"They're not fatal," Babette said. "I mean, a ham sandwich can be fatal if you choke on it. I read the directions. One night I gave Max three. He was a bit flushed in the face. But he didn't die. Right now I could give him *ten* Viagras."

"Did you administer it to your husband the same way you administered it to mine?"

"No. I—well, you know how men don't like to admit?"

"Oh, I know."

"I crushed them up and put them in his borscht."

"I see. Just one or two final questions, Ms. Van Anka. How did it occur to you to administer the Viagra to my—to the President in this way?"

"I couldn't get to his soup. The Secret Service sees you putting powder in the President's soup and they open fire. I have a friend who does it this way, with the moisturizer. She said it worked. It worked. Well, up to a point."

"Thank you, Ms. Van Anka. No further questions at this time. Reserve the right to recall the witness."

Beth looked down at her laptop.

PUT IT IN MY SOUP AND I'LL SHOOT YOU.

☆ · ☆ · ☆

"Do we believe her that she ground up only three pills?" Beth said. "I wouldn't put it past her to feed the whole bottle into a blender."

"Yes," Boyce said. "I think for once she was actually telling the truth. But Grayson said he had three hundred milligrams' worth in him. That leaves three more pills unaccounted for. Did he have a prescription?"

"Are you kidding? Every time the White House doctors give a president a Tylenol, it's front-page news. He would never have gotten a prescription."

"Did you ever see any in his toilet kit?"

"I never went into his toilet kit."

"You didn't?"

"Not after I found a twelve-pack of rubbers in it."

"Twelve-pack? When did he have time to run the country? But assuming he had the pills—who gave them to him?"

Beth thought. "It would have to be someone he trusted. Trusted absolutely."

She said the name.

"We've got to be sure. If we get him up there on the stand and he says no, it'll look like we're just fishing. And we can't subpoena eighty of his best friends and ask them if they were slipping the President hard-on pills on the sly. They'd lie anyway, and who's to contradict them?"

"The advantage of this witness," Beth said, "is that he can't lie under oath."

☆ · ☆ · ☆

"Defense calls Damon Blowwell."

Damon Blowwell seemed uncharacteristically subdued. Normally he looked like a pit bull who hadn't been fed in three days.

Beth asked that he be given the oath again, even though he was still technically bound by the first.

"Mr. Blowwell, you are a born-again Christian, are you not?"

"I am."

"And you have just taken an oath swearing, before God, that the evidence you give will be truthful, is that about correct?"

"I'm not a liar, if that's what you are implying."

BACK OFF, Boyce typed. GIVE HIM ROOM.

"I'm implying exactly the opposite, Mr. Blowwell. I have only one question to ask you today. Did my husband ask you to provide him with Viagra?"

Blowwell's lower lip disappeared into the upper. Every fiber in the man's mortal body wanted to say no, but the soul that he had rededicated to the Risen Lord was whispering, *The truth shall set ye free.*

"He might have." It hung there for a second or two before he added, "Yes, he did. He did."

Murmurmurmur.

"And how much did you provide him with?"

"One bottle."

"Containing approximately how many pills?"

"One hundred, I believe."

"Did you do this on one occasion, or more?"

"Yes."

"How many occasions, approximately?"

"Half a dozen. More, maybe."

Murmurmurmurmur.

"So you provided him with as many as six hundred, or more, pills?"

"That would be correct."

"And approximately when did you last fill the President's prescription, as it were?"

"It would have been about the middle of September."

"A few weeks before he died?"

"That's correct."

Blowwell's expression, for the first time that anyone could recall in public, took on a look of terrible pain. No one could remember ever before seeing Damon Blowwell look vulnerable. The man was crumpling.

"It was an accident, Damon," Beth said tenderly. "There's no need to blame yourself."

"Objection," said Sandy Clintick, almost reluctantly.

"Sustained. Mrs. MacMann," said Judge Dutch, "if you have a question for the witness, ask it."

"No further questions for the witness, Your Honor. Thank you, Mr. Blowwell."

"Yes, ma'am. I—want to add something."

Judge Dutch said, "Very well, Mr. Blowwell."

"I want to apologize to Mrs. MacMann."

Chapter 37

For the sake of what remained of the national dignity, the exhumation of President Kenneth MacMann was carried out under wraps during the hours of two and five A.M. This did not deter the TV networks from providing live coverage of the event, consisting of telephoto nightvision lenses aimed at a dark tent with soldiers standing in front of it while commentators passed the time by speculating about what was going on inside.

"For an operation like this, Tom, they would use, probably, a backhoe, in conjunction with—there would be a backup backhoe, in the event the primary backhoe was for whatever reason unable to dig, or malfunctioned."

"How deep is the President buried?"

"My information is that the President is between six and eight vertical feet beneath the stone *plaza* that was erected, the one that was placed over him after the burial."

"So they have to go through that first, correct?"

"Yes, and that's tough Vermont granite, of course."

"Once they've gotten the casket to the surface, do they—what happens then?"

"We're told that the casket, which is within a bronze outer casket, to prevent—that everything, the inner and outer caskets, will be loaded onto a military transport and taken to the National Institutes of Health."

"No more Bethesda Naval autopsies."

"No. And of course it is ironic that the NIH, where this second autopsy will be performed, under the supervision of a special master of evidence appointed by the court and *six* independent pathologists and toxicologists, none of them connected with the armed services, is practically right across the *street* from Bethesda Naval Hospital."

"One thing I'm not clear on—why wasn't the President embalmed?"

"It's standard procedure in cases of murder or suspicious death, Tom, *not* to embalm. In case they have to exhume the body for further medical testing. If you embalm a body, that's it as far as further toxicology testing goes."

"Talk to us for a moment about formaldehyde. . . ."

☆ · ☆ · ☆

"Did you watch?" Boyce said. *"Honestly?"*

"I was working on my concluding argument."

"You won't have to give one if the tox report comes out the way it should."

"I . . ."

"What is it? Did he kick?"

"No. Nothing. Just a procedural point I was going to ask you about. I've forgotten. I'll ask you about it when I see you. When will they know?"

"Possibly this afternoon. Toxicologists are a pain in the ass. They love to take forever. They know everything's hanging on them, so they get to be the center of attention. Did you see the *Times*?"

"I've given up newspapers."

"You might want to check out the front page of today's. There's a poll."

"Has the procedure"—the word Beth used for exhumation—"caused my remaining four percent of supporters to hate me?"

"Quite the opposite. Your numbers are up, as you'd put it. Seventy-five percent feel the government owes you an apology. That's quite a reversal. You should be pleased."

Beth sighed. "Yes, that's nice."

"You've gone from being Lady Bethmac to Wronged Woman. You're not happy?"

"My husband is on a metal table somewhere. You're facing five years for saving me from myself. Having created the mother of all scandals, I'm about to become a mother and haven't the slightest confidence that I won't screw that up, too. 'Happy' isn't quite the word for what I feel right now. I better get back to my concluding argument. Just in case Dr. Grayson really was gaga on morphine and hallucinating the whole thing."

"Whatever happens, you're going to be a brilliant mother. You're going to be the mother of all mothers. Do you know why?"

"No idea."

"To make up for screwing up everything else in your life. Including my life."

"That's pretty good motivation."

☆ · ☆ · ☆

"Folks," CBS News anchorman Dan Rather told his viewers, looking as if he might, finally, have a fatal nosebleed on live television, "this case has got more evolutions than a species in the Galápagos. We are told that a Dr. Laftos Crogenos, chief pathologist of the team that has performed the second autopsy on the remains of President MacMann, will be making an announcement shortly. Bob, that name, Laftos Crogenos, has more vowels in it than a bowl of alphabet soup after buzzards have finished picking out all the consonants. What do we know about him?"

"Dan, Dr. Crogenos is Greek, originally. But he is a *naturalized* American citizen—"

"So his sympathies, naturally, would be above question?"

"There's apparently a *saying,* Dan, in the pathology community, that there *are* no nationalities around an autopsy table."

"Good. That's what Americans at this point need to hear."

"Dr. Crogenos has been for many years chairman of the Department of Forensic Medicine at Johns Hopkins medical school. He has performed over fifteen *thousand* autopsies and is considered to be one of the best pathologists in the *world*. In the words of one colleague, this man can open you up from stem to stern with his eyes closed."

"This is no roadkill armadillo on Route 77 north of Corpus Christi he's working on, but a former president of the United States of America."

"There he is now. Dr. Crogenos is approaching the podium, accompanied by the five other medical examiners. . . ."

"How does he look to you, Bob? What can we say from his expression?"

"Dan, it can't be *easy* examining the corpse of a, well, *any* corpse. Especially one that's been in the ground for over a year. But this one in particular, with the whole world watching over your shoulder, as it were. It has to be *tremendous* pressure."

"I'd be jumpier than a coked-up Mexican who's just found half a *cucaracha* in his guacamole. Let's hear what he has to say."

Dr. Crogenos's statement took less than five minutes to read. As he spoke, his face was bathed in thousands of flashes. It was done with as much dignity as could be mustered. He announced that the President had been killed by a "probably accidental" overdose of sildenafil citrate. There was evidence of "moderately advanced" coronary heart disease. An estimated 300 milligrams of Viagra had put too great a strain on the heart, bringing about lethal cardiac arrhythmia. The penile epidermis showed traces of sildenafil citrate as well as ingredients commonly found in high-end brands of moisturizing cream. There was no evidence of an epidural hematoma. The bruise on his forehead, though pronounced, had not been fatal.

At this point, Dr. Crogenos looked at his colleagues and sighed. If the Republic lasted a thousand years, schoolchildren in ages hence would remember President Kenneth MacMann as vividly as, if not more vividly than, Presidents Washington, Lincoln, and Roosevelt. His place in history was assured.

Chapter 38

*B*oyce's cell phone rang.

"Hello, Counselor."

It was Sandy Clintick.

"I won't bother asking you how you got this number," he said. "But it's extremely unlisted. To what do I owe this pleasure? Are you ready to move to dismiss the indictment of my client?"

"Your former client. You're no longer representing Mrs. MacMann."

"So you're calling to apologize on behalf of the federal government, for entrapping me in the jury-tampering case?"

Sandy Clintick laughed. "No, that wasn't on my agenda. I don't have any involvement in that case. But," she added, "it's one I'd frankly *love* to try."

"I'll bet you would. For what it's worth, I'm glad you're not. You're not as good as me, but you're up there."

"When the biggest narcissist in the law tells me I'm almost in his league, I feel lavishly complimented."

"No, Alan Crudman is the biggest narcissist in the law. I'm second."

"Shall I get to the point, or shall we continue to sniff each other?"

"By all means. Fire away."

"I'm weighing whether to move to dismiss."

"Oh, come on, Sandy. I can hear the mob outside your window with torches and pitchforks, chanting, 'Justice!' "

"I have insulated windows."

"I also read that you now have a U.S. marshals bodyguard. Don't worry, after the first coupla dozen death threats, you get used to them. I get Christmas card death threats."

"I'm thrilled to be in your league, Boyce. The reason I'm weighing whether to dismiss is there's something still bothering me."

"What would that be?"

"The Grayson deposition."

"The Crogenos autopsy supports everything that he said."

"There was something else in it that bothered me. At the end, when he asks Beth to forgive him."

"Yes?" Boyce said cautiously.

"She did. Just like that."

"She's a forgiving type."

"I don't buy that. Her life became hell because of what he did. No one is that forgiving. Even Jesus Christ would have needed to think about it for five seconds before saying, Okay, let bygones be bygones."

"She's a mensch. It's why I fell in love with her back in law school."

"Some mensch. She dumped you for that asshole."

"Please, you're speaking of the dead."

"I think I know what happened the night of September twenty-eight. And I'm pretty sure you do, too."

"So move to dismiss."

"I'll weigh it."

"Look, if it's my ass you still want, don't sweat it. I'm going down. Even Alan Crudman couldn't get me off."

"It's some consolation, I admit."

"Look on the bright side. After I spend five years in prison being made love to by passionate weight lifters with AIDS, they'll disbar me. You'll never have to face me again in a courtroom."

"I'm feeling better and better."

"Let it go," Boyce said.

"I'll weigh it." She hung up.

Boyce considered whether to tell Beth about the call. He decided against it.

☆ · ☆ · ☆

The next morning, shortly after 10:00 A.M., the deputy attorney general of the United States rose and went to the podium in Judge Umin's courtroom. The mood was, as Dan Rather put it, "more electric than a drenched cat with its tail stuck in a socket."

"If it please the court," she began, "the United States respectfully moves that the court dismiss the indictment in *United States* versus *Elizabeth MacMann,* by reason of new developments that show that justice requires that."

The courtroom exploded.

Beth sat gravely in her seat, expressionless. Boyce, watching from his hotel room, was similarly calm. His eyes bored in on Beth.

Judge Dutch said, "In view of the prosecutor's motion to dismiss, I—"

Beth rose. "If it please the court, Your Honor, may the defendant in this case make a statement at this time?"

Oh shit, Boyce thought.

"I was about to make a ruling on the prosecution's motion," said Judge Dutch, as if to say, *"If you will just remain seated and quiet, Mrs. MacMann, I'll have you out of here in three minutes."*

Sandy Clintick looked at her. The entire world—some billion-plus viewers, at any rate—was looking at Beth.

"I am aware of that, Your Honor. But the defendant would like to make a statement *before* you rule on the motion." She added, "So that the court may be fully informed."

Judge Dutch sat back wearily with the air of a reasonable man surrendering to an unreasonable world, glasses beginning to fog. "Very well, Mrs. MacMann. Proceed."

"Thank you, Your Honor. I . . ." She paused. "Am not sure where to begin, so I will begin with an apology. To the people of the United States. To this court. Even to my attorney, Mr. Baylor. For not telling the truth about what happened that night."

The nosebleed that had been building for decades finally burst from Dan Rather. Mercifully, it was kept from his viewers.

Judge Dutch's eyes disappeared for the last time behind the pea-soup fog of his glasses.

"Not last," Beth continued, "I apologize to the United States Secret Service and the Federal Bureau of Investigation. Terrible accusations were laid at their doorsteps, on my behalf. I—not Mr. Baylor—bear the full moral responsibility for those accusations, and I hereby retract them."

Beth looked down, swallowed, and continued. "I threw the historical . . . object at the President that night. The spittoon."

The courtroom stirred.

"In fact, I threw it at him hard. This happened at a moment of emotional . . . Oh, to hell with it . . . excuse me, Your Honor. I was furious with him. I knew what he'd been doing. And if I had killed him, I cannot say to you here and now that I would have regretted it at the time."

She continued, "But I was certain, somehow, that I had *not* killed him. And it was to that certainty that I clung throughout the investigation and"—she sighed—"subsequent events. I cannot justify that certainty. I cannot excuse the accusations that were made in my defense."

Beth's hand moved abruptly to her stomach. She winced.

"Mr. Baylor, genuinely believing in my innocence, defended me to the utmost of his ability. Which, in the case of Boyce Baylor, is pretty utmost. He now faces the possibility of prison and professional ruin. If my debt to the American people is exceeded by any other, it is by my debt to him. For without Mr. Baylor's interventions, however zealous, the result of these proceedings might very well have been otherwise. Perhaps, on balance, that would have been for the best, at least for the country's sake. At any rate, now this court knows the full truth of what happened in the White House that night. And can make such disposition," Beth concluded, sitting down, "as it deems fitting."

She sat down and folded her hands on her lap.

There was no murmuring. Even normally garrulous television commentators said nothing.

At length, Judge Dutch removed his glasses and cleared his throat. He looked toward the clerk of the court, then at Beth. He hesitated for several long seconds, then spoke.

"Motion is granted."

He turned to the jury. "The jury is discharged. On behalf of the people of the United States, I would like to extend gratitude for your service in what I know have been trying circumstances."

With that he said, "Court is adjourned," and brought down his gavel on the Trial of the Millennium.

Epilogue

ive days before *United States* v. *Boyce Baylor et al.* was scheduled
to go to trial, a trial that in the opinion of most legal observers would be
a "slam dunk" for the prosecution, Boyce's co-defendants, Felicio Andaluz and Ramon Martinez, escaped from the U.S. Detention Center
in Fairfax, Virginia, during a game of basketball with other inmates.
This was highly embarrassing to the government and forced a delay in
the start of Boyce's trial.

From Boyce's point of view, it was a welcome delay, allowing him
time to be with Beth when she gave birth. Her pregnancy had been the
most media-covered gestation since an actress had appeared nude and
immensely gibbous on the cover of *Vanity Fair* magazine. Their daughter, Ilsa Tyler Baylor, weighed six pounds ten ounces, exactly—a fact
The Washington Post pointed out—the weight of the infamous Paul Revere silver spittoon. Chatting with reporters outside the hospital, Boyce
was good-humored enough to remark that he hoped his new daughter
would soon be too heavy for her mother to throw at him.

The investigation into the disappearance of Felicio and his colleague
proved inconclusive. They had, simply, vanished.

One night, rocking his newborn daughter to sleep, Boyce received a
telephone call. After listening to what Felicio had to say, he in turn
called a reporter friend. The friend had already won two Pulitzer Prizes
for his investigative reporting but was by no means averse to having a
third. With the information that Boyce vouchsafed him, he went to

work and in six weeks, on the eve of the start of Boyce's rescheduled trial for conspiracy to commit jury tampering, brought out the first in a series of articles, thoroughly if somewhat anonymously sourced, stating that Felicio Andaluz was a longtime agent of the U.S. Central Intelligence Agency. Furthermore, it had been the CIA that had so deftly arranged his and Mr. Martinez's escape from the detention facility. The CIA had been most eager not to have one of its prize agents, one fairly teeming with sensitive information about its operations in Latin America, take the stand in a federal court case.

The CIA naturally had "no comment" on the articles. But in the aftermath of the trial, public opinion was sensitive to any suggestion that the government had been up to yet more covert mischief.

The Justice Department found itself assailed by the media, demanding to know why, if one branch of the government was secretly springing from jail a set of defendants in the same trial, another branch of the government should so assiduously pursue the remaining defendant.

High-level meetings were held.

At length it was announced that the government would nolle prosequi in the case of *U.S.* v. *Baylor et al.* In plain English, this means: *I am not going to touch this with a ten-foot pole.*

The stated justification given was that Messrs. Andaluz and Martinez had agreed to cooperate with the government and testify against Boyce Baylor. (Untrue.) In their absence, the government now felt that it had insufficient grounds to continue against him. But what about the videotape of him plotting away happily to pollute the jury? The spokesman bravely cleared his throat and said that the tape was "open to subjective interpretation."

The nolle was greeted with approval by the over 85 percent of the American people who said they were suffering from Trial of the Millennium–related exhaustion.

The Ethics Panel of the District of Columbia Bar Association convened to determine whether there had been ethical violations sufficiently grievous to warrant disbarring Boyce from continuing to practice law. The hearings were closed but were reported in the press to be "heated." There was a certain amount of harrumphing on the nation's editorial pages about the "ridiculous" spectacle of lawyers declaring each other morally unfit.

On the eve of what was said to be a "close" vote, Boyce himself, in a brief statement given on his front steps while holding his infant daughter, announced that he was retiring from the law, as he put it, "to improve humanity by reducing the number of lawyers by one."

"Won't you miss it?" asked one reporter.

"You mean, honestly?"

The United States v. *Van Anka* lasted less than two weeks. Nick Naylor, Babette's publicist, held press conferences every afternoon after the day's proceedings, to say how enormously satisfied the Van Anka camp was with how it was all going. A number of famous actors testified on Babette's behalf, as well as the Israeli defense minister and two former prime ministers. It took the jury five hours to find her guilty of perjury. The judge (not Judge Dutch) sentenced her to one and a half years in a minimum-security facility near Los Angeles, so that she could be near her agent. She'd be out in four months, pounds thinner and looking fabulous.

Her divorce from Max was complicated by the fact that Max was now a fugitive from U.S. justice living in Indonesia and Switzerland. Though not a divorce attorney per se, Alan Crudman represented her in the matter and, after ingeniously—as even Boyce admitted—managing to attach the assets of his offshore holding companies in the Netherlands, brought him to a bargaining table in Taiwan and to a settlement that was described by the *Financial Times* as "a lulu."

Wiley P. Sinclair disappeared once again and then several years later was given Chinese citizenship. His behind-the-scenes maneuvering to help China win sponsorship of the Olympics came to public light when he was decorated by the Prime Minister and awarded the title "Hero of the Revolution." He is said to live comfortably in Beijing and to maintain a summer residence in Hangchow. Occasionally, dressed as an elderly Chinese woman, he travels to Las Vegas.

Some thirty-eight books have been written so far about the trial, sixteen of them by the jurors. *Juror Number Eighteen* is generally considered to be the least tedious.

Judge Dutch Umin received plaudits for his handling of the Trial of the Millennium. He declined President Harold Farkley's nomination to the Supreme Court, saying that when he reached retirement age, he planned to accept an outstanding offer to be curator of the Institute for Dutch Still Life.

Harold Farkley was overwhelmingly defeated in his bid to be reelected president, confirming in everyone's mind that he was fundamentally second-rate and that he never would have achieved the number one job in government had it not been for the fact that his predecessor had died in, as one columnist put it, "pathetic" circumstances.

His opponent ran on a platform of restoring dignity to the White House. He announced that his first piece of legislation would be the Lincoln Bedroom Protection Act, barring presidents from turning the once sacred second-floor room overlooking the South Lawn into, as he put it, "a by-the-hour motel for political donors."

He also pledged to reduce the size of government.

Acknowledgments

I am once again in the debt of Dr. David Williams, MC, USNR. Compliments and duty, *Sir!*

Steve "Dutch" Umin of Williams and Connolly was patiently and endlessly helpful and so far has yet to submit a bill. Let the record show that he finally threw up his hands over my implacable legal solecisms and should not be held accountable thereunto. Thereof? Whatever.

Before he got mad at me for something I wrote about his client, Monica Lewinsky, Plato Cacheris provided the spittoon.

C. Boyden Gray bought me a shad-roe lunch and chuckled at the idea, a reassuring sound from a tough grader and Establishmento.

The combined hourly bill of these three distinguished attorneys, a sum equivalent to the gross domestic product of the sultanate of Brunei, is worth it, so if you have killed anyone or swindled shareholders or fought with the Taliban, call them. They're in the book.

Lincoln Caplan of the Yale Law School's journal *Legal Affairs,* in whose pages some of this first appeared, showed once again that he is a peerless editor, to say nothing of friend.

Thomas Jackson gave precociously good advice for a young man.

John Tierney was as ever generous with his wisdom and enthusiasm.

Thanks, also, to the keen eyes of Gregory Zorthian and William F. Buckley Jr.

Special thanks to Sona Vogel for her relentlessly superb copyediting and fact checking.

President George "41" Bush kindly provided certain details of life on the second floor of the White House residence.

Affectionate thanks, once again, to Amanda "Binky" Urban of International Creative Management. Again, if you have killed someone or swindled stockholders or fought with the Taliban, call her—after you call the lawyers.

I am again in deep debt to my editor, Jonathan Karp of Random House. This is our fifth collaboration. He has now said "no" 1,278 times. But this makes it sweet when he says "yes." Thank you, my very dear Mr. Karp.

Last but never leastly: wife Lucy, daughter Caitlin, and son Conor, who put up with the author. Once again, I am left wondering why anyone would marry a writer or want one for a dad.

And finally the faithful Hound Jake, who barked at everything.

—*Blue Hill*
September 9, 2001

About the Type

This book was set in Bembo, a typeface based on an old-style Roman face that was used for Cardinal Bembo's tract *De Aetna* in 1495. Bembo was cut by Francisco Griffo in the early sixteenth century. The Lanston Monotype Company of Philadelphia brought the well-proportioned letterforms of Bembo to the United States in the 1930s.

——